"Arla, if you love me you must go away at once," he said sternly coming toward the girl again, and now he was within the range of the next room and Sherrill had to shrink further back into the shadow again lest Carter should see her.

Suddenly she saw him stoop, put both arms about the other girl, draw her close to him, and put his lips down on hers, hungrily, passionately, kissing her and devouring her with his eyes, just as he had sometimes on rare and precious occasions done to Sherrill!

Sherrill clutched her bridal flowers and shivered as she shrank into the shadow and tried to shut the sight out by closing her eyes. . . .

Tyndale House books by Grace Livingston Hill.
Check with your area bookstore for these best-sellers.

COLLECTOR'S CHOICE SERIES

1. *The Christmas Bride*
2. *In Tune with Wedding Bells*
3. *Partners*
4. *The Strange Proposal*

LIVING BOOKS®

1 *Where Two Ways Met*
2 *Bright Arrows*
3 *A Girl To Come Home To*
4 *Amorelle*
5 *Kerry*
6 *All Through the Night*
7 *The Best Man*
8 *Ariel Custer*
9 *The Girl of the Woods*
10 *Crimson Roses*
11 *More Than Conqueror*
12 *Head of the House*
14 *Stranger within the Gates*
15 *Marigold*
16 *Rainbow Cottage*
17 *Maris*
18 *Brentwood*
19 *Daphne Deane*
20 *The Substitute Guest*
21 *The War Romance of the Salvation Army*
22 *Rose Galbraith*
23 *Time of the Singing of Birds*
24 *By Way of the Silverthorns*
25 *Sunrise*
26 *The Seventh Hour*
27 *April Gold*
28 *White Orchids*
29 *Homing*
30 *Matched Pearls*
32 *Coming Through the Rye*
33 *Happiness Hill*
34 *The Patch of Blue*
36 *Patricia*
37 *Silver Wings*
38 *Spice Box*
39 *The Search*
40 *The Tryst*
41 *Blue Ruin*
42 *A New Name*
43 *Dawn of the Morning*
44 *The Beloved Stranger*
60 *Miranda*
61 *Mystery Flowers*
63 *The Man of the Desert*
64 *Miss Lavinia's Call*
77 *The Ransom*
78 *Found Treasure*
79 *The Big Blue Soldier*
80 *The Challengers*
81 *Duskin*
82 *The White Flower*
83 *Marcia Schuyler*
84 *Cloudy Jewel*
85 *Crimson Mountain*
86 *The Mystery of Mary*
87 *Out of the Storm*
88 *Phoebe Deane*
89 *Re-Creations*
90 *Sound of the Trumpet*
91 *A Voice in the Wilderness*
92 *The Honeymoon House*
93 *Katharine's Yesterday*

CLASSICS SERIES

1. *Crimson Roses*
2. *The Enchanted Barn*
3. *Happiness Hill*
4. *Patricia*
5. *Silver Wings*

Grace Livingston Hill

THE BELOVED STRANGER

LIVING BOOKS ®
Tyndale House Publishers, Inc.
Wheaton, Illinois

This Tyndale House book
by Grace Livingston Hill
contains the complete text
of the original hardcover edition.
NOT ONE WORD
HAS BEEN OMITTED.

Printing History
J.B. Lippincott edition published 1933
Tyndale House edition/1992

Library of Congress Catalog Card Number 92-61575
ISBN 0-8423-0303-0

Printed in the United States of America

99 98 97 96 95 94 93 92
8 7 6 5 4 3 2 1

SHERRILL stood before the long mirror and surveyed herself critically in her bridal array.

Rich creamy satin shimmering, sheathing her slender self, drifting down in luscious waves across the old Chinese blue of the priceless rug on which she stood! Misty white veil like a cloud about her shoulders, caught by the frosty cap of rare lace about her sweet forehead, clasped by the wreath of orange blossoms in their thick green and white perfection, flowers born to nestle in soft mists of tulle and deepen the whiteness, the only flower utterly at home with rich old lace.

Sherrill stooped to the marble shelf beneath the tall mirror and picked up a hand glass turning herself this way and that to get a glimpse on every side. There seemed to be no possible fault to be found anywhere. The whole costume was a work of art.

"It's lovely, isn't it, Gemmie?" she said brightly to the elderly woman who had served her aunt for thirty years as maid. "Now, hand me the bouquet. I want to see how it all looks together. It isn't fair not to be able to get the effect one's self after taking all this trouble to make it a pleasant sight for other people."

The old servant smiled.

"What quaint things you do say, Miss Sherry!" she said as she untied the box containing the bridal bouquet. "But don't you think maybe you should leave the flowers in the box till you get to the church? They might get a bit crushed."

"No, Gemmie, I'll be very careful. I want to see how pretty they look with the dress and everything. Aren't they lovely?"

She took the great sheaf of roses gracefully on one arm and posed, laughing brightly into the mirror, the tip of one silver slipper advancing beneath the ivory satin, her eyes like two stars, her lips in the curves of a lovely mischievous child; then advancing the other silver shod foot she hummed a bar of the wedding march.

"Now, am I quite all right, Gemmie?" she asked again.

"You are the prettiest bride I ever set eyes on," said the woman looking at the sweet fair girl wistfully. "Ef I'd had a daughter I could have asked no better for her than that she should look like you in her wedding dress," and Gemmie wiped a furtive tear from one corner of her eye over the thought of the daughter she never had had.

"There, there, Gemmie, don't go to getting sentimental!" cried Sherrill with a quick little catch in her own breath, and a wistful sudden longing in her breast for the mother she never had known. "Now, I'm quite all right, Gemmie, and you're to run right down and get Stanley to take you over to the church. I want you to be sure and get the seat I picked out for you, where you can see everything every minute. I'm depending on you, you know, to tell me every detail afterward,—and, Gemmie, don't forget the funny things too. I wouldn't want to miss them you know. Be sure to describe how

Miss Hollister looks in her funny old bonnet with the ostrich plume."

"Oh, now Miss Sherrill, I couldn't be looking after things like that when you was getting married," rebuked the woman.

"Oh, yes, you could, Gemmie, you've got the loveliest sense of humor! And I want to know *everything*! Nobody else will understand, but you do, so now run away quick!"

"But I couldn't be leaving you alone," protested the woman with distress in her voice. "It'll be plenty of time for me to be going after you have left. Your Aunt Pat said for me to stay by you."

"You have, Gemmie, you've stayed as long as I had need of you, and just everything is done. You couldn't put another touch to me anywhere, and I'd rather know you are on your way to that nice seat I asked the tall dark usher to put you in. So please go, Gemmie, right away! The fact is, Gemmie, I'd really like just a few minutes alone all by myself before I go. I've been so busy I couldn't get calm, and I need to look into my own eyes and say good bye to myself before I stop being a girl and become a married woman. It really is a kind of scary thing you know Gemmie, now that I'm this close to it. I don't know how I ever had the courage to promise I'd do it!" and she laughed a gay little trill full of joyous anticipation.

"You poor lamb!" said the older woman with sudden yearning in her voice; the old, anticipating and pitying the trials of the young. "I do hope he'll be good to you."

"Be good to me!" exclaimed Sherrill gayly. "Who? Carter? Why of course, Gemmie. He's wonderful to me. He's almost ridiculous he's so careful of me. I'm just wondering how it's going to be to have someone always fussing over me when I've been on my own for so many years. Why, you know, Gemmie, these last six months I've been with Aunt Pat are the first time I've had anybody who really cared where I went or what I did since my mother died when I was ten years old. So you don't need to worry about me. There, now, you've spread that train out just as smooth as can be, please go at once. I'm getting very nervous about you, really Gemmie!"

"But I'll be needed, Miss Sherry, to help you down to the car when it comes for you."

"No, you won't, Gemmie. Just send that little new waitress up to the door to knock when the car is ready. I can catch up my own train and carry it perfectly well. I don't want to be preened and spread out like a peacock. It'll be bad enough when I get to the church and have to be in a parade. Truly, Gemmie, I want to be alone now."

The woman reluctantly went away at last, and Sherrill locked her door and went back to her mirror, watching herself as she advanced slowly, silver step after silver step, in time to the softly hummed Lohengrin. But when she was near to the glass Sherrill's eyes looked straight into their own depths long and earnestly.

"Am I really glad," she thought to herself, "that I'm going out of myself into a grown up married person? Am I perfectly sure that I'm not just a bit frightened at it all? Of course Carter McArthur is the handsomest man I ever met, the most brilliant talker, the most courteous gentleman, and I've been crazy about him ever since I first met him. Of course he treats me just like a queen, and I trust him absolutely. I know he'll always be just the same graceful lover all my life. And yet, somehow, I feel all of a sudden just the least bit scared. Does any girl *ever* know any man *perfectly?*"

She looked deep into her own eyes and wondered. If she only had a mother to talk to these last few minutes!

Of course there was Aunt Pat. But Aunt Pat had never been married. How could Aunt Pat know how a girl felt the last few minutes before the ceremony? And Aunt Pat was on her way to the church now. She was all crippled up with rheumatism and wanted to get there in a leisurely way and not have to get out of the car before a gaping crowd. She had planned to slip in the side door and wait in the vestry room till almost time for the ceremony and then have one of her numerous nephews, summoned to the old house for the occasion to be ushers, bring her in. Aunt Pat wouldn't have understood anyhow. She was a good sport with a great sense of humor, but she wouldn't have understood this queer feeling Sherrill was experiencing.

When one stopped to think of it, right on the brink of doing it, it was a rather awful thing to just give your life up to the keeping of another! She hadn't known Carter but six short months. Of course he was wonderful. Everybody said he was wonderful, and he had always been so to her. Her heart thrilled even now at the thought of him, the way he called her "Beautiful!" bending down and just touching her forehead with his lips, as though she were almost too sacred to touch lightly. The way his hair waved above his forehead. The slow way he smiled, and the light that came in his hazel eyes when he looked at her. They thrilled her tremendously. Oh, there wasn't any doubt in her mind whatever but that she was deeply in love with him. She didn't question that for an instant. It was just the thought of merging her life into his and always being a part of him. No, it wasn't that either, for that thrilled her too with an exquisite kind of joy, to think of never having to be separated from him any more. What was it that sent a quiver of fear through her heart just at this last minute alone? She couldn't tell.

She had tried to talk to Gemmie about it once the day before, and Gemmie had said all girls felt "queer" at the thought of being married. All nice girls that is. Sherrill couldn't see why that had anything to do with the matter. It wasn't a matter of nicety. Gemmie was talking about a shrinking shyness probably and it wasn't that at all. It was a great awesomeness at the thought of the miracle of two lives wrought into one, two souls putting aside all others and becoming one perfect life.

It made Sherrill feel suddenly so unworthy to have been chosen, so childish and immature for such a wonder. One must be so perfect to have a right to be a part of such a great union. And Carter was so wonderful! Such a super-man!

Suddenly she dropped upon one silken knee and bowed her lovely mist-veiled head.

"Dear God," she prayed softly, long lashes lying on velvet cheeks, gold tendrils of hair glinting out from under lacy cap, "O, dear God, make me good enough for him!" and then, hesitantly in a quick little frightened breath, "Keep me from making any awful mistakes!"

Then having shriven her ignorant young soul, she buried her face softly, gently, in the baby roses of her bouquet and drew a long happy breath; feeling her fright and burden roll away, her happy heart spring up to meet the great new change that was about to come upon her life.

She came softly to her feet, the great bouquet still in her clasp, and glanced hurriedly at the little turquoise enamel clock on her dressing table. There was plenty of time. She had promised to show herself to Mary the cook after she was dressed. Mary had broken her knee cap the week before and was confined to her couch. She had mourned distressedly that she could not see Miss Sherrill in her wedding dress. So Sherrill had promised her. It had been one of the reasons why she had got rid of Gemmie. She knew Gemmie would protest at her going about in her wedding veil for a mere servant!

But there was no reason in the world why she couldn't do it. Most of the people of the house were gone to the church. The bridesmaids left just before Gemmie, and Aunt Pat before them. Herself had watched the ushers leave while Gemmie was fixing her veil. Of course they had to be there ages before anyone else.

The bridesmaids and maid-of-honor had the next two rooms to her own, with only her deep closet between, and there were doors opening from room to room so that all the rooms were connected around the circle and back to Aunt Pat's room which was across the hall from her own. It had been one of the idiosyncrasies of the old lady that in case of burglars it would be nice to be able to go from room to room without going into the hall.

So the rooms were arranged in a wide horseshoe with the back hall behind the top of the loop, the middle room being a sitting room or library, with three bedrooms on either side. Nothing would be easier than for her to go swiftly, lightly, through the two rooms beyond her own, and through the door at the farther end of the second room into the back hall that led to the servants' quarters. That would save her going through the front hall and being seen by any prying servants set to keep track of her till she reached the church. It was a beautiful idea to let old Mary see how she looked, and why shouldn't she do it?

Stepping quickly over to the door that separated her room from the next she slid the bolt back, and turned the knob cautiously, listening; then swung the door noiselessly open.

Yes, it was as she supposed, the girls were gone. The room was dimly lit by the two wall sconces over the dressing table. She could see Linda's street shoes with the tan stockings stuffed into them standing across the room near the bureau. She knew them by the curious cross straps of the sandal-like fastening. Linda's hat was on the bed, with the jacket of her silk ensemble half covering it. Linda was always careless, and of course the maids were too busy to have been in here yet to clear up. The closet door was open and she saw Cassie's suitcase yawning wide open on the floor where Cassie had left it in her haste. The white initials, C.A.B. cried out a greeting as she crept stealthily by. Cassie had been late in arriving. She always was. And there was Carol's lovely imported fitted bag open on the dressing table, all speaking of the haste of their owners.

Betty and Doris and Jane had been put in the second room, with Rena, the maid of honor whom Aunt Pat had wanted her to ask because she was the daughter of an old friend. It was rather funny having a maid of honor whom one hadn't met, for she hadn't arrived yet when Sherrill had gone to her room to dress, but assurance had come over the telephone that she was on her way in spite of a flat tire, so there had been nothing to worry about. Who or what Rena was like did not matter. She would be wholly engaged in eying her dear bridegroom's face. What did it matter who maid-of-honored her, so Aunt Pat was pleased?

Sherrill paused as she stepped into this second room. It was absolutely dark, but strangely enough the door to the left, opening into the middle room had been left open. That was curious. Hadn't Carter been put in there to dress? Surely that was the arrangement, to save him coming garbed all the way from the city!

But of course he was gone long ago! She had heard

him arrange to be early at the church to meet the best man who had been making some last arrangements about their stateroom on the ship. That was it! Carter had gone, and the girls, probably not even knowing that he occupied that room, had gone out that way through what they supposed was the sitting room instead of using the other door into the hall.

So Sherrill, her soft train swung lightly over her arm, the mist of lace gathered into the billow that Gemmie had arranged for her convenience in going down stairs, and the great sheaf of roses and valley-lilies held gracefully over her other arm stepped confidently into the room. She looked furtively toward the open door where a brilliant overhead light was burning, sure that the room was empty, unless some servant was hovering about watching for her to appear.

She hesitated, stepping lightly, the soft satin making no sound of going more than if she had been a bit of thistle down. Then suddenly she stopped short and held her breath, for she had come in full sight of the great gilt-framed pier glass that was set between the two windows at the back of the room, and in it was mirrored the full length figure of her bridegroom arranging his tie with impatient fingers and staring critically into the glass, just as she had been doing but a moment before.

A great wave of tenderness swept over her for him, a kind of guilty joy that she could have this last vision of him as himself before their lives merged; a picture that she felt would live with her throughout the long years of life.

How dear he looked! How shining his dark hair, the wave over his forehead! There wasn't any man, not *any* man, *any*where as handsome—and *good,* she breathed softly to herself—as Carter, *her man!*

She held herself back into the shadow, held her very

breath lest he should turn and see her there, for—wasn't there a tradition that it was bad luck for the bride to show herself in her wedding garments to the groom before he saw her first in the church? Softly she withdrew one foot and swayed a little farther away from the patch of light in the doorway. He would be gone in just a minute of course and then she could go on and give Mary her glimpse and hurry back without being seen by anyone. She dared not retreat further lest he should hear her step and find out that she had been watching him. It was fun to be here and see him when he didn't know. But sometime, O sometime in the dear future that was ahead of them, she would tell him how she had watched him, and loved him, and how all the little fright that had clutched her heart a few minutes before had been melted away by this dear glimpse of him.

Sometime, when he was in one of those gentle moods, and they were all alone—they had had so little time actually alone of late! There had always been so many other things to be done!—But sometime, soon perhaps, when he was giving her soft kisses on her eyelids, and in the palm of her hand as he held her fingers back with his own strong ones, then she would draw him down with his face close to hers and tell him how she had watched him, and loved him—!

But—! What was happening? The door of the back hall, that was set next to the nearest window was opening slowly, without sound, and a face was appearing in the opening! Could it be a servant, mistaken her way? How blundering! How annoyed he would be to have his privacy broken in upon!

And then the face came into the light and she started. It was a face she had seen before, a really pretty face, if the make-up on it had not been so startling. There was something almost haggard about it too, and wistful, and the eyes were frightened, pleading eyes. They scanned the room hurriedly and rested upon the man, who still stood with his back to the room and his face to the mirror. Then the girl stepped stealthily within the room and closed the door as noiselessly as she had opened it.

Who was it? Sherrill held her breath and stared. Then swift memory brought the answer. Why, that was Miss Prentiss, Carter's stenographer! But surely, no one had invited her! Carter had said she was comparatively new in the office. He had not put her name on the list. How dared she follow him here? Had something come up at the last minute, some business matter that she felt he must know about before he left for his trip to Europe? But surely, no one could have directed her to follow him to the room where he was dressing!

This all went swiftly through Sherrill's mind as she stood that instant and watched the expression on the girl's face, that hungry desperate look, and something warned her with uncanny prescience. So Sherrill stood holding that foolish bouquet of baby roses and swinging lily-bells during what seemed an eon of time, till suddenly Carter McArthur saw something in the mirror and swung around, a frozen look of horror and anger on his handsome face, and faced the other girl.

"What are you doing here, Arla?" he rumbled in an angry whisper, and his bride, standing within the shadow trembled so that all the little lily-bells swayed in the dark and trembled with her. She had never heard him speak in a voice like that. She shivered a little, and a sudden thought like a dart swept through her. Was it conceivable that he would ever speak so to her? But—of course this intruder ought to be rebuked!

"I have come because I cannot let this thing go on!" said the girl in a desperate voice. "I have tried to do as you told me. O, I have tried with all my might—" and her voice broke in a helpless little sob, "but I can't do it. It isn't *right!*"

"Be still can't you? You will rouse the house. Do you want to bring disgrace upon us all?"

"If that is the only way," said the girl desperately, lifting lovely darkly circled eyes to his face, and suddenly putting her hands up with a caressing motion and stealing them around his neck; desperate clinging arms that held him fast.

"I can't give you up, Cart! I can't! I *can't!* You promised me so long ago you would marry me, and you've always been putting me off—and now—*this! I can't!*"

"Hush!" said the man sternly with a note of desperation in his voice. "You are making me hate you, don't you know that? Don't you know that no good whatever can come of this either for me or yourself? How did you get here anyway? Have you no shame? Who saw you? Tell me quick!"

"Nobody saw me—" breathed the girl between sobs, "I came up the fire escape and along the back hall. This was the room I came to that day to take dictation for you when you had a sprained ankle and had to stay out here. Don't you remember? Oh, Cart! You told me then that some day you and I would have a house just like this. Have you forgotten how you kissed my fingers, and the palm of my hand when they all had gone away and left us to work?"

"Hush!" said the man, his face stern with agony. "No, I haven't forgotten! You know I haven't forgotten! I've explained it all to you over and over again. I thought you were reasonable. I thought you understood that this was necessary in order to save all that I have worked so hard to gain."

"Oh, but Cart! I've tried to, but I can't! I cannot give you up!"

"You won't have to give me up," he soothed impatiently. "We'll see each other every day as soon as I get back from this trip. We'll really be closer together than if we were married, for there'll be nothing to hinder us having good times whenever we like. No household cares or anything. And really, a man's secretary is nearer—"

There came a sharp imperative tap on the door of the sitting room. McArthur started and pushed the weeping girl from him into a corner.

"Yes?" he said harshly going over to the door. "Has the car come for me? Well, say I'll be there in just a minute. There is plenty of time by my watch. But I'll be right down."

There was a painful silence. Sherrill could see the other girl shrinking behind a curtain, could hear the painful breathing as she struggled to keep back the sobs, could see the strained attitude of Carter McArthur as he stood stiffly in the middle of the room glaring toward the frail girl.

"Arla, if you love me you must go away at once," he said sternly coming toward the girl again, and now he was within the range of the next room and Sherrill had to shrink further back into the shadow again lest he should see her.

Suddenly she saw him stoop, put both arms about the other girl, draw her close to him, and put his lips down on hers, hungrily, passionately, kissing her and devouring her with his eyes, just as he had sometimes on rare and precious occasions done to Sherrill! Sherrill clutched her bridal flowers and shivered as she shrank into the shadow and tried to shut the sight out by closing her eyes, yet could not.

A great awful cold had come down upon her heart, caught it with an icy hand, and was slowly squeezing it to death. She wanted to cry out, as in a nightmare, and waken herself; prove that this was only a hideous dream, yet something was stopping her voice and holding her quiet. It must not be that he should hear her, or see her! It must never happen that she should be drawn into this dreadful scene. She must keep very still and it would pass. This awful delirium would pass, and her right mind would return! She was going pretty soon to the church to be married to this man, and all this would be forgotten, and she would be telling him sometime how she had watched him and loved him as he prepared to go forth and meet her, her dear bridegroom! He would be kissing *her* fingers, and *her* eyelids this way—But no! She was going crazy! That would never happen! A great wall had come down between them. She knew in her heart that now she would never, never tell him! He would never take her in his arms again, or kiss her lips or eyelids, or call her his! That was over forever. A dream that could not come true.

Then an impassioned voice broke the stillness and cut through to the depths of her being. It was his voice with that beloved quality she knew so well!

"O, my darling, my darling! I can't stand it to see you suffer so! There will never be any girl like you to me. Why can't you understand?"

"Then if that is so," broke out the weeping girl lifting her head with sudden hope, "come with me now! We can get out the way I came and no one will see us. Let us go away! Leave her and leave the business, and everything. No one will see us! Come!"

The man groaned.

"You *will* not understand!" he murmured impatiently. "It is not possible! Do you want to see me ruined? This girl is rich! Her fortune and the connection with her family will save me. Sometime later there may come a time when I could go with you, but not now!"

Then into the midst of the awfulness there swung a sweet-toned silver sound, a clock just outside the door striking the hour in unmistakable terms, and Carter McArthur started away from the girl, fairly flinging her in his haste, till she huddled down on her knees in the corner sobbing.

"Shut up, can't you!" said the man wildly as he rushed over to the mirror and began to brush the powder marks from his otherwise immaculate coat, "Can't you see you're goading me to desperation? I've *got* to go *instantly!* I'm going to be late!"

"And what about me?" wailed the girl. "Would you rather I took poison and lay down in this room to die? Wouldn't that be a nice thing to meet you when you came back from the church?"

But with a last desperate brush of his coat Carter snapped out the light, and swung out into the upper hall, slamming the door significantly behind him, and hurrying down the stairs with brisk steps that tried to sound gay for the benefit of the servants in the hall below.

The girl's voice died away into a helpless little frightened sob, and then all was still.

And Sherrill stood there in the utter darkness trying to think, trying to gather her scattered senses and realize what had happened; what might happen next. That something cataclysmic had just taken place that would change all her after life she knew; but just for that first instant or two after she heard her bridegroom's footsteps go down the stairs and out the front door she had not got her bearings. It was all that she could do just then to stand still and clutch her great bouquet while the earth reeled under her trembling feet.

The next instant she heard a sound, soft, scarcely perceptible to any but preternaturally quickened senses, that brought her back to the present, the necessity of the moment and the shortness of time.

The sound was the tiniest possible hint of stirring garments and a stealthy step from the corner where the weeping girl had been flung when the angry frightened bridegroom made his hasty exit.

Instantly Sherrill was in possession of herself and reaching forward accurately with accustomed fingers, touched the electric switch that sent a flood of light into the sitting room.

Then Sherrill in her white robes stepped to the doorway and confronted the frightened, cowering, blinking interloper, who fell back against the wall, her hands outspread and groping for the door, her eyes growing wide with horror as she caught the full version of her lover's bride.

FOR just an instant they faced one another, the bride in her beauty, and her woe-begone rival, and in spite of her Sherrill could not help thinking how pretty this other girl was. Even though she had been crying and there were tears on her lashes. She was not a girl whom crying made hideous. It rather gave her the sweet dewy look of a child in trouble.

She stood wide-eyed, horror and fear on her face, the soft gold of her hair just showing beneath a chic little hat. She was dressed in a stylish street suit of dark blue with slim correct shoes and long wristed wrinkled white doeskin gloves. Even as she stood, her arms outspread and groping for refuge against the unfriendly wall, she presented an interesting picture. Sherrill could not help feeling sorry for her. There was nothing arrogant about her now. Just the look of a frightened child at bay among enemies.

"How long have you known him?" asked Sherrill trying to keep her voice from trembling.

The other girl burst forth in an anguished tone, her

hands going quickly to her throat which moved convulsively:

"Ever since we were kids!" she said with a choking sob at the end of her words. "Always we've been crazy about each other, even in High School. Then after he got started up in the city he sent for me to be his secretary so we could be nearer to each other till we could afford to get married. It has never been any different till you came. It was you—*you* who took him away from me—!" and the girl buried her hands in the drabbled little handkerchief and gave a great sob that seemed to come from the depths of her being.

Sherrill felt a sudden impulse to put her face down in her lovely roses and sob too. It somehow seemed to be herself and not this other girl who was sobbing over there against the wall. Oh, how could this great disaster have befallen them both? Carter! Her matchless lover! This girl's lover too! How could this thing be?

"No," she said, very white and still, her voice almost toneless and unsteady, "I never took him away from you. I never knew there was such a person as you!"

"Well, you took him!" sobbed the other girl, "and there's nothing left for me but to kill myself!" and another great sob burst forth.

"Nonsense!" said Sherrill sharply. "Don't talk that way! That's terrible. You don't get anywhere talking like that! Hush! Somebody will hear you! We've got to be sensible and think what to do!"

"Do?" said Arla dropping her hands from her face and flashing a look of scorn at the girl in bridal array. "What is there to do? Oh, perhaps you mean how you can get rid of me the easiest way? I don't see why I should make it easy for you I'm sure, but I suppose I will. I'll go away and not make any more trouble of course. I suppose I knew that when I came, but I *had* to come! Oh!—" and she gave another deep sob and turned her head away for an instant, then back to finish her sentence, "and you will go out to the church to marry him. It is easy enough for you to say 'hush' when you are going to marry him!"

"Marry him!" said Sherrill, sudden horror in her voice, "I could never marry him after *this!* Could *you?"*

"Oh, yes," said the girl in a quivering, hopeless voice, "I'd marry him if I got the chance! You can't love him the way I do or you would too. I'd marry him if I had to go through hell to do it!"

Sherrill quivered at the words. She was watching this other girl, thinking fast, and sudden determination came into her face.

"Then you shall!" she said in a low clear voice of determination. "You may get taken at your word. You may have to go through hell for it. But I won't be responsible for that. If you feel that way about it you shall marry him!"

The other girl looked up with frightened eyes.

"What do you mean?"

"I mean you shall marry him! Now! To-night!"

"But how could I?" she asked dully. "That would be impossible."

"No, it is not impossible. Come! Quick. We have got to work fast! Hark! There comes somebody to the door. Come with me! Don't make a sound!"

Sherrill snapped the light off and grasping the gloved hand of the girl she pulled her after her through the dimly lighted middle rooms and inside her own door, which she swiftly closed behind her sliding the bolt.

"Now!" she said drawing a breath of relief, "We've got to work like lightning! Take off your gloves and hat and dress just as fast as you can!"

Sherrill's hands were busy with the fastening of her veil. Carefully she searched out the hairpins that held it and lifted it off, laying it in a great billow upon the bed, her hands at once searching for the fastening of her own bridal robe.

"But what are you going to do?" asked the other girl staring at her wildly though she began automatically to pull off her long gloves.

"I'm going to put these things on you," said Sherrill, pulling off her dress over her head frantically. *"Hurry,* won't you? The car is probably out there waiting now. They'll begin to get suspicious if we are a long time. Take off your hat quick! And your dress! Will it just pull over your head? Hurry I tell you! What kind of stockings have you got on? Tan ones? That won't do. Here, I've got another pair of silver ones in the drawer. I always have two pairs in case of a run. Sit down there and peel yours off quick! I wonder if my slippers will fit you. You'll have to try them anyway, for we couldn't get any others!"

Sherrill kicked her silver slippers off, and groped in the closet, bringing out an old pair of black satin ones, and stepping into them hurriedly. The jeweled buckles glinted wickedly.

Her mind was working rapidly now. She dashed to her suitcase and rooted out a certain green taffeta evening gown, a recent purchase, one that she had especially liked, and she had planned to take with her, in case anything should delay her trunk. She dropped it over her own head, pulling it down with hurried hands and a bitter thought of what pleasure she had taken in it when she bought it. If she had known—Ah, *if she had known!* But there was no time for sentiment.

The other girl was fitting on the silver stockings and shoes, her hands moving slowly, uncertainly.

"Here, let me fasten those garters!" said Sherrill almost compassionately. "You really must work faster than this!

Stand up. Can you manage to walk in those shoes? They're a bit long aren't they? My foot is long and slim. Stand up quick and take off that dark slip. Here, here's the white slip," and she slid it over the golden head of the other girl. Queer their hair was the same color! Sherrill's mind was so keyed up that she thought of little painful things that at another time would not have attracted her attention.

"But I can't do this!" said Arla Prentiss suddenly backing away from the lovely folds of ivory satin that Sherrill was holding for her to slip into. "I couldn't ever get away with it! Cart would kill me if I tried to do a thing like this!"

"Well, you were talking about killing yourself a few minutes ago," said Sherrill sharply, wondering at herself as she said it, "it would be only a choice of deaths in that case, wouldn't it? For mercy's sake stand still so I won't muss your hair! This dress has *got* to go on you, and mighty quick, too!"

"But I couldn't get away with a thing like this!" babbled Arla as she emerged from the sweeping folds of satin and found herself clothed in a wedding garment, drifting away in an awesome train such as her wildest dreams had never pictured.

"Oh, yes, you could," said Sherrill, snapping the fastenings firmly into place and smoothing down the skirt hurriedly. "All you've got to do is to walk up the aisle and say yes to things."

"Oh, I *couldn't!*" said Arla in sudden terror. "Why, they would know the minute I reached the church that it wasn't you! They would never let it get even as far as walking up the aisle. They would *mob* me! They would *drive me out—!*" she paused with a great sob and sank down to the chair again.

"Get up!" said Sherrill standing over her fiercely.

"You'll ruin that dress! Hark! There is someone coming to the door! Hush! Yes? Are you calling for me?" Sherrill spoke in a pleasant casual tone. "Is the car ready for me? You say it's been ready ten minutes? Oh, well," she laughed a high little unnatural trill, "that's all right! They always expect a bride to be late. Well, tell the man I'll be down in a minute or two now!"

The maid retreated down the stairs and Sherrill flew over to the bed and took up the wedding veil carefully.

"Now, stand there in front of the mirror and watch," she commanded as she held the lace cap high and brought it down accurately around the golden head. "Stand still please. I've got to do this in just a second. And now listen to me."

"But I can't! I can't really!" protested the substitute bride wildly. "I couldn't let you do this for me!"

"You've *got to!*" said Sherrill commandingly. "I didn't get up any of this mess, and it's up to you to put this wedding through. Now listen! The man who is to take me—*you* in—is a stranger to me. His name is Nathan Vane. He's a second cousin of my mother's family and he's never seen me. He hadn't arrived yet when I came up to dress. Neither had the maid-of-honor, and she's a stranger to me too. Her name is Rena Scott. They'll both be waiting at the door for you and will be the only ones who will have a chance to talk to you. All you'll have to do will be to smile and take his arm and go up the aisle. This is the step we're taking"—Sherrill stood away and went slowly forward. "You'll see how the others do it. You're clever, I can see. And when you get up there all you've got to do is answer the questions, and say things over after the minister, only using your *own* name instead of mine. Ten to one nobody will notice. You can speak in a low voice. The maid of honor will take your bouquet and you'll need to put out your left hand for the ring. Here! You must have the diamond too!" and Sherrill slipped her beautiful diamond engagement ring off her finger and put it on Arla's.

"Oh," gasped Arla, "you're wonderful! I *can't* let you do all this!"

"Hold your head still!" commanded Sherrill. "This orange wreath droops a little too much over that ear. There! Isn't that right? Really, you look a lot like me! I doubt if even the bridegroom will know the difference at first, wedding veils make such a change in one!"

"Oh, but"—gasped Arla, "Carter *will* know me. I'm *sure* he will! And suppose, suppose he should make a scene!"

"He won't!" said Sherrill sharply. "He hasn't the nerve!" she added cryptically, and suddenly knew that it was true and she had never known it before.

"But if he should!"

"He won't!" said Sherrill more surely, "And if he does we'll all be in it, so you won't be alone."

"Oh! Will you be there too?" Arla said it in a tone of wonder and relief.

"Why, of course," said Sherrill in the tone of a mother reproving a child. "I'll be there, perhaps before you are."

"Oh, why don't you go *with* me?"

"That would be a situation wouldn't it?" commented Sherrill sarcastically. "Former bride and substitute bride arrive together! For heaven's sake don't weep on that satin, it's bad luck! And don't talk about it any more or you'll have me crying too, and that would be just too bad! Here! Take your bouquet. No, hold it on this arm, and your veil and train over the other, now! All set? I'm turning off this light, and you must go out and walk right down the steps quickly. They are all caterer's people out there, they won't know the difference. You really look a lot like me. For mercy's sake don't look as if you were going to your own funeral. Put on a smile and *wear it all the evening*. And listen! You tell Mr. McArthur as soon as you get in the car on the way back with him, that if he plays any tricks or doesn't treat you right, or doesn't bring you back smiling to your reception, that I'll tell everybody here the whole truth! I'll tell it to everybody that knows him! And I mean what I say!"

"Oh!" gasped Arla, with a dubious lifting of the trouble in her eyes, and then, *"Oh!* Do we *have to come back* for the *reception!* Can't we just disappear?"

"If you disappear the whole story will come out in the papers to-morrow morning! I'll see to that!" threatened Sherrill ominously. "I'm not going to be made a fool of. But if you come back and act like sane people and go away in the usual manner, it will just be a good joke that we have put over for reasons of our own, see? Now go, quick! We mustn't get them all worked up because you are so late!"

Sherrill snapped out the light and threw open the door, stepping back into the shadow herself and watching breathlessly as Arla took the first few hesitating steps. Then as she grew more confident, stepping off down the hall, disappearing down the stairs, Sherrill closed the door and went over to the window which overlooked the front door.

The front steps were a blaze of light, and she could see quite plainly the caterer's man who was acting as footman, standing by and helping a vision in white into the car. The door slammed shut, and the car drove away with a flourish. Sherrill watched till it swept around the curve, and went toward the gateway. Then she snapped on a tiny bed light and gathered in haste a few things, her black velvet evening wrap, her pearl evening bag, a small sheet of note paper and her gold pencil. She would have to write a note to Aunt Pat. Her mind was racing on ahead! The keys to her own little car! Where had she put them? Oh, yes, in the drawer of her desk. Had she forgotten anything?

The bride's car had barely turned into the street ere Sherrill went with swift quiet steps back through those two rooms again, into the back hall, cautiously out through the window that Arla had left open, onto the fire escape, and down into the side yard.

It was but the work of a moment to unlock her door of the garage. Fortunately the chauffeur was not there. He had taken Aunt Pat of course, and everybody who would have known her was at the church. With trembling fingers she started her car, backed out the service drive and whirled away to the church.

She threaded her way between the big cars parked as far as she could see either way from the church. Could she manage to get hidden somewhere before the service really began?

Breathlessly she drove her car into a tiny place on the side street perilously near to a fire plug, and recklessly threw open her door. The police would be too busy out in the main avenue to notice perhaps, and anyway she could explain to them afterwards. Even if she did have to pay a fine she must get into that church.

A hatless young man in a trim blue serge suit was strolling by as she plunged forth from her car, and fortunately, for she caught the heel of her slipper in the billowy taffeta that was much too long for driving a car, and would have gone headlong if he had not caught her.

"I beg your pardon," he said pleasantly as he set her upon her feet again, "Are you hurt?"

"Oh, no!" said Sherrill, smiling agitatedly. "Thank you so much. You saved me from a bad fall. I was just in a terrible hurry," and she turned frantic eyes toward the looming side of the church across the street.

The young man continued to keep a protective arm about her and eye her anxiously.

"You're sure you're not hurt?" he asked again. "You didn't strike your head against the running board?"

"No!" she gasped breathlessly, trying to draw away, "I'm quite all right. But please, I must hurry. I am late now."

"Where do you want to go?" he asked, shifting his hand to her elbow and taking a forward step with her.

"Over there!" she motioned frantically, "to the church. I must get in before the ceremony begins."

"You ought to wait until you get your breath," he urged.

"I can't! I've *got* to get there!" and she tried to pull away from him and fly across the street. But he kept easy pace with her, helping her up to the curb.

"Don't you want to go around to the front door?" he said as she turned toward the side entrance.

"No!" she said, her heart beating so fast that it almost choked her. "This little side door. I want to get up to the choir loft."

"Well, I'm coming with you!" he announced fairly lifting her up the steps. "You're all shaken up from that fall. You're trembling! Can I take you to your friends? You're not fit to be alone."

"I'm—all—right!" panted Sherrill fetching a watery smile and finding the tears right at hand.

"Don't hurry!" he commanded, circling her waist impersonally with a strong arm and fairly lifting her up the narrow winding stair that led to the choir loft, "You've plenty of time. Don't you hear? Those are the preliminary chords to the wedding march. The bride must be just at the door! Take it slow and easy!"

They arrived at the top of the stair in an empty choir loft. It was a church of formal arrangement, with the organ console down out of sight somewhere and the choir high above the congregation, visible only when standing to sing, and then only to one who dared to look aloft.

The whole quiet place was fully screened by plumy palms, and great feathery tropical ferns, and not even a stray from the street had discovered this vantage point from which to watch the ceremony. They had it all to themselves. No curious eyes could watch the face of the agonized bride-that-was-to-have-been.

Sherrill nestled in wearily against the wall behind the thickest palm, where yet she could peer through and see everything. She thanked her unknown friend pantingly with a hasty fervor, and then forgot he was still beside her.

Breathlessly she leaned forward looking down, catching a glimpse of the bridegroom as he stood tall and handsome beside the best man, a smile of expectancy upon his face. Her bridegroom, watching for *her* to come! Her heart contracted and a spasm of pain passed over her face. She mustn't, O, she mustn't cry! This wasn't *her wedding!* This was something she must nerve herself to go through. This was something tragic that must move aright or all the future would be chaos.

Then she remembered and her eyes turned tragically, alertly down the aisle to the front door, her hand unconsciously pressed against her heart in a quick little frantic motion.

Yes, the bride had arrived! Of course she might have known that or the wedding march would not be ringing out its first stately measures! Yes, there was the huddle of rainbow-colored dresses that were the bridesmaids. How glad she was that none of them were really intimate friends. All of them new friends from Aunt Pat's circle of acquaintances. Her own girlhood friends were all too poor or too far away to be summoned. The first of them, the pink ones, were stepping forward now, slowly differentiating themselves from the mass of color, beginning the procession with measured, stilled thread; and back in the far dimness of the hall silhouetted against the darkness of the out-of-doors she could see the mist of whiteness that must be the bride, with the tall dark cousin beside her. Yes, the bride had come. Sherrill's secret fear that she might somehow lose her nerve and escape on the way to the church was unfounded. This girl really wanted Carter enough to go through this awful ordeal to get him! Besides, a girl couldn't very well run away and hope to escape detection in a bridal outfit. Sherrill felt a hysterical laugh coming to her lips that changed into a quiver of tears, and a little shiver that ran down her back. And then suddenly she felt that strong arm again just under her elbow, supporting her, just as her knees began to manifest a tendency to crumble under her.

"Oh, thank you!" she breathed softly letting her weight rest on his arm. "I'm—a little—nervous—I guess!"

"You aren't fit to stand!" he whispered. "I wonder if I couldn't find you a chair down there in the back room?"

She shook her head.

"It wouldn't be worth while," she answered, "the ceremony will soon be over. You are very kind, but I'll be all right."

He adjusted his arm so it would better support her, and somehow it helped and calmed her to feel him standing there. She had no idea how he looked or who he was. She hadn't really looked at him. She just knew he was kind, and that he was a stranger who didn't know a thing about her awful predicament. If he had been a friend who knew she couldn't have stood him there. But it was like being alone with herself to have him staying there so comfortingly. After it was over she would never likely see him again. She hoped he would never know who she was nor anything about it. She hadn't really thought anything about him as a personality. He was just something by the way to lean upon in her extremity.

The pink bridesmaids were half way up the middle aisle now, the green at the formal distance behind, the violet just entering past the first rank of seats with the blue waiting behind. Their faces wore the set smile of automatons endeavoring to do their best to keep the step. There was no evidence so far that either the wedding party or the audience had discovered anything unusual about this wedding or unexpected about the bride. She suddenly gasped at the thought of the gigantic fraud which she was about to perpetrate. Had she a right to do this? But it was too late to think about that now.

Sherrill's eyes went back to the bridegroom standing there waiting, his immaculate back as straight and conventional as if nothing out of the ordinary had occurred a half hour before. She remembered with a stab of pain the powder that he had brushed from his left lapel. Was there any trace of it left? She had a sudden sick faint feeling as if she would like to lay her head down and close her eyes. She reeled just a tiny bit, and the young man by her side shifted his arms, putting the right one unobtrusively about her so that he could the better steady her, and putting his left hand across to support her elbow. She cast him a brief little flicker of a smile of gratitude, but her eyes went swiftly back to the slow procession that was advancing up the aisle, so slow it seemed to her like the march of the centuries.

The bride was standing in the doorway now, just behind the yellow-clad maid-of-honor, her hand lying on the arm of the distant cousin, her train adjusted perfectly; no sign on the face of the maid-of-honor that she had noticed it was the wrong bride whom she had just prepared for her appearance. They didn't know it yet! Nobody knew what was about to happen except herself! The thought was overwhelming!

Suddenly her eyes were caught by the little figure in gray down in the front seat. Aunt Pat! Poor Aunt Pat! What would she think? And after all her kindness, and the money she had spent to make this wedding a perfect one of its kind! She must do something about Aunt Pat at once!

Her trembling fingers sought the catch of her hand bag and brought out pencil and paper. The young man by her side watched her curiously, sympathetically. Who was this lovely girl? What had stirred her so deeply? Had she perhaps cared for the bridegroom herself, and not felt able to face the audience during the ceremony? Or was the bride her sister, dearly beloved, whom she could not bear to part from? They truly resembled one another, gold hair, blue eyes, at least he was pretty sure this one's eyes were blue, as much as he could judge by the brief glimpse he had had of them here in the dimness of the gallery.

She was looking about for some place to lay her paper, and there was none, because the gallery rail was completely smothered in palms.

"Here!" he said softly, sensing her need, and drew out a broad smooth leather note book from his pocket, holding it firmly before her, his other arm still about her.

So Sherrill wrote rapidly, with tense trembling fingers:

> *"Dear Aunt Pat:*
>
> *I'm not getting married to-night. Please be a good sport and don't let them suspect you didn't know. Please, dearest."*
>
> *Sherrill.*

The young man beside her had to hold the note book very firmly. He couldn't exactly help seeing the hastily scrawled words, though he tried not to, he really did. He was an honorable young man. But he was also by this time very much in sympathy with this unknown lovely girl. However, he treated the whole affair in the most matter of fact way.

"You want that delivered?" he whispered.

"Oh, would you be so good?"

"Which one? The little old lady in gray right down here?"

"Oh, how did you know?" Sherrill met his sympathetic gaze in passing wonder.

"I saw you looking down at her," he answered with a boyish grin. "You want her to read it before she leaves the church?"

"Oh, yes, please! Could you do it do you think?"

"Of course," he answered with confidence. "Do you happen to know if there is a door at the foot of these stairs opening into the church?"

"Yes, there is," said Sherrill.

"Well, there's no one else in the seat all across to the side aisle. I don't know why I couldn't slide in there without being noticed while the prayer is going on."

"Oh, could you do that?" said Sherrill with great relief in her eyes, and looking down quickly toward the front seat that stretched a vacant length across to the flower-garlanded aisle. "Would you mind? It would be wonderful! But, there's a ribbon across the seat."

He grinned again socially.

"It would take more than a ribbon to keep me out of a seat I wanted to get into. Are you all right if I leave you for a minute?"

"Of course!" said Sherrill drawing herself up and

trying to look self sufficient. "Oh, I can never thank you enough!"

"Forget it!" said the young man. "Well, I'd better hurry down and reconnoiter. *Sure* you're all right?"

"Sure," she smiled tremulously.

He was gone, and Sherrill realized that she felt utterly inadequate without him. But suddenly she knew that the procession had arrived at the altar and disposed itself in conventional array. Startled she looked down upon them. Did nobody know yet? She should have been watching Carter's face. But of course he would have had his back to her. She could not have told what he was feeling from just his back could she?

She moved a little farther and could see his face now between the next two palms, and it was white as death, white and frightened! Did she imagine it? No, she felt sure. He had swung half reluctantly around into his place beside Arla, but he lifted his hand to his mouth as if to steady his lips and she could see that his hand trembled. Didn't the audience see that? They would. They could not help it. But they would likely lay it to the traditional nervousness all bridegrooms were supposed to feel. Still, *Carter!* He was always so utterly confident, so at his ease anywhere. How could they credit him with ordinary nervousness?

But the ceremony was proceeding now, *her* bridegroom, Carter McArthur, getting married to *another* girl, and there she was above him, unseen, watching.

"Dearly beloved, we are gathered together in the sight of God and in the presence of this company to join together this man and this woman in the bonds of holy matrimony—"

A great wrench came to Sherrill's heart as she looked down and realized that but for a trifling accident she would even now be standing down there in that white dress and that veil getting married! If she had not tried to go through those two rooms without being seen, if she had not planned to go and show herself to Mary—poor Mary who was lying on her bed even now thinking she was forgotten—if just such a little trifle as that had not been, she would be down there with Carter now, blissfully happy, being bound to him forever on this earth as long as they both should live. So irrevocable!

For an instant as she thought of it her heart contracted. Why did she do this awful thing, this thing which would separate her forever from the man she loved so dearly? She could have slipped back into her room unseen, the other girl would have gone away, afraid to do anything else, she could have gone to the church and nobody would ever have been the wiser. She would have been Mrs. McArthur. Then what could Arla Prentiss do? Even if she had taken her life few would have ever heard of it.

But she Sherrill Cameron, even if she were Sherrill McArthur, would never have been happy. She knew that, even as she looked down into the white face of the staring, stony-eyed bridegroom. For between her and any possibility of joy there would always have come that look on his face when he had kissed the other girl, and told her he would always love her best. She never could have laughed down nor forgotten that look. How many other girls had he said that to, she wondered? Was Arla, too, deceived about it? She evidently thought, that she, Sherrill, was her only rival. But there might have been others too. Oh, if one couldn't trust a man what was the joy of marriage? If one were not the only one enthroned in a man's heart why bind oneself to his footsteps for life? Sherrill had old-fashioned simple ideas and standards of love and marriage. But Sherrill was wondering if she would ever be able to trust *any* living man again, since Carter who had always seemed such a paragon of perfection had proved himself so false and weak! No, she could never have married him, not after seeing him with Arla. Oh, were all men like that?

And there he was getting married to the other girl, and not doing a thing about it! She was sure he knew now, and he was making no protest.

And then suddenly she saw her own heart and knew that somewhere back in her mind she had been harboring the hope that he would do something. That he would somehow—she didn't know how for it wasn't reasonable—find a way to stop this marriage and explain all the wrong, and that joy would find its way through sorrow! But he wasn't doing a thing! He didn't dare do a thing! Fear, stark and ugly was written upon his face. He *knew* himself to be guilty. He was standing there before the assembled multitude, the "dearly beloved" of the service, and not one of them knew a thing about what was happening but himself, and he knew, and he *wasn't doing a thing!* He *didn't dare!*

And then, just down below her in the front seat a little motion attracted her eyes. A white ribbon lifted and a figure slid beneath. A young man in a blue serge suit with a pleasant face had glided so quietly into the seat beside the little gray lady with the white laces that nobody around her seemed to have even noticed. He was handing her a folded paper and whispering unobtrusively a word in her ear. Aunt Pat had her note now and in a moment she would know the truth! How would Aunt Pat take it? She was perfectly capable of rising in her delicate little might and putting a stop to the service. How awful it would be for everybody if she did that! Perhaps the note ought to have been held up until the service was over.

Then even with the thought came that frightful challenge. Was it only last night at the rehearsal that they had joked over it?

"Therefore if any man can show just cause why they may not lawfully be joined together, let him now declare it, or else hereafter forever hold his peace."

Her eyes were fastened on Aunt Pat in terror! What if Aunt Pat should arise and say she knew a just cause! Oh, why had she sent that note down so soon? If she could only recall it!

But Aunt Pat was sitting serenely with the note in her hand, reading it, and a look of satisfaction was on her lips, the kind a nice house cat might wear when she had just successfully evaded detection in licking the creamy frosting from a huge cake. Actually, Aunt Pat was looking up with a smile on her strong old face and a twinkle in her bright old eyes. It was almost as if she were *pleased!* The young man in the blue serge who had delivered the note was nowhere in sight, and yet she couldn't remember seeing him slip out again, though the white ribbon was swaying a little as if it had recently been stirred.

That deathly stillness settled down over the audience, an audible stillness, even above the voice of the organ undertone; and Sherrill, puzzling over Aunt Pat, turned fascinated eyes toward her erstwhile lover. How was he standing this challenge? Whichever girl he thought was standing beside him, surely he could not take this calmly. Oh, if she might only look in his face and see his innocence written there! Yet she knew that could never be!

But she was not prepared for the haggard look she saw on his face, a terror such as a criminal at bay might wear when about to face an angry mob who desired to hang him. The look in his eyes was awful! All their gay brilliancy gone! Only fear, uncertainty, a holding of the breath to listen! His hands were working nervously. She felt almost a contemptuous pity for him, and then a wrenching of the heart again. Her lover, to have come to such a place as that! Almost she groaned aloud, and looked toward the radiant bride, for radiant she really seemed to be, carrying out her part perfectly. Sherrill had felt she could do it. She was clever, and she had an overwhelming love!

And yet in spite of her horror over what was happening, somehow as she looked down there it seemed to be her own self that was standing there in that white satin garb and veil about to take sweet solemn vows upon her. What had she done to put her bright hopes out of her life forever! Oh, hadn't she been too hasty? Might there not have been some other explanation than the only obvious one? Ought she perhaps to have gone in and confronted those two in each other's arms?

Then suddenly the girl down there before the altar spoke, and her voice was clear and ringing. The great church full of people held their breath again to catch every syllable:

"I, Arla, take thee, Carter,—"

Sherrill felt her breath coming in slow gasps, felt as if someone were stifling her. She strained her ears to hear, on through that long paragraph that she had learned so carefully by heart, her lips moving unconsciously to form the words ere she heard them. And Arla was speaking them well, clearly, with a triumphant ring to them, like a call to the lover she had lost. Could he fail to understand and answer? Sherrill pressed her hands hard upon her aching heart and tried to take deep breaths to keep her senses from swimming off away from her.

Again she had a feeling as if that girl down there was herself; yet she was here looking on!

And now it was the bridegroom's turn!

Sherrill closed her eyes and focussed every sense upon the words. Would he respond? Would he do something or would he let it go on? For now he surely knew!

His voice was low, husky, she could scarcely hear the words above the tender music that she herself had planned to accompany the troth they were plighting. Afterwards she fancied it must have been by some fine inner sense rather than the hearing of her ears that she knew what he was saying, for he spoke like one who was afraid!

"I Carter, take thee, *Arla—!*"

A-h-h! He had said it. He knew now and he had accepted it! He was taking the words deliberately upon his lips. Shamedly, perhaps, like one driven to it, but he had taken them. Her lover was marrying another girl! He had not even tried to do anything about it!

With a little gasp like a deep driven sob she dropped upon her knees and hid her face in her hands, while the gallery in which she knelt reeled away into space, and she suddenly seemed to be hurled as from a parapet by the hands of her erstwhile bridegroom, down, down into infinite space with darkness growing all about her. Ah! She had been foolish! Why had she not known that this would happen to her? Love like hers could not be broken, torn from its roots ruthlessly, without awful consequences. How had she thought she could go through this and live through it? Was this the end? Was she about to die, shamelessly, and all the world know that she had a broken heart?

Ahh!

A breath of fresh air came sharply into her face from an opening door just as she was about to touch an awful depth, a strong arm lifted her upon her feet, and a glass of cool water was pressed to her lips.

"I thought this might be refreshing," a friendly casual voice said, not at all as if anything unusual were happening.

She drank the water gratefully, and afterward she wondered if it were only fancy that she seemed to remember clinging to a hand. But of course that could not have been.

He looked down at her smiling, as if he might have been a brother.

"Now, do you feel you have to stay up here till this performance is ended and all the people escorted out below?" he asked pleasantly, "or would you like to slip down now and get your car out of traffic before things get thick? You look awfully tired to me, but if you feel you should stay I'll bring up a chair."

"Oh," said Sherrill bewilderedly, "Is it,—Are they almost—?"

She leaned forward to look.

"Just about over I fancy," said the man who was steadying her so efficiently.

And as if to verify his words the voice of the clergyman came clearly:

"I pronounce you husband and wife. . . . Whom therefore God hath joined together, let no man put asunder."

She shuddered and shrank back. The man could feel her tremble as he supported her.

"This would be a good time if you are going to slip away," he whispered. "There is just the brief prayer and then the procession out is rather rapid. I fancy traffic will thicken up quickly after they are out. Or, would you rather wait until they are all gone?"

"Oh, no!" said Sherrill anxiously, "I must get back to the house if possible before they get there!"

"Then we should go at once!"

She cast one more glance down at the two who stood with clasped hands and bowed heads, and rapidly reviewed what was to come.

After this prayer there was the kiss!

She shivered! No, she did not want to see Arla lift her radiant head for that kiss. She had watched him kiss her once that night, she could not stand it again.

"Yes! Let us go quickly!" she whispered hurriedly with one last lingering glance, and then stumbled toward the stairs.

Out in the cool darkness with a little breeze blowing in her face and the bright kind stars looking down Sherrill came to herself fully again, her mind racing on to what was before her.

She was glad for the strong arm that still helped her across the street, but she felt the strength coming into her own feet again.

"I can't ever be grateful enough to you," she said as they reached the car, and she suddenly realized that she had treated him as if he were a mere letter carrier or a drink of water, "you have done a lot for me tonight. If I had more time I would try to make you understand how grateful I am."

"You needn't do that," he said gently. "You just needed a friend for a few minutes and I'm glad I happened by. I wonder if there isn't something more I could do? I'm going to drive you home of course if you'll let me, for you really shouldn't try yourself, believe me. Or is there some friend you would prefer whom I could summon?"

"Oh, no," she said looking frightened, "I don't want *any*one I know. I want to get back before they miss me—And really, I think I could drive. Still if you don't mind, it *would* be a great help. But I hate to take more of your time."

"I'd love to," he said heartily. "I haven't another thing to do this evening. In fact I'm a stranger in town and was wondering what I could do to pass the time until I could reasonably retire."

"You seem to have been just sent here to help in a time of need," she said simply as he put her into the car and then took the wheel himself.

"I certainly am glad," he said. "Now, which way? Couldn't we take a short cut somewhere and keep away from this mob of cars?"

"Yes," said Sherrill roused now fully to the moment. "Turn to the left here and go down that back street."

"I wonder," he said as they whirled away from the church with the triumphant notes of the wedding march breaking ruthlessly into their conversation, "if there wouldn't be some way I could serve you the rest of the evening? I'm wholeheartedly at your service if there is any way in which just a mere, may I say friend, can help out somewhere?"

"Oh," said Sherrill giving him a startled look in the

semi-darkness, "you're really wonderfully kind. But—I hate to suggest any more, and—it's such a silly thing!—"

"Please," said the young man earnestly, "just consider me an old friend for the evening, won't you, and ask what you would ask if I were."

Sherrill was still a second, giving him a troubled look.

"Well, then—would you consider it a great bore to go back with me to that reception and sort of hang around with me a while? Just as if you were an old friend who had been invited to the wedding? You see, I—Well, I'm afraid I'll have to explain."

"You needn't if you don't want to," said the young man promptly. "I'll be delighted to go without explanations. Just give me my cue and I'll take any part you assign me if I can help you in any way. Only, how the dickens am I going to a swell wedding reception in a blue serge suit?"

"Oh," said Sherrill blankly. "Of course, I hadn't thought of that. And I suppose there wouldn't be any place open near here where we could rent some evening things? Well, of course it was a foolish idea, and I oughtn't to have suggested it. I'll go through the thing all right alone I'm sure. I'm feeling better every minute."

"No," said the young man, "It *wasn't* and *you're not!* I've got a perfectly good dress suit and all the fixings in a suitcase up in my room in the hotel and it's just around that corner there. If you think it wouldn't make you too late I could just park you outside a minute and run up and get the suitcase. Then I could put it on in the garage or somewhere couldn't I? Or would it be better for me to get dressed in the conventional manner and take a taxi back?"

"Oh," laughed Sherrill nervously. "Why, we'll stop at the hotel of course. It won't take you long, and they can't have started home yet, can they?"

"They haven't got the bride and groom into their car yet, if you ask me," said the young man blithely. "I doubt if they're out at the front door to judge by that music. I've sort of been humming it inside since we started. You know there's always delay getting the cars started. Here's the hotel. Shall I really stop and get my things?"

While she waited before the hotel she put back her head and closed her eyes, her mind racing ahead to the things she had to do. The worst nightmare of the evening was yet to come, and for an instant as she faced it she almost had a wild thought of leaving the whole thing, kind young man and all and racing off into the world somewhere to hide. Only of course she knew she wouldn't do it. She couldn't leave Aunt Pat like that!

And then almost incredibly the young man was back with a suitcase in his hand.

"I had luck," he explained as he swung himself into the car, "I just caught the elevator going up with a man to the top floor. I had only to unlock my door, snatch up my suitcase and lock the door again, so I caught the elevator coming back. I call that service. How about it?"

"You certainly made record time," said Sherrill. "Now turn right at the next corner and go straight till I tell you to turn."

They were out in a quiet street and making good time when she spoke again.

"I've got to tell you the situation," she said gravely, "or you won't understand what it's all about and why I want you to help. You see, this was *my* wedding tonight."

"Your wedding?" He turned a startled face toward her.

"Yes, and I doubt whether very many have taken it in yet that I wasn't the bride."

"But,—why—how—when—?"

"Yes, of course," explained Sherrill. "It all happened less than an hour ago. I was all dressed to go to the church and I happened to find out about *her*. I—saw them together—saying good bye—"

She caught her breath trying to steady her voice and keep the tears back, and he said gently:

"Don't tell me if that makes it harder. I'll get the idea all right. You want me to hang around and be an old friend, is that the idea?"

"That's it," said Sherrill, "I thought if I just had *some*body—somebody they all *didn't know*—somebody they could think had been an old friend back in my home in the west before I came here, it wouldn't be so hard."

"I understand perfectly," he said, "I am your very special oldest friend, and I'll do my noblest to help you carry off the situation." His voice was gravely tender and respectful, and somehow it gave her great relief to know he would stand by her for the evening.

"You are wonderful," she said in a shaky little voice. "But, I never thought, is there,—have you a wife or, or—somebody who would mind you doing that for a stranger?"

He laughed blithely, as if he were glad about it.

"No, I haven't a wife. I haven't even somebody. Nothing to worry about in that direction. Though I wouldn't think much of them even if I had if they would mind lending me for such an occasion."

"Well, I guess I'm not worth much that I'm letting you do it, but things are almost getting me. I was pretty tired and excited when it happened, and then you know it was less than an hour ago, and kind of sudden."

"Less than an hour ago!" said the young man appalled.

"Why, how did you work it to get the other girl there all dressed up?"

"I waited till he had started to the church. I guess I was dazed at first and didn't know what to do. I just dragged her into my room and made her put on the wedding things, and sent her off in the car. You see the man who was to give me away was a distant cousin who didn't know me, had been late in arriving, and the maid-of-honor was a friend of my aunt's who had never seen me, either."

"But didn't the bridegroom know?"

"Not until he saw her coming up the aisle, or—I'm not sure *when* he knew, but—" there came that piteous catch in her voice again, "I don't know just *when* he knew, but he accepted it all right. He—used *her name* in the service, not mine. I haven't thought much yet about what I did. But I guess it was a rather dreadful thing to do. Still—I don't know what else I could have done. The wedding was all there, and *I* couldn't marry him, could I? Perhaps you think I am a very terrible girl. Perhaps you won't want to pose as my friend now you know."

He could hear that the tears were very near to the surface now and he hastened to say earnestly:

"I think you are a very brave and wonderful girl."

"Here's where we turn," she said breathlessly, "and I think that's their car down two blocks away. They have to go in the front drive, but we'll go on around here to the service entrance. Then we can get in before they see us."

"And by the way, oughtn't I know your name?" he said quietly. "Mine is Graham Copeland, and you can call me 'Gray' for short. It will sound more schoolmatish won't it? All my friends call me Gray."

"Thank you," said Sherrill gravely. "And I'm Sherrill

Cameron. That was my aunt Pat you took the note down to. She is Miss Catherwood. She didn't know either. I had to write and tell her."

"I couldn't help seeing some of the words," he admitted. "Will she stand by you?"

"I—don't know—!" Sherrill hesitated, "I thought I saw a twinkle in her eye, but it may have been indignation. She's rather severe in her judgments. She may turn me right out of the house after it's over. But if I can only get through the evening without shaming her, I won't care. She's been so very kind to me. I know this will be hard for her to bear. She stands very high in the community and is very proud. But she'll be nice to you. And then, there'll be the bridesmaids and ushers. I'll introduce the rest of them. You won't be expected to know everybody. Here we are, and that's the first car just coming into the drive now! Oh, we're in plenty of time! Just leave the car right here. This is out of the way. Yes, lock it. Now, come, we'll go up the fire escape if you don't mind, and then we won't have to explain ourselves."

Swiftly they stole up the iron stairs, Sherrill ahead, reaching down a guiding hand in the dark, giggling a little, nervously, as they stepped inside the window. Then she scuttled him down the back hall, opened a door to a small room that had been fixed up for the occasion as a dressing room, showed him how to find the front stairs, and directed him where to meet her as soon as he was ready.

Back through the two dim rooms where she had so recently come face to face with catastrophe, she hurried; only they were not in confusion now. The maids had been there straightening up. There were no traces of Cassie's suitcase nor Linda's street shoes. All was in immaculate order, the door thrown open to accommodate the expected crowds.

Sherrill slipped into her own room and fastened both doors.

Here too were signs of straightening. Her suitcase was closed, the closet doors and bureau drawers shut, everything put carefully away. But this room of course was not to be used for the guests. It was where the bride was expected to dress for going away.

Sherrill dashed to the dressing table and tried to obliterate as far as possible the traces of the past hour's experience from her face. She didn't care personally how she looked, but she did not want the assembled multitude to remark on her ghastly appearance. If she must go through this evening she would do it gallantly.

She waited long enough to possess herself of a great ostrich fan that just matched the green of her frock. It would be wonderful to hide behind if need came, and give her a brave outfit. Then she put on the gorgeous necklace of emeralds, with three long pendants of emeralds and diamonds, a family heirloom that Aunt Pat had given her just that day. She must have something to replace the bridal pearls that were hers no longer. There were some rings and bracelets too. She hadn't had much time to get acquainted with them. She fingered them over and chose one luscious square cut emerald for her finger. Her hands also should go bravely, not missing the diamond which she had worn for the past four months.

She slipped the magnificent ring on her finger, closed her eyes for a second taking a deep breath, then hurried down stairs.

There were sounds of approach at the front of the house, gay chatter of bridesmaids disembarking from their respective cars. Aunt Pat was just entering the front door leaning on Gemmie's arm. Off in the far corner of the great reception room to the right she could see Carter with his bride huddled under the bower of palms and flowers like a pair of frightened fowls between the clearing of two storms. The bride had her back toward the hall and was talking earnestly. Carter was half turned away too, casting furtive frantic glances behind him, an ungroomly scowl upon his handsome brow. Poor Arla! Her hell had probably begun!

Sherrill unfurled her green fan and went bravely forward to meet Aunt Pat.

GEMMIE gave Sherrill a frightened scrutinizing glance, took the old lady's wrap and scarf and fled, casting another worried puzzled look behind her.

Sherrill took her aunt's arm. The old lady was smiling affably, but there was an inscrutable look about her. Sherrill couldn't tell whether it held disapproval or not. It was a mask, she could see that.

"What's her name? Who is she?" demanded the old lady out of the side of her mouth, without moving her lips or disturbing her smile. She was steering Sherrill straight toward the bridal bower. Sherrill had to speak quickly, keeping her own lips in a smile that she was far from feeling.

"She's his secretary, Arla Prentiss. He's known her for years."

"H'm! The puppy!" grunted the old lady under her smile, and then raising her voice a little. "Come, let's get this line in order! Where's this bride and groom? Mrs. McArthur, Mr. McArthur—" her voice was smooth, even, jovial and yet frigid, if such a combination can be imagined. Just as if she had not been calling the groom "Carter" for the past six weeks!

The bride and groom swung around to face her, the bride with a heightened color and a quick lifting of her chin as of one who expects a rebuff, the groom with every bit of color drained from his handsome face, and points of steel in his sulky eyes.

"I'm sure I hope you'll both be very happy," said Aunt Pat with a grimly humorous twist of her smile, implying perhaps that they didn't deserve to be, and then with just a tinge of the Catherwood haughtiness she took her place in the line as had been arranged.

Now had come the most trying moment for Sherrill, the one spot in the program that she hadn't been able to think out ahead. It was as if she had blindly shut her eyes to the necessity of speaking to these two, unable to prepare the right words of formal greeting, unable to school her expression. And here she was facing them with that silly smile upon her lips and nothing in her heart to say but horror at the situation, which such a brief time ago had been so different!

And then, just as a strange constriction came in her throat to stop any words she might try to form with her cold dumb lips, and her smile seemed to her to be fading out across the room and getting hopelessly away from her forever, she felt a touch upon her arm, and there miraculously was Copeland, meticulously arrayed in evening garb, a cheery grin upon his face, and gay words upon his lips:

"Is this where you want me to be, Sherrill?"

The ice melted from Sherrill's heart, her frightened throat relaxed, fear fled away and the smile danced back into her eyes. He had come in just the nick of time. A warm feeling of gratitude flowed around her heart and her voice returned with a delightful little lilt.

"Oh, is that you, Gray? How did you manage to get back so soon? Yes, this is just where I want you. Let me introduce you to the bride, Mrs. McArthur, my friend Mr. Copeland of Chicago. Mr. McArthur, Graham."

Arla eyed the two keenly.

"Were you old schoolmates?" she asked the stranger brightly, "Carter and I went to school together from kindergarten up through senior high."

"Well, not exactly schoolmates," answered Copeland with an amused glance at Sherrill, "but we're pretty good friends, aren't we, Sherrill?" He cast a look of deep admiration and understanding toward the girl in green and she answered with a glowing look.

"I should say!" she rippled a little laugh. "But come, Graham, they're all arriving in a bunch, and you've got to meet the bridesmaids and ushers. Here, come over to Aunt Pat first!" and they swung away from the astounded bridal couple with formal smiles.

"Aunt Pat, I want you to know Mr. Graham Copeland of Chicago. He's been a really wonderful friend to me. She's Miss Catherwood, Gray. I've told you about her."

"And why haven't I been told about *him* before?" asked Aunt Pat as she took the young man's hand and gave him a keen quick friendly look. Then, as her old eyes twinkled, "Oh, I have met him before, haven't I? You had a blue coat on when I saw you last!" and her lips twisted into what would have been called a grin if she had been a few years younger.

"You're one of the conspirators in this practical joke we're playing, I suppose?" And her eyes searched his again.

"I trust I'm a harmless one, at least," he said gracefully.

And then there came a sudden influx of bridesmaids,

preening their feathers and chattering like a lot of magpies.

They gushed into the room and seemed to fill it with their light and color and jubilant noise.

"Sherrill Cameron! Whatever did you put over on us?"

"Oh, Sherrill, you fraud! All these weeks and we thinking *you* were the bride!"

"What was the idea, Sherrill? Did you expect us to fall over in a faint when we saw another bride?"

"But we all thought it was you for the longest time!"

"I didn't!" said Linda, "I knew when she got out of her car that there was something different about her!"

"Sh!"

Into the midst of the bevy of voices, came Sherrill's clear controlled one, sweet, almost merry, though Aunt Pat turned a keen ear and a keen eye on her and knew she was under great strain:

"Girls! Girls! For pity's sake! Hush with your questions! Come and meet the bride, and then get into the receiving line quick! Don't you see the guests are beginning to arrive?"

The girls turned dizzily about, as Sherrill with a smile almost like her own natural one, approached the bride:

"Arla—" the name slipped off her tongue glibly, for somehow with Aunt Pat and Graham Copeland in the background she felt more at her ease, "Arla—" The bride turned in quick astonishment to hear herself addressed so familiarly, "let me introduce your bridesmaids. This is Linda Winters, and Doris Graeme—"

She went on down the row, speaking their names with more and more confidence, and suddenly the best man, who had been on some errand of his office, loomed frowning beside her.

"And oh, here's the best man! Carter, you'll have to

make the rest of the introductions. I simply must get these girls into place! Here come all the ushers too! I'll leave you to introduce them to your wife!" She said it crisply and moved away to make room for them, pushing the laughing bridesmaids before her and arranging them, with room for the ushers between, though every one knew as well as she did where they ought to stand, having rehearsed it only the night before.

Then Sherrill slid behind them back to her place by Aunt Pat and the stranger, a place that had *not* been rehearsed the night before.

It was a hard place, a trying place, the worst place she could have been. She knew that when she chose it. But she had to face the music, and knew it was better to do it merrily at the head of the line than skulking at the foot where there would be plenty of time for explanations and questions.

So as the crowd of guests surged into the big lovely room, filled with curiosity and excitement, and ready to pull any secret one might have from the air and waft it to the world, it was Sherrill who stood at the head of the line in her lettuce green taffeta, the little frock she had bought as a whimsie at the last minute, her second best silver slippers, and the gorgeous Catherwood emeralds blazing on her neck and arms and finger. She was wafting her great feather fan graciously, and by her side was a handsome stranger! Would wonders never cease? The guests stepped in, gave one eager avid glance and hastened to the fray.

Aunt Pat was next the stranger, smiling her cat-in-the-cream smile, with twinkles in her eyes and a grim look of satisfaction.

"You ought to be at the head of the line, Aunt Pat," demurred Sherrill. "I really don't belong in this line at all."

"Stay where you are!" commanded the old lady. "This is *your* wedding not mine. Run it the way you please. I'm only here to lend atmosphere." She said it from one corner of her mouth and she twinkled at the stranger. She was standing next to the bride and groom but she hadn't addressed two words to them since her congratulations. However, they were getting on fairly well with the best man and maid of honor on the other side, and the stage was set for the great oncoming crowd.

Mrs. Battersea with her ultra-modern daughter-in-law in the wake headed the procession, with the Reamers, the Hayworths and the Buells just behind. They represented the least intimate of the guests, the ones who would really be hard to satisfy. Sherrill with a furtive glance up at the tall stranger by her side, aware of his kindly reassuring grin, felt a sudden influx of power in herself to go through this ordeal. It helped too, to realize that several others were having an ordeal also. It probably wasn't just what this stranger would have chosen to do, to play his part in this strange pageant, and she was sure Aunt Pat hated it all, though she was entering into the scene with a zest as if she enjoyed it. Aunt Pat hated publicity like a serpent.

And there were the bride and groom. One could scarcely expect them to enjoy this performance. Sherrill cast them a furtive glance. The bride was a game little thing. She was holding her head high and conversing bravely with all those chattering bridesmaids, who kept surging out of line to get a word with her. And Carter, well, Carter had always been able to adjust himself to his surroundings pretty well, but there was a strained white look about him. Oh, whatever he might have felt for either of his prospective brides, it was scarcely likely that he was enjoying this reception. It was most probable that he would give all he possessed to have a nice hole open in the floor and let him and his Arla through out of sight.

So Sherrill drew a deep breath, summoned a smile, and greeted Mrs. Battersea, sweeping up in purple chiffon with orchids on her ample breast.

"Now, Sherrill, my dear," said the playful lady, "what does this all mean? You've got to give us a full explanation of everything."

"Why, it was just that we thought this would be a pleasant way to do things," smiled Sherrill, "Don't you think it was a real surprise? Mrs. Battersea, do let me introduce my friend Mr. Copeland of Chicago. Oh, Mrs. Reamer, I'm so glad you got well in time to come—!"

Suddenly Sherrill felt a thrill of triumph. She was getting away with it! Actually she was! Mrs. Battersea had been not only held at bay, but entirely sidetracked by this new young man introduced into the picture. She closed her mouth on the question that had been just ready to pop out and fixed her eyes on Copeland, a new fatuous smile quickly adjusted, as she passed with avidity to the inquisition of this stranger. Here was she, the first in the line, and it was obviously up to her to get accurate information concerning him and convey it as rapidly as possible to the gathering assembly. Sherrill could see out of the tail of her eye this typical Battersea attitude, even as the guest put up her lorgnette to inspect the young man. She felt a pang of pity for her new friend. Did he realize what he was letting himself in for when he promised to stand by her through this? Oh, but what a help he was! How his very presence had changed the attitude that might have been, the attitude of pity for a cast off bride! And, too, he had brought in an element of mystery, of speculation. She could see how avidly

Mrs. Battersea was drinking in the possibilities as she approached.

But Sherrill drew another breath of relief. The young man by her side would be equal to it. She need not worry.

And there too was Aunt Pat! She would not let the first comer linger too long with the new lion of the occasion.

Even with the thought, she heard the woman's first question, and saw Aunt Pat instantly, capably, if grimly, take over the Battersea woman. Whether Aunt Pat was going to forgive Sherrill afterward or not for making such a mess of a beautiful stately wedding which she had financed, she would be loyal now and defend her own whether right or wrong. That was Aunt Pat.

Yes, those two could be depended upon.

And then came Mrs. Reamer fairly bursting with curiosity, and Sherrill was able to smile and greet her with a gracious merriment that surprised herself, and then interrupt the second question with, "Oh, but you haven't met my friend Mr. Copeland of Chicago yet. Graham, this is Mrs. Reamer, one of our nearest neighbors."

The Haywards and Buells were mercifully pressing forward, eager to get in their questions, and Sherrill thankfully handed over Mrs. Reamer to Copeland who dealt with her merrily. So with a lighter heart and well turned phrases she met the next onslaught, marveling that this terrible ordeal was really going forward so gayly, and presently she began to feel the thrill that always comes sooner or later to one who is accomplishing a difficult task successfully.

She was on a strain of course, like one who pilots an airship through the unchartered skies for the first time perhaps, yet she knew that when she got back to earth and her nerves were less taut there was bound to be a reaction. Just now the main thing was to keep sailing and not let anyone suspect how frightened and sick at heart she really was; how utterly humiliated and cast out she felt, with another bride standing there beside the man who was to have been her husband. And he smiling and shaking hands, and withal deporting himself as if he were quite satisfied. She stole a glance at him now and again between hand shakes and introductions, and perceived that he did not appear greatly distraught. His assurance seemed to have returned to him, the whiteness was leaving his lips, his eyes were no longer deep moldering angry fires. He really seemed to be having a good time. Of course he too was playing a part, and there was no telling what his real feelings were. Equally of course he was caught in the tide of the hour and had to carry out his part or bolt and bear the consequences of publicity of which she had warned him. She remembered that he had always been a good actor.

But there was another actor in the line who utterly amazed her. Arla, the bride, filled her part graciously, with a little tilt triumphant to her pretty chin, a glint of pride in her big blue eyes, an air of being to the manor born that was wholly surprising. There she stood in borrowed bridal attire, beside a reluctant bridegroom, wearing another girl's engagement ring, and a wedding ring that was not purchased for her, bearing another girl's roses and lilies, standing under a bower that did not belong to her; and yet she was carrying it all off in the most delightfully natural way. To look at her one would never suspect that an hour ago she had been pleading with her lover to run away with her and leave another girl to wait in vain for him at the church. Well, perhaps she deserved to have her hour of triumph. She certainly was getting all she possibly could out of it. One would never suspect to look at her that she was a girl who had threatened just a little while before to kill herself. She looked the ideal radiant bride.

Sherrill's eyes went back to the face of her former lover for just an instant. It was lit with one of his most charming smiles as he greeted one of his old friends. How she had loved that smile! How like a knife twisting in her heart was the sight of it now! Every line of his face, every motion of his slim white hands, the pose of his fine athletic body, so familiar and so beloved, how the sight of them suddenly hurt her! He was not hers any more! He belonged to another girl! Her mind and soul writhed within her as the thought pierced home to her consciousness with more poignancy than it had yet done. He belonged to another!

But there was something worse than even that. It was that he never really had been what she thought him. There never had existed the Carter McArthur whom she had loved or all this could not have happened.

For an instant it all swept over her how terrible it was going to be to face the devastation in her own life after this evening was over.

Then more people swarmed in and she put aside her thoughts and faced them with a frozen smile upon her face, wondering why everybody did not see what agony she was suffering. She must not look at him again, not think about him, she told herself breathlessly as she faced her eager guests and tried to say more pleasant nothings.

At last there came a lull in the stream of guests and Copeland turned to her confidentially, the gay smile upon his lips, but a graver tone to his voice:

"I'm wondering what you've done about the license? Anything? It might make trouble for all concerned if that's not attended to to-night before they leave. I don't know what your law is in this state, but I'm sure it ought to be looked into right away. I'm a lawyer you know and I can't help thinking of those things."

Sherrill turned a startled face toward him.

"Mercy, no! I never thought of it. We had a license of course. Wouldn't that do?"

He shook his head slightly.

"I'm afraid not. Do you know where the license was got? If we could get hold of the man—"

"Yes, I went along. But the office would be closed to-night wouldn't it?"

"I suppose so. Still if we knew the man's name he might be willing, if there were sufficient inducement, to come over here at once and straighten things out for us."

"Oh, that would be wonderful! Perhaps he'd come for twenty-five dollars, or even fifty. I'd offer him fifty if necessary. It would be dreadful to have that kind of trouble."

Her eyes were full of distress.

"There, don't look so troubled," he said putting on his grin again. "Remember you're a good little sport. This can all be straightened out I'm sure. If you could just give me a clue to find that man. You don't know his name I suppose?"

"Yes, I do," said Sherrill eagerly. "His mail was brought in while we were there and I saw the name on the letters. Afterwards, too, somebody called him by it so I am sure it was he. The name was Asahel Becker. I remembered it because it was so queer. Maybe we could find it in the telephone book. But would he have his stamps and papers and seals and things? Could he get them do you think if we offered him enough?"

"It's worth trying. If you will tell me where I can telephone without being heard by this mob I'll see what I can do."

"There's a booth in the back of the hall under the stairs, but I'll go with you of course."

"No, please, if you are willing to trust me, I think I can handle this without you. You have been taking an awful beating and this is just one thing you don't need to do. Just give me the full names, all three. Here, write them on the card so I won't make a mistake, and then you stay right here and *don't worry!* If I need you I'll come for you."

He gave her a reassuring smile and was gone. Sherrill found she was trembling from head to foot, her lips trembling too. She put up an unsteady hand to cover them. Oh, she must not give way! She must snap out of this. She must not remember yesterday when she went joyously to get that license,—and how her beautiful romance was all turned to dust and ashes!

Just then the three elderly Markham sisters hove in sight moving in a body, fairly bristling with question marks and exclamation points, and she had plenty to do again baffling them, with no Copeland there beside her to help.

But blessed Aunt Pat turned in to help and soon had drawn the attention of all three.

"And this other bride," said the eldest sister, Matilda by name, leveling her gaze on Arla as if she were a museum piece, and then bringing it back to Aunt Pat's face again. "Did you say she was a relative too? A close relative?"

"Yes, in a way," said Aunt Pat grimly, "but not so close. Quite distant in fact. It's on the Adamses side of the family you know."

Sherrill gasped softly and almost gave a hysterical giggle, just catching herself in time.

"Indeed!" said Miss Markham giving the bride another appraising glance, "I wasn't aware there were Adamses in your family. Then she's not a Catherwood?"

"Oh, no!" said Aunt Pat with pursed lips, "In fact," and her voice sounded almost like a chuckle, "the relationship was several generations back."

"Ohh!" sighed the inquisitor lowering her lorgnette and losing interest. "Well, she seems to be quite attractive anyway."

"Yes, isn't she? Now let me introduce you—"

But suddenly Sherrill saw Copeland coming toward her and her eyes sought his anxiously.

"You must be desperately tired," he said in a low tone as he stepped into the line beside her, "couldn't we run away outside for just a minute and get you into the open air?"

"Oh, yes!" said Sherrill gratefully, "Come through here."

She led him to the long French window just behind the line, open to the garden terrace, and they stepped out and went down the walk where pale moonlight from a young moon was just beginning to make itself felt.

"It's all right," he assured her comfortably, drawing her arm within his own. "He'll be here shortly with all his papers and things. He didn't want to do it at first, but finally snapped at the bait I offered him and promised to be here within the hour. Now, had you thought where we can take him?"

"Yes," said Sherrill, "up in that little room where you dressed. That is quite out of the way of all guests and,—" she stopped short in the walk and looked up at her escort with troubled eyes, "we'll have to tell them—the bride and groom—won't we?" Her gaze turned back toward the house anxiously. He could see how she was dreading the ordeal.

"Not yet," he said quickly, "not till our man comes.

Then I'll just give the tip to the best man to ask them to come upstairs. You leave that to me. I'll attend to it all. You've had enough worry."

"You are so kind!" she murmured, beginning to walk along by his side again.

He laid his hand gently over hers that rested on his arm.

"I'm glad if I can help. And by the way I told this Mr. Becker to come to the side entrance and ask for me, and I took the liberty of asking the butler to keep an eye out for him and let me know at once."

"Oh, thank you," she said, "I don't know what I should have done without you!"

"I am honored to be allowed to help," he said, glad that she had not taken away her hand from his touch, although he was not quite sure she was aware of it, she seemed so distraught. "As far as I am concerned," he went on brightly, "if it weren't that you are taking such a beating I'd be having the time of my life!"

Sherrill gave him a quick convulsive laugh that seemed very near to tears.

"Oh, if it weren't all so very terrible," she responded wistfully, "I'd think it was almost fun, you're being so splendid!"

"You're a brave girl!" said Copeland almost reverently.

They had reached the end of the garden walk.

"I suppose we ought to go back in there," said Sherrill with a little shiver of dislike. "They'll be wondering where we are."

They turned and walked silently back a few steps, when suddenly a bevy of young people broke forth hilariously from the house swinging around the corner from the front piazza and evidently bound for the garden.

"Oh!" said Sherrill shrinking back, "We've got to meet them!"

"Isn't there some place we can hide for a minute until they have passed?" asked Copeland with a swift glance at their surroundings, "Here, how about this?" and he swung aside the tall branches of privet that bordered the path around the house and the hedge.

Sherrill stepped in and Copeland after her and the branches swung together behind them shutting them in together. There was not much space, for it happened that the opening in the hedge had been near the servants' entrance door, and the hedge curved about across the end, and at the other end it rose nearly twelve feet against the end of the side piazza where they had come out. It made a little room of fragrant green, scarcely large enough for them to stand together in, with the ivy-covered stone wall of the house behind them.

There in the sweet semi-darkness of the spring night, where even frail new moonlight could not enter except by reflection, and with only a few stars above, they stood, face to face, quietly, while the noisy throng of guests trooped by and rollicked down to the garden.

Sherrill's face was lifted slightly and seemed a pale picture made of moonlight, so sweet and sad and tired and almost desperate there in the little green haven. Copeland looking down suddenly put out his arms and drew her close to him, just as a mother might have drawn a little troubled child, it seemed to her. Drew her close and held her so for an instant. She let her head lie still against his shoulder, startled at the sweetness that enwrapt her. Then softly she began to cry, her slim body shaking with the stifled sobs, the tears coming in a torrent. It was so sweet to find sympathy even with a stranger.

Softly he stooped and kissed her drenched eyelids,

kissing the tears away, then paused and looked down at her reverently.

"Forgive me!" he said tenderly in a low whisper, "I had no right to do that—now! I'm only a stranger to you! But—I wanted to comfort you!"

She was very still in his arms for a moment and then she whispered so softly that he had to bend to hear her: "You *aren't* a stranger, and—you *do*—comfort me!"

Suddenly above their heads there arose a clatter inside the window of the butler's pantry.

"Quick, get those pattie shells! The people are coming out to the dining room. We must begin to serve!"

Dishes began to rattle, trays to clatter, a fork fell with a silvery resonance. The swinging door fell back and let in another clatter from the kitchen. Hard cold facts of life began to fall upon the two who had been so set apart for the moment.

"We must go back at once!" said Sherrill making hasty dabs at her eyes with her scrap of lace handkerchief.

"Of course," said Copeland offering a large cool square of immaculate linen.

Then he took her hand and led her gravely out into the moonlight, pulled her arm possessively through his and accommodated his step to hers.

When they came to the long window where they had escaped a few minutes before he looked down at her.

"Are you all right?" he asked softly.

"All right!" she answered with a brave little catch in her breath, and smiled up at him.

He still held her hand and he gave it a warm pressure before he let her go. Then they stepped inside the room and saw the end of the long line of guests progressing slowly down the hall and Aunt Pat hovering behind them looking this way and that, out the front door, and into the vacated library. It was evident she was looking for Sherrill for as they came forward her brow cleared, she smiled a relieved smile, and came to meet them.

Just an instant she lingered by Sherrill's side as Copeland stepped to the dining room door to look over the heads of the throng and reconnoitre for seats for them all.

"I don't know how you have planned," said the old lady in something that sounded like a low growl, "nor how long this ridiculous performance has been going on, but I thought I'd remind you that it will be necessary for that girl to have some baggage if you expect to carry this thing out. I don't want to interfere with your plans, but there's that second suitcase, the one that wasn't marked that we had sent up. It hasn't been returned yet you know. I suppose you'll have to see that she has things enough to be decent on ship board, unless she has time enough to get some of her own. But if you let that lace evening dress, or that shell-pink chiffon go I'll never forgive you. It's bad enough to lose the going-away outfit, but I suppose there isn't any way out of that. A couple of evening dresses and some sport things ought to see her through. Don't be a fool and give up everything!" and Miss Catherwood with her head in the air and a set smile on her aristocratic face swept on to the dining room.

Sherrill stood startled, looking after her doubtfully. Did that mean that Aunt Pat was angry? Angry yet going to stand by till it was all over to the last detail? Or did it mean that she understood the awful situation better than Sherrill knew? She was a canny old lady. How wonderfully she had stood and met that line of hungry gossip mongers! But yet, she might still be angry. Very angry! To be the talk of the town when she had done so much to make this wedding perfect in every way. To have people wondering and gossiping about them! It would be dreadful for Aunt Pat!

Sherrill had a sudden vision of what it might be to face an infuriated Aunt Pat and explain everything after it was all over, and she had that panicky impulse once more to flee away into the world and shirk it,—never come back any more. But of course she knew she never would do that!

Then Copeland touched her on the arm.

"Please, do we follow the rest, or what?" and she perceived that they two were left alone in the room, with only the end of the procession surging away from them toward the dining room.

Sherrill giggled nervously.

"I haven't much head, have I?" she said. "I've got to go upstairs a minute or two and put some things in a suitcase. It won't take long. Perhaps I'd better go now."

"Yes," said Copeland thoughtfully. "Now would be a good time. I'll wait here at the foot of the stairs for you."

She flew up the stairs with a quick smile back at her helper. He was marvelous! It could not be that he was an absolute stranger! It seemed as if she had known him always. Here she had almost laid bare her heart to him and he had taken it all so calmly and done everything needful, just as if he understood all the details. No brother could have been tenderer, more careful of her. She remembered his lips on her eyelids and her breath came quickly. How gentle he had been!

She hurried to her own room and miraculously found Gemmie there before her, the suitcase in her hand.

"Your Aunt Pat thought you might be wanting this," said the woman respectfully, no hint of her former surprise in her eyes, no suggestion that aught was different from what it had been when the old servant left her there in her wedding dress ready to go to the church.

"Oh, yes!" said Sherrill in relief. "You'll help me, won't you, Gemmie?"

With half frenzied fingers Sherrill went to work, laying out things from her suitcase and bags, separating them into two piles upon the bed. The black satin evening dress, the orchid, and the yellow, those ought to be enough. Aunt Pat wasn't especially crazy about any of those. She put aside the things that were marked with her own initials, not one of those should go. She shut her lips tight and drew in a sharp little breath of pain.

Gemmie seemed to understand. She gathered those things up quickly and put them away in the bureau drawers. Gemmie's powers of selection were even keener than Sherrill's.

It did not take long, three or four minutes, and Gemmie's skillful fingers did the rest.

"There, now, Miss Sherrill, I can manage," she said. "You run back. They'll be missing you."

It was as if Gemmie was also a conspirator.

"Thank you, Gemmie dear!" said Sherrill with a catch in her voice like a sob, and closed the door quickly behind her.

Copeland was waiting at the foot of the stairs and they found places saved for them close to the bride's table, a little table for two, and the eyes of all upon them as they sat down.

Sherrill saw the Markham sisters looking eagerly from Copeland to herself and back again, and nodding their heads violently to one another as they swept in large mouthfuls of creamed mushrooms and chicken salad. She had an impulse to put her head down on the table and laugh, or cry. She knew she was getting very near to the limit of her self control.

But Copeland knew it also, and managed to keep her busy telling him who the different people were.

After all the ordeal was soon over, even to the cutting of the wedding cake by a bride very much at her ease, and enjoying her privileges to the last degree. If Arla never was happy again she was to-night.

And then after all the matter of the license which loomed like a peril in Sherrill's thoughts was arranged so easily. Just a quiet word from the butler to Copeland, a quiet sign from Copeland to the best man. Sherrill had put money in her little pearl evening bag which she slipped to Copeland as they went upstairs together while the bride was throwing Sherrill's bouquet to the noisy clamoring bridesmaids down in the hall. Sherrill and Copeland were presumably escorting the bride and groom to their rooms to change into traveling garb, and no one noticed them enter the little room off the back hall where the representative of the law was waiting.

Just a few quiet questions from the grizzly old man who had come to make the legal part right, and who looked at them as only three more in the long procession that came to him day by day. They waited, those five, the best man doing his best not to seem too curious about it all, while those important seals were placed, and the proper signature affixed, and then Sherrill hurried the bride away to dress. A frightened almost tearful bride now, afraid of her, Sherrill was sure.

Almost the last lap of this terrible race she was running! There would be one more. She would have to face Aunt Pat, but that she dared not think about yet. This present session with the bride who had taken her place was going to be perhaps the hardest of all.

SHERRILL led her white bride through the two middle rooms again, hurriedly, silently, remembering with sharp thrills of pain all that had happened earlier in the evening. She dreaded intensely the moment when they two would be shut in together again. One would have to say something. One could not be absolutely silent, and somehow her tongue felt heavy and her brain refused to think.

But Gemmie was there! Dear Gemmie! Ah! She had forgotten Gemmie! What a relief! Gemmie with her most professional air of dignity.

The frightened little bride did not feel relief however at her presence. She faltered at the doorway and gave Sherrill a pitiful look of protest. Sherrill drew her inside and fastened the door, feeling suddenly an infinite pity for this girl among strangers in a role that belonged to another.

"Oh, here is Gemmie!" she said gently. "She will help you off with the veil and dress. Gemmie knows how to do it without mussing your hair."

Arla submitted herself to Gemmie's ministrations and

Sherrill hovered about looking over the neatly packed suitcase, and the great white box that Gemmie had set forth on the bed.

"Oh, you have the box ready for the wedding dress, haven't you, Gemmie?" said Sherrill feeling she must break this awful silence that seemed to pervade the room. "That's all right. Gemmie will fold it for you and get it all ready to be sent to whatever address you say."

"Oh," began Arla, with a hesitant glance toward Gemmie and then looking Sherrill almost haughtily in the eye, "I couldn't think of keeping it. I really couldn't!"

"Certainly you will take it," said Sherrill sternly. "It is your wedding dress! *You* were married in it. *I* wouldn't want it you know."

Arla answered with a quick-drawn startled "Oh!" of comprehension. Then she added, "And I'm afraid I wouldn't either!"

Over Sherrill's face there passed a swift look of sympathy.

"I see," she said quietly. "You wouldn't want it of course. I'm sorry. You are right. I'll keep it."

Arla was silent until she was freed from the white veil and sheathing satin, but when Gemmie brought forth the dark slip and lovely tailored going-away costume that Sherrill had prepared for herself she suddenly spoke with determination:

"No," she said with a little haughty lifting of her pretty chin, "I will wear my own things away. Where are they? Did somebody take them away?"

"They are here," said Sherrill, a certain new respect in her voice that had not been there before. "But—you are perfectly welcome to the other dress. I think it would fit you. We are about the same size."

"No," said Arla determinedly, "I prefer to wear my

own dress. It is new and quite all right. Wouldn't you prefer to wear your own things?" She asked the question almost fiercely.

"I suppose I would," said Sherrill meekly. "And I remember your dress. It was very pretty. But I just wanted you to feel you were perfectly welcome to wear the other."

"Thank you," said Arla in a choking voice, "but there is no need. You have done enough. You really have been rather wonderful, and I want you to know that I appreciate it all."

Gemmie, skillfully folding the rich satin, managed somehow to give the impression that she was not there, and presently took herself conveniently out of the room.

Sherrill looked up pleasantly.

"That's all right," she said with a wan smile, "and now listen! I've packed some things for you in this suitcase. I think there will be enough to carry you through the trip."

"That wouldn't be necessary either," said the other girl coldly, "I can get some things somewhere."

"I'm afraid not," said Sherrill. "You'll barely have time to make the boat train. The ship sails at midnight. You might be able to stop for a few personal things if you don't live too far out of the way, but you'd have to hurry awfully. You couldn't take more than five minutes to get them, and you couldn't possibly pack for a trip to Europe in that time."

"Then I can get along without things!" said the bride with a sob in her voice.

"Don't be silly!" said Sherrill in a friendly voice. "You can't make the trip into an endurance test. You've got to have the right things of course. You're on your wedding trip you know, and there may be people on board that Carter knows. You've got to look right."

She wondered at herself as she said all this coolly to this other girl who was taking the trip in her place. It was just like a terrible dream that she was going through. A wild thought that perhaps it was a dream passed through her weary mind. Perhaps she would presently wake up and find that none of all this nightmare was true. Perhaps there wasn't any Arla, and Carter had never been untrue!

Idle thoughts of course! She pushed them frantically from her and tried to talk practically.

"I haven't put much in, just some sports things and three little evening dresses. Necessary under things and accessories of course. Some slippers too, and there's a heavy coat for the deck. The bag is fitted with toilet articles. You won't need to stop for any of your own unless you feel you must."

"Oh, I feel like a criminal!" the bride said suddenly, and sank into a chair with her golden head bowed and her face in her hands, sobbing.

"Nonsense!" said Sherrill under the same impulse with which she might have dashed cold water in the girl's face if she had been fainting. "Brace up! You've got through the worst! For pity's sake don't get red eyes and spoil it all. Remember you've got to go down stairs and smile at everybody yet. Stop it! Quick!"

She offered a clean handkerchief.

"Now look here! Be sensible! Things aren't just as either you or I would have had them if we'd had our choice! But we've got this thing to go through with now, and we're not going to pass out just at the last minute. Be a good sport and finish your dressing. There isn't a whole lot of time you know. Say, that is a pretty frock! I hadn't noticed it closely before. It certainly is attractive. Come, get it fastened and I'll find your shoes and stockings."

Arla accepted the handkerchief and essayed to repair

the damages on her face, but her whole slender body was quivering.

"I've—taken your—hus—band—," she began with trembling lips.

"You have not!" said Sherrill with flashing eyes. "He's *not my* husband, thank goodness!"

"You'd—have—been—happpp-py—" sobbed Arla, "if—you—just—hadn't—found—out—! It would have been much bbbet-ter if I had kkkkilled myself!"

"Don't you suppose I'd have found out eventually that he was that sort? And what good would your killing yourself have been? Haven't you any sense at all? For pity's sake stop crying! *You're* not to blame." Sherrill was frantic. The girl seemed to be going all to pieces.

"Yes I am! I've taken your husband—!" went on Arla getting a fresh start on sobs, "and I've taken your wedding away from you, and now you want me to take your clothes—*And I can't do it!"*

"Fiddlesticks!" said Sherrill earnestly. "I tell you I don't *want* your husband, and if anybody wanted a frantic wedding such as this has been they are welcome to it. As for the clothes, they're all new and have never become a part of me. I'm glad to have you have them, and anyway you've *got* to, to carry out this thing right! Now stop being a baby and get your shoes on. I tell you the time is going fast. Listen! I *want* you to have those things. I really do! And I *want* you to have just as good a time as you can. Don't you believe it?"

"Oh, you're wonderful!" said Arla suddenly jumping up and flinging her slender young arms around Sherrill's neck, "I just love you! And to think I thought you were so different! Oh, if I'd known you were like this I wouldn't have come here! I really wouldn't!"

"Well, I'm glad you came!" said Sherrill fiercely. "I didn't know it but I guess I really am. Of course I'm not having a particularly heavenly time out of it, but I'm sure in my heart that you've probably done me a great favor, and some day when I get over the shock I'll thank you for it!"

"Oh, but I wouldn't have wanted to hurt you," sighed Arla, her red lips still quivering, "I really wouldn't. I've always been—well—decent—!"

"That's all right!" said Sherrill blinking her own tears back. "And I wouldn't have wanted to hurt you either. There! Let's let it go at that and be friendly. Now, please, powder your nose and brisk up. *Smile!* That's it!"

Just then Gemmie came back, a big warm coat over her arm, richly furred as to collar and sleeves.

"It's getting late, Mrs. McArthur!" she suggested officially, and presented Arla's chic little hat and doeskin gloves with a look of approbation toward them. Gemmie had decided that the substitute bride must be a lady. At least she knew how to buy the right clothes.

Arla paused at the door as Gemmie stepped off down the hall to direct the man who had come to take the suitcase, and whispered to Sherrill:

"I'll never forget what you've done for me! *Never!*" she said huskily.

"That's all right," said Sherrill almost tenderly as she looked at the pretty shrinking girl before her, "I'm just sorry you couldn't have had a regular wedding instead of one all messed up with other things like this."

"Oh, but I never could have afforded a wedding like this!" sighed Arla wistfully.

"Well, it might at least have been peaceful," said Sherrill with a tinge of bitterness in her voice, "But never mind. It's over now, and I hope a good happy life for you has begun. Try not to think much about the past. Try to make yours a happy marriage if it can be done."

They passed on together down the hall to the head of

the stairs where Carter McArthur and his best man stood waiting, and as she saw her bridegroom standing there so handsome and smiling and altogether just what a happy bridegroom ought to look like there came to Arla new strength. She lost her sorrowful humility and became the radiant bride again. That was her *husband* standing there waiting for her! *Her* husband, not another girl's! Only a short walk down the stairs now, a dash to the car, and she would be out and free from all this awfulness, and into a new life. She might be going into hell, but she was going with him, and it was what she had chosen.

Then suddenly, as Arla's hand was drawn within the arm of her bridegroom and they walked smilingly down the stairs with measured tread, Sherrill, falling in behind, felt greatly alone and lost. A sinking feeling came over her. Was she going to fall? That would be dreadful, now when it was almost over. Must she walk down those steps alone? Couldn't she just slip back to her room and stay there till they were all gone?

But just as she faltered at the top step she felt a hand under her arm and a pleasant voice said in her ear:

"Well, is it all over now but the shouting?" and she looked up to see the cheerful grin of Copeland.

She had forgotten his existence in the last few tense minutes, but he had been waiting, had seen her weakness, and was there just at the right moment.

"Did anybody ever before pick up a friend like you right out of the street in the dark night?" she asked suddenly, lifting grateful eyes to his face.

"Why, I thought it was *I* who picked *you* up!" he answered quickly with a warm smile.

"Well, anyway you have been wonderful!"

"I'm only too glad if I have been able to live up to the specifications," he said earnestly, and finished with his delightful grin again.

The people down in the hall looking up said to one another:

"Look at those two! They look as if it was *their* wedding, don't they? Who *is* he do you suppose, and where has he been all this time?"

Sherrill stood with the rest on the wide front veranda watching the bride and groom dash across to their beribboned car which awaited them. She even threw a few of the pink rose petals wherewith the guests were hilariously pelting the bridal couple. Even now at this last moment, when she was watching another girl go away with her bridegroom, she must smile and keep up appearances; although her knees felt weak and the tears were dangerously near.

Mrs. Battersea had stationed herself and her lorgnette in the forefront, and fixed her eagle eye especially on Sherrill. If there was still any more light on the peculiar happening of the evening to be gleaned from a view of the original bride off her guard, at this last minute, she meant to get it.

Sherrill suddenly visioned her and it had the effect of making her give a little hysterical giggle. Then Copeland's hand on her arm steadied her again, and she flashed a grateful smile up to meet his pleasant grin.

Mrs. Battersea dropped her lorgnette, deciding that of course this was the other lover appeared just at the last minute, only *how* did they get that other girl?

They were all gone at last. The last guest had joked Aunt Pat on her wonderful surprise wedding, the last bridesmaid had taken her little box of wedding cake to sleep on and stolen noisily away. Just Aunt Pat and Sherrill and Copeland left standing alone in the wide front hall as the last car whirled away.

Copeland had stayed to the end, as if he were a part of the household, stayed close by Sherrill, taken the burden of the last conversations upon himself as if he had the right, made every second of those last trying minutes just as easy for her as possible, kept up a light patter of brilliant conversation filling in all the spots that needed tiding over.

"And now," said he turning to the hostess as the last car whirled down the lighted driveway, "I have to thank you, Miss Catherwood, for a most delightful evening. Sherrill, it's been wonderful to have had this time with you. I must be getting on my way. I think your butler is bringing my things."

Just then the butler came toward them bearing Graham Copeland's suitcase and high hat. Sherrill looked up in surprise. With what ease he had arranged everything so that there would be no unpleasant pauses for explanation.

But Aunt Pat swung around upon him with a quick searching look at Sherrill.

"Why, where are you staying?" she asked cordially.

"I'm at the Wiltshire," he answered quickly, "I hadn't time to get into proper garb before the ceremony, so I brought my things up here and Sherrill very kindly gave me a place to dress."

"Well, then why don't you just stay here to-night? It's pretty late I guess. We've plenty of rooms now you know," and she gave him a little friendly smile that she gave only to an honored few whom she liked.

"Thank you," he said with an amused twinkle at Sherrill, "that would be delightful, but I've an appointment quite early in the morning, and my briefcase is at the hotel. I think I'd better go back to my room. But I certainly appreciate the invitation."

"Well, then, you'll be with us to dinner to-morrow night surely. That is, unless you and Sherry have made other plans."

"I certainly wish I could," said the young man wistfully, "but unfortunately I am obliged to take the noon train for Washington to meet another appointment which is quite important."

Aunt Pat looked disappointed.

"I wonder," said the young man hesitantly, "I'm not sure how long I shall be obliged to stay in Washington, several days likely as I have some important records to look up at the Patent Office, but I shall be passing through the city on my way to New York some time next week probably. Would I be presuming if I stopped off and called on you both?"

"Presuming?" said Aunt Pat with a keen look at Sherrill. "Well, not so far as I know," and she gave one of her quaint little chuckles.

"I do hope you can," said Sherrill earnestly with a look that left no doubt of her wish in the matter.

His eyes searched hers gravely for an instant and then he said as though he had received a royal command:

"Then I shall surely be here if it is at all possible. I'll call up and find out if it is convenient."

"Of course it'll be convenient!" said the old lady, *"I'm* always at home whether anybody else is or not, and *I'll* be glad to see you."

He bowed a gracious thanks, then turned to Sherrill as if reluctant to relinquish his office of assistant.

"I'll hope you'll be—" he hesitated, then finished earnestly, "all right."

There was something in his eyes that brought a warm little comforted feeling around her heart.

"Oh, yes!" she answered fervently. "Thank you! You were—It was wonderful having you here!" she finished with heightened color.

"Oh, but you're not going that way!" said the old

lady. "Gemmie, tell Stanley to bring the car around and take Mr. Copeland—"

A moment more and he was gone and Sherrill had a sudden feeling of being left alone in a troublous world.

Now she must have it out with Aunt Pat!

Slowly she turned away from the door and faced the old lady, all her lovely buoyant spirits gone, just a weary troubled little girl who looked as if she wanted to cry.

"WELL," said Aunt Pat with grim satisfaction in her voice, "you never did anything in your life that pleased me so much!"

"Oh, you darling Aunt Pat!" said Sherrill her face glowing with sudden relief, and quick tears brimming unbidden into her eyes.

"Why certainly!" said the old lady crisply. "You know I never did like that Carter McArthur. Now, come upstairs to my room and tell me all about it!"

"Oh, but aren't you too tired to-night, Aunt Pat?" asked Sherrill, struggling under the shock of relief.

"Bosh!" said Aunt Pat. "You know neither you nor I will sleep a wink till we've had it out. Run get your kimono on. I suppose you gave the grand new one to that little washed-out piece. Of course she had to have it. But put on your old one with the blue butterflies. I like that one best anyway. Gemmie,—" raising her voice to the faithful maid who was never far away, "Send up two plates of *every*thing to my room. *Every*thing, I said. We're hungry as bears. Neither of us ate as much as a bird while that mob was here. No, you needn't worry,

Gemmie, it won't hurt me this time of night at all. I'm as chipper as a squirrel, and if I've stood this evening and all the weeks before it I certainly can stand one good meal before I sleep. The fact is Gemmie, things have come out my way to-night, and I don't think anything could very well hurt me just now."

"Yes, Ma'am!" said Gemmie with a happy glance toward Sherrill.

A general air of good cheer pervaded Aunt Pat's room when Sherrill, in her old kimono of shell pink satin with blue butterflies fluttering over it, and her comfortable old slippers with the lamb's wool lining and pink feather edges, arrived and was established in a big stuffed chair at one side of the open fire. Aunt Pat with her silver hair in soft ringlets around her shoulders, sat on the other side of the fire robed in dove gray quilted silk.

Gemmie brought two little tables and two heaping trays of food, and left them with the lights turned low. The firelight flickered over the two, the young face and the old one.

"Now," said Aunt Pat, "Who *is* he?"

Sherrill looked up puzzled.

"The other one, I mean. You certainly picked a winner this time if I may be permitted a little slang. He seems to be the key to the whole situation. Begin with him! Where have you been keeping him all this time? And why haven't I been told about him before? Is he an old schoolmate, to quote Mrs. Battersea, and how long have you known him?"

"I haven't!" said Sherrill with a sound of panic in her voice.

"You *haven't?"* asked her aunt with a forkful of chicken salad paused half way to her mouth. "What do you mean, you haven't? You certainly seemed to know him pretty well, and he you."

"But I don't, Aunt Pat. I don't really know him at all."

"But—where did you meet him?"

"On the street."

"On the street! When?"

"To-night."

"Mercy!" said Aunt Pat with a half grin. "Explain yourself. You're not the kind of girl that goes around picking up men on the street."

"No!" said Sherrill with a choke of tears in her voice. "But I did this time. I really did. At least—he says he picked me up. You see, I fell into his arms!"

"Mmmm!" said Aunt Pat enjoying her supper and scenting romance. "Go on. That sounds interesting."

"Why, you see it was this way. I parked my car in a hurry to get up into the gallery and when I went to get out I caught my toe in one of those long ruffles, or else I stepped on it, anyway, I fell headlong out on the pavement. Or at least I would have if this man hadn't been there and caught me. I guess I was so excited I didn't really realize that I was pretty well shaken up. Perhaps I struck my head, I'm not sure. It felt dizzy and queer afterward. But he stood me up and brushed me off and insisted on going across the road with me. I guess I must have been unsteady on my feet for when he found I wanted to go upstairs to the gallery he almost carried me up, and he was very nice and helpful. He took that note down to you and then got me a drink of water."

"H'm!" said Aunt Pat with satisfaction. "He's what I call a real man. Nice face! Makes me think of your father when he was young. I couldn't make out how you'd take up with that little pretty-face McArthur nincompoop after seeing a man like this one."

"Why, Aunt Pat!" said Sherrill in astonishment, "I never knew you felt that way about Carter! You never said you did!"

"What was the use of saying? You were determined to have him. But go on. How did this Graham fellow get up here, and how did he get to calling you by your first name, and you him?"

"Well, you see, I slipped out just before the ceremony was over. He said I wasn't fit to drive, he'd either drive himself or get some friend if I said so. But I was in a hurry so I let him drive. I wasn't thinking about formalities then. I knew I ought to get back home quickly. Anyhow he was so respectful I knew he was all right."

"H'm! There are respectful crooks sometimes! But never mind, go on."

"But really Aunt Pat, I don't know what you'll think of me! I haven't had time before this to think what a dreadful thing it was I did, a total stranger, but it didn't seem so then. It seemed just a desperate spot in life. You'd let a stranger pull you out of the street when a mad dog was coming or something like that. I'm afraid you'll be horrified at me. But he was really very kind. He offered to do anything in the world, said he was a stranger in town with the evening to pass, before he met a business appointment in the morning, and if there was any way at all he could help—"

"For mercy's sake, child, stop apologizing and tell things as they happened. I'm not arraigning you."

"Well, I let him come home with me. I knew it would be easier if there was someone that everybody didn't know, and I let him come."

"H'm!" said the old lady with a thoughtful smile that the firelight showed off to perfection. "Well, he certainly was clever enough. But how did he get a dinner coat?"

"Oh, we stopped at the hotel and got his suitcase. He'd been to a dinner the night before in Cleveland. I let him dress in the little room at the end of the back hall.

We came in up the fire escape just before the first car arrived."

"H'm! Clever pair!" commented the old lady as she took delicate bites of her creamed mushrooms. "Well, now get back to your story. How long have you known about this other girl, Artie, was that her name?"

"Arla."

"Silly name! But go on. How long has this double business been going on?"

"I don't know," said Sherrill wearily, "always I guess."

"I mean when did you find it out?"

"Just after you left the house for the church," answered the girl with downcast eyes. Now she was at the beginning of the real story, and it suddenly seemed to her as if she could not possibly tell that part.

The old lady gave her a startled look. She knew that they were now come to the crux of the matter. Sherrill had been so brave up to this point and had carried matters off with such a spirit that she had somehow hoped that Sherrill was not so hard hit. Hoped against hope perhaps, that the final discovery was but the culmination of long suspicions.

"You don't say!" said the old lady, her usual serio-comic manner quite shaken. "But how? I don't see what—How—!"

Sherrill shut her eyes and drew a quick deep breath, then began.

"I was all ready. So I made Gemmie hurry on to the church. I wanted her to be there to see it all, and I wanted to go and see Mary the cook. I'd promised her to come after I got dressed. I knew Gemmie would try to stop me so I wouldn't let her wait as she wanted to. As soon as she was gone I unlocked my door into the next room, and went softly through toward the back hall."

Sherrill had to stop for another deep breath. It seemed as though she was about to go through the whole terrible experience again.

"Well?" said the old lady sharply laying down her fork with a click on the china plate.

"As I stepped into the end room which was dark," she began again trying to steady her voice, "I saw that the door into the middle room was open and the light streaming across the floor. I listened for an instant but heard nothing. I was afraid some of those strange servants would be snooping about. Then I stepped softly forward and saw Carter standing before the long mirror arranging his tie."

"Yes?" said the old lady breathlessly.

"I watched him just a second. I didn't want to stir lest he would hear me, and I wanted him to see me first as I came up the aisle—"

Sherrill's voice trailed away sorrowfully. Then she gathered strength again.

"But while I watched him I saw the door beside the mirror open noiselessly, and that girl came in!"

"H'm!" said Aunt Pat allowing herself another bite of oyster pattie, but keeping her eyes speculatively on her niece. "She must have come up the fire escape or somebody would have seen her."

"She did," said Sherrill wearily, putting her head back and closing her eyes for an instant. Somehow the whole thing suddenly overwhelmed and sickened her again. It seemed she could not go on.

"Well?" said the old lady impatiently. "Did she see you?"

"No." Sherrill's voice was almost toneless. "No, but—"

"There! there! child! I know it's hard, but it's got to

be told once, and then we'll close it over forever if you say so."

"Oh, I know," said Sherrill, sitting up and taking up her tale with a little shudder that seemed to shake her whole slender self.

"No, she didn't see me. She was looking at him. She went straight to him and began to talk, and I could see by his whole attitude that they were old friends. He was shocked when he saw her, and very angry. He ordered her out and scolded her, but she pled with him. It was really heart breaking. Just as if he had been nothing to me. I couldn't help feeling sorry for her, though I thought her—Oh, at first I thought her the lowest of the low. Then I recognized her as his secretary, and of course I guess I thought still less of her, because she would have known that he was engaged."

"Yes, of course!" said Aunt Pat in a spritely tone. "Well, what else?"

"Well, she began pleading with him to go away with her. She reminded him that he had promised to marry her, and in his answer he acknowledged that he had, but oh, Aunt Pat! It is too dreadful to tell!"

"That's all right, Sherrill, get it out of your system. No way to do that like telling it all, making a clean sweep of it! Besides, sometime you'll want to look back on it and remember that you had the assent of someone else that you did the right thing. Even though you're sure you're right there will come times when you will question yourself perhaps."

"I know!" said Sherrill quickly with that sharp intake of breath that shows some thought has hurt, "I have already!" Her aunt gave her a sharp keen look.

"Poor kiddie!" she said gently.

"Oh, I know I never could have married him," went on Sherrill heart-brokenly. "Only it is so dreadful to have my life all upset in one awful minute that way! To know in a flash that everything you've ever counted on and trusted in a person had no foundation whatever! That he simply wasn't in the least what I had thought him. Why, Aunt Pat, he had the nerve to tell her that it didn't matter if he was marrying someone else, that wouldn't hinder their relation. He reminded her that after he got home from the wedding trip he would spend far more time with her than with me, and that whenever he wanted to get away for a few days it would be entirely possible! Oh, Aunt Pat—it was too dreadful—! And I standing there not daring to breathe! Oh!" Sherrill put her face down in her hands and shook with suppressed sobs.

"The dirty little puppy!" said Aunt Pat setting down her plate with a ring on the table. Then she got up from her big chair and came across to Sherrill laying a frail roseleaf hand on her bowed head.

"You poor dear little girl!" she said tenderly, more tenderly than Sherrill had ever heard her speak before.

For a moment then the tears had full sway, let loose by the unusual gentleness of the old lady's voice, till they threatened to engulf her. Then suddenly Sherrill lifted her face all wet with tears, and drew Aunt Pat's hand to her lips kissing it again and again.

"Oh, Aunt Pat! It's so wonderful of you to take it this way! You've done so much to make this a wonderful wedding, spent all this money, and then had it finish in a terrible scandal like this!"

"It's not a scandal!" protested the old lady. "You carried it off like a thoroughbred and nobody will ever know what happened. You were the bravest girl I ever knew. You are like your father, Sherrill." Her tone was very gentle now, and soft. It hardly sounded like herself, and her sharp old eyes were misted with sweet tears.

"And why wouldn't I take it this way, I should like to know when I was pleased to pieces at what had happened?"

Then suddenly she straightened up, marched back to her seat and took up her plate again. Her eyes were snapping now, and her tone was far from gentle as she said:

"But it was far too good a thing to happen to Carter McArthur. He ought to have been tarred and feathered! He deserves the scorn of the community! Go on. Tell me the rest! What excuse did he offer?"

"Oh, he said things about his business. He said he couldn't marry her, he had to marry influence and money! Aunt Pat, he seemed to think I had money, though I've told him I was poor, and that you were giving me my wedding. Or else, maybe he was just lying to her, I don't know—"

"Well," said Aunt Pat setting her lips wryly, "I suppose I'm to blame for that. I thought the thing was inevitable and I told him myself that you would be pretty well fixed after I was gone. He likely was figuring to borrow money or something."

Sherrill's head dropped again and she gave a sound like a groan.

"There! There! Stop that, child!" said the old lady briskly. "He isn't worth it."

"I know it," moaned Sherrill, "but I'm so ashamed that I loved a man like that!"

"You didn't!" said her aunt. "You loved a man you'd made up in your own imagination. Come, tell me the rest and then eat your supper or you'll be sick and then what'll Mrs. Battersea say?"

Sherrill gave a hysterical little giggle and lifting her head wiped away the tears.

"Well, then someone came to the door and told him

the car was waiting and it was late, and he got frantic. He told her to go away and then she threatened to kill herself, and suddenly he took her in his arms and kissed her—just the way he used to kiss me Aunt Pat—! Oh, it was awful. His arms went around her as if he was hungry for her! Oh, there was no doubt about how he felt toward her, not a bit! And then he kissed her again and suddenly threw her from him into the corner, turned out the light in the room, and went away slamming the door hard behind him."

"The poor fool!" commented Aunt Pat under her breath.

"I stood quite still holding my breath," went on Sherrill, "till suddenly I heard her move, and then I reached out and flashed on both lights in both rooms and she saw me."

"What happened?" The old lady's eyes were large with interest.

"I believe I asked her how long she had known him," said Sherrill wearily, "and she said *always,* that they had grown up and gone to school together, and then he had sent for her to come here and be his secretary till he could afford to marry her—"

"A beast! That's what he is!" murmured Aunt Pat. "A sleek little beast!"

"She said it was not until I came that he turned away from her. She said awful things to me. She said it was all my fault, that I had everything and she had nothing but him, and I had ruined her life and there was nothing for her to do but kill herself! And when I told her to hush, that there wasn't much time and we had to do something, she thought I meant that she was to get away quietly so no one would know. She raved, Aunt Pat! She said it was all right for me, that I was going to marry him. And when I told her that of course I couldn't marry him now, and asked her if she would marry a man like that she said she'd marry him if she had to go through hell with him!"

Aunt Pat's face hardened, though there was a mist across her eyes which she brushed impatiently away.

"Poor little fool!" she commented.

"So I dragged her into my room and made her put on my dress and veil. I guess that is all. She couldn't believe me at first. She said she couldn't do that, that he would kill her, but I told her to tell him that if he didn't treat her right, if he didn't go through the evening in the conventional way, or if he tried to throw it up to her afterward, that I would tell the whole world what he had done."

"Great work!" breathed Aunt Pat. "Sherry, you certainly had your head about you! And you certainly seemed to know your man better than I thought you did."

"Oh, Aunt Pat, it seems so awful for me to be sitting here talking about Carter when just a few hours before I thought he was so wonderful!"

"Yes, I know!" mused Aunt Pat with a faraway look. "I had that experience too once, ages ago before you were born."

"You did?" Sherrill looked up with wonder in her eyes.

"Yes," said Aunt Pat with a strangely tender look in her face, "I did. I was engaged to a young hypocrite once, and thought he was the angel Gabriel till I got my eyes open. Sometime I'll tell you all about it. There isn't anybody living now that knows the story but myself. I thought I was heartbroken forever, and when my grandmother told me that he just wasn't the man God had meant for me, and that He probably had somebody a great deal better waiting somewhere I got very angry at her. But that turned out to be true too, and I did have another lover who was a real man later. It wasn't his fault that we never married. Nor mine either. He died saving a little child's life. But the memory of him has been better for me all my life than if I'd married that first little selfish whiffet. So don't let yourself think that the end of the world has come, Sherrill."

Sherrill sat looking at the old lady and trying to reconstruct her ideas of her, wondering at the mellowing and sharpness that were combined in her dear whimsical old face.

"There, now, child, you've told enough!" said the old lady briskly. "Eat your supper and go to bed. Tomorrow you may tell me about everything else. We've had enough for to-night. I'll talk while you eat now. What do you want to do next? Go to Europe?"

"Oh, not Europe!" Sherrill shrank visibly.

"Of course not!" snapped the old lady with triumph in her eyes. "We'll go some place a great deal more interesting."

"I don't think I want to go anywhere," said Sherrill sadly. "I guess I had better just stay here and let people see I'm not moping. That is if I can get away with it."

"Of course you can!" lilted the old lady. "We'll have the time of our lives. They'll see!"

"The only place I'd want to go anyway would be out west by and by, back to my teaching. I'd like to earn money enough to pay you for this awful wedding, Aunt Pat!"

"Stuff and nonsense!" fumed the old lady. "If you mention that again I'll disinherit you! You hurt me, Sherrill!"

"Oh, forgive me, Aunt Pat! But you've been so wonderful!"

"Well, that's no way to reward me. Go away when

I'm just congratulating myself that I've got you all to myself for a while. Of course I don't fool myself into thinking I can keep you always. You're too good looking for that. And there are a few real men left in the world even in this age. They are not all Carter McArthurs. But at least let me have the comfort of your companionship until one comes along!"

"You dear Aunt Pat!"

"There's another thing we've got to consider tomorrow," said the old lady meditatively. "What are you going to do with those wedding presents?"

Sherrill lifted her face aghast at the thought.

"Oh, mercy! I never thought about them. How terrible! What could one do?"

"Oh, send most of them back. Send Carter those *his* friends sent. Don't bother about it to-night. We'll work it out. You run along to bed now, and don't think another thing about it."

Ten minutes later Sherrill was back in her own room.

Gemmie had been there and removed every trace and suggestion of wedding from the place. Sherrill's best old dresses hung in the closet, Sherrill's old dependable brushes and things were on the bureau. It might have been the night before she ever met Carter McArthur as far as her surroundings suggested.

She cast a quick look of relief about her, and went forward to the mirror and stood there, looking into her own eyes, just as she had done when she was ready for her marriage. Looked at her real self and tried to make it seem true that this awful thing had happened to her, Sherrill Cameron! And then suddenly her eyes wandered away from the deep sorrowful thoughts that she found in her mirrored eyes, with an unthinking glance at her slim white neck, and she started. Why! Where was her emerald necklace? She hadn't taken it off when she put on her kimono. She was sure she had not. She would have remembered undoing the intricate old clasp!

Frantically she searched her bureau drawers. Had Gemmie taken it away? Surely not. She went to the little secret drawer where she usually kept her valuable trinkets. Ah! There was the box it had come in! And yes, the ring and bracelets were there! She remembered taking them off. But not the necklace! Where could the necklace be? Perhaps it had come unfastened and dropped in the big chair while she was eating her supper!

She stepped across the hall quickly and tapped at the door of her aunt's room.

"Aunt Pat, may I come in a minute?" she called, and upon receiving permission she burst into the room excitedly:

"Aunt Pat! I've lost my emerald necklace! Could I have dropped it in your room?"

FOR a moment Sherrill and Aunt Pat stood facing one another, taking in the full significance of the loss from every side. Sherrill knew just how much that necklace was prized in the family. Aunt Pat had told her the story of its purchase at a fabulous price by an ancestor who had bought it from royalty for his girl bride. It had come down to Aunt Pat and been treasured by her and kept most preciously. Rare emeralds, of master workmanship in their cutting and exquisite setting! Sherrill stood appalled, aghast, facing the possibility that it was hopelessly gone.

"Oh, Aunt Pat!" she moaned. "You oughtn't to have given it to me! I—I'm—not fit—to have anything rare!—Either man or treasure—!" she added with a great sob, her lips trembling. "It—seems—I—can't—keep—*any*thing!"

Aunt Pat broke into a roguish grin.

"I hope you didn't call that man rare, Sherrill Cameron!" she chuckled, "and for sweet pity's sake, if you ever do find a real man don't put him on a level with mere jewels! Now, take that look off your face and use your head a little. Where did you have that necklace last? You wore it this evening, I know, for I noticed with great satisfaction that you were not wearing that ornate trinket your would-be bridegroom gave you."

"Oh, I thought I had it on when I came in here!" groaned Sherrill. "I just can't remember! I'm sure I didn't take it off anywhere! At least I can't remember doing it."

She rushed suddenly to the big chair where she had been sitting for the last hour and pulled out the cushions frantically, running her hands down in the folds of the upholstery, but discovering nothing but a lost pair of scissors.

She turned on the overhead lights and got down on her knees searching earnestly, but there was no green translucent gleam of emeralds.

Meanwhile Aunt Pat stood thinking, a canny look in her old eyes.

"Now look here, Sherrill," she said suddenly, whirling round upon the frantic girl, "you haven't lost your soul you know and we are still alive and well. Emeralds are just emeralds after all. Get some poise! Get up off that floor and go quietly down stairs! Look just casually wherever you remember to have been. Just walk over the same places. Don't do any wild pawing around, just merely look in the obvious places. Don't make a noise and don't say anything to the servants if any of them are up. I don't think they are. Gemmie thought they were gone to bed. I just sent Gemmie away. Then if you don't find it come up to me."

Sherrill made a little dismal moan.

"Oh, for mercy's sake!" said Aunt Pat impatiently. "It isn't as if you hadn't had a chance to wear them once anyway, and one doesn't wear emeralds, such emeralds, around every day. You won't miss them much in the long run even if you never find them. Now stop your hysterics and run down stairs, but don't make any noise!"

Sherrill cast a tearful look at her aunt and hurried away, stopping at her own room to get a little flashlight she kept in her desk.

Step by step she retraced the evening in an agony of memory. It wasn't just her losing the emeralds forever, it was Aunt Pat losing the pleasure of her having them. It was—well, something else, a horrible haunting fear that appeared and disappeared on the horizon of her mind and gripped her heart like a clutching hand.

When she came in her search to the long French window out which she and Copeland had passed to the garden such a little while before she paused and hesitated, catching her breath at a new memory. If it came to that *there* would be something she couldn't tell Aunt Pat! She couldn't hope to make her understand about that kiss! Oh! A long shudder went through her weary body and every taut nerve hurt like the toothache. How was she to explain it to herself? And yet—!

She unfastened the window with a shaking hand and touching the spring of her flash went carefully over the piazza, and inch by inch down the walk where they had passed, not forgetting the grassy edges on either side. On her way back she stopped and her cheeks grew hot in the dark as she held back the branches of privet and stepped within that cool green quiet hiding place. Oh, if she could but find it here! If only it had fallen under the shrubs. It would have been very easy for it to come unfastened while he held her in his arms. If only she might find it and be set free from that haunting fear. Just to know that he was all right. Just to be *sure—!* She felt again the pressure of his arms about her, so gentle, the touch of his lips upon her eyelids. It had rested and comforted her so. It hadn't seemed wrong. Yet of course he was an utter stranger!

But she searched the quiet hiding place in vain. There was no answering gleam to the little light that went searching so infallibly and at last she had to come in and give it up. There was utter dejection in her attitude when she came back to Aunt Pat, her lip trembling, her eyes filled with large unshed tears, that haunting fear in their depths. For of course she could not help but realize that that moment when he held her in his arms would have been a most opportune time for a crook to get the emeralds.

"There isn't a sign of them anywhere!" she said.

"Well," said Aunt Pat, "You can't do anything more to-night. Get to bed. You look worn to a thread. I declare, for anybody who went through the evening like a soldier you certainly have collapsed in a hurry. Lose a bridegroom, and take it calmly. Lost a bauble and go all to pieces! Well go to bed and forget it child! Perhaps we'll find it in the morning."

"But Aunt Pat!" said Sherrill, standing tragically with clasped hands under the soft light from the old alabaster chandelier, with her gold hair like a halo crowning her, "Oh, Aunt Pat! You *don't* suppose—*he*—took it, do you?"

"He?" said the old lady sharply whirling on her niece. "Whom do you mean? Your precious renegade bridegroom? No, I hadn't thought of him. I doubt if he had the nerve to do it. Still, it's not out of the thinking."

"Oh, Aunt Pat! Not Carter! I didn't mean Carter." She said astonished, "Of course he wouldn't do a thing like that!"

"Why of course?" snapped Aunt Pat grimly. "He knew the value of those stones, didn't he? And according to his own confession he needed money didn't he? If he would steal a girl's love and fling it away why not steal another girl's necklace? Deception is deception in whatever form you find it, little girl! However, I suppose Carter McArthur had enough on his hands this evening for one occasion and he likely wouldn't have had the time to stage another trick. But I hope you are not trying to suspect that poor innocent bystander that you dragged into your service this evening!"

"He was a *stranger!"* said Sherrill with white anxious lips and frightened eyes.

"H'm! Did he act to you like a crook, Sherrill Cameron?"

"No, Aunt Pat! He was wonderful! But—"

"Well, no more buts about it. Of course he had nothing to do with it. I know a true man when I see him if I am an old maid, and I won't have a man like that suspected in my house! You don't really mean to say you haven't any more discernment than that, do you?"

"No," said Sherrill managing a shaky smile, "I'm sure he is all right, but I was afraid *you* would think—"

"There! I thought as much! You thought *I* had no sense. Well go to bed. We're both dead for sleep. And don't think another thing about this to-night! Mind me!"

"But—oughtn't I to call the police?"

"What for? And have them demand a list of our guests and insult every one of them? No emeralds are worth the losing of friends! Besides, nobody can do anything about it to-night anyway. Now get to bed. Scat!"

Sherrill broke into a little hysterical laugh and rushing up to her aunt threw her arms around her neck and gave her a tender kiss.

"You are just wonderful!" she whispered into her ear, and then hurried back to her room.

Before her mirror she stood again looking sternly into

her own eyes. Such sorrowful tired eyes as looked back at her; such a chastened little face, utterly humble.

Somehow as she stood facing her present situation it seemed weeks, almost years, since she had stood there in wedding satin facing married life like an unknown country through which she had to travel. If she had known when she stood there smiling with her wedding bouquet in her arms, and her wedding veil, blossom-wreathed, on her head, that all this was to be, how would the laughter have died on her lips! How trivial would have seemed her faint fears! Had those fears been a sort of premonition of what was to happen in a few minutes, she wondered? She had read of such things, and perhaps they were in the air like radio sounds waiting to be picked up!

Oh, what a night! What an ending to all that lovely preparation! The tears welled suddenly into her eyes and a great feeling of being overwhelmed came over her anew. Dust and ashes! How had all the beauty of her life faded in a few short minutes! And how was she to face the long desert of the future?

Ah! To have lifted the goblet of Life to her lips, and suddenly to have had it snatched from her without even a single sip! How was she going to bear it all?

It was like coming up to a great stone wall and not being able to scale it, a stone wall on every side, and not even a desire left to try and get over it. All that she really wanted just now was to drop down and sleep and forget.

Well, that was just what she had promised Aunt Pat she would do, but even the effort seemed too much.

She turned from the mirror, too tired even to cry, and saw that Gemmie had laid out one of her plain simple night robes, nothing new and smart, just an old soft well worn gown out of her pleasant thoughtless past. Gratefully she crept into it and got into her bed.

She was too tired to think, too burdened to toss and weep. All she wanted was to sink down into oblivion; and that was just what happened. Tired Nature pulled a curtain about her and she drifted away into deep sleep.

But it was not a peaceful sleep. There were troublous times and buffetings. She was having to drive her car very fast over a rough wild road in a storm, and her wedding veil kept blowing over her eyes and getting tangled in her steering wheel. Carter seemed to be standing somewhere ahead in the darkness waiting for her with a terrible frown on his handsome face, the frown he had worn when he first saw Arla enter that door. She was late for her wedding and out of breath. She seemed to be lost on a wild prairie, and was afraid, terribly afraid!

Over and over she dreamed this with variations. Sometimes it was snowing and the sleet stung her cheeks, and shriveled the lilies of the bouquet in her lap, but she had to go on until she finally arrived at a strange dark rendezvous in an unknown country, and plunged out of her car letting it run away into the darkness without her. She groped about in the night to find her wedding, but there was only a closed and darkened church. She was filled with despair till a stranger, whom yet she seemed to have known all her life, came out of the shadows and helped her home. A stranger who kissed her gently when he left her at her door.

A great gust of perfume from many flowers was wafted out into the passageway as the steward threw open the door and ushered in Arla and Carter McArthur. Flowers everywhere! Sherrill's flowers!

Arla stepped back and closed her eyes quickly as if she had been struck in the face. Carter frowned angrily. He stepped inside and looked at the array. Flowers, fruit, confectionery! A hunted look passed over his face. This all represented what he had lost in the other bride. Popularity, wealth, influence! He began to examine the cards of the friends who had sent them. Sherrill's friends. All Sherrill's friends. None of his represented except the big basket of fruit from his underpaid office. He looked at it contemptuously. Smelton with his six children and sick wife, Johnny Farr the errand boy with a widowed mother, Miss Gaye the assistant secretary who wore bargain counter clothes and chewed incessant gum. Arla! Arla? Had Arla contributed to that basket of fruit too? He cast a quick look at her, his wife, swaying there in the doorway looking white and miserable. Could it be possible that those poor wretches had asked Arla to contribute to a voyage gift for her rival? He had a passing sense of what it might have meant to her to be asked. The whiteness of her face showed she was not enjoying the festive array. Just for an instant he forgot his own annoyance and realized sharply what all this might have been to her. And yet how well she had gone through with it! So confidently, almost radiantly. It had been maddening to have her so confident, when she had dared to interfere, yet somehow it had also stirred his pride in her. After all she was beautiful. No one could deny that! But she had gone beyond all limits in coming there to the house and precipitating this disaster. Yes, disaster! It meant destruction to his well laid financial plans. And no matter how lovely this unsought bride might be, how well she might carry off her position as his wife, that could not offset the fact that he had in himself no position for her to carry off. It had all been a big bluff dependent on Miss Patricia Catherwood's fortune. And what he was to do now remained to be seen. However crazy he might always have been about Arla, that did not alter the fact that he cared for money and position more than he cared for any living woman. And he had in his mind the comfortable realization that he could always get the adoration of another girl if one failed him, or became for the time unwise.

Arla rallied her self-control and quietly entered in the wake of the bags, drifting unobserved into a corner until the steward had left and they were alone.

Carter readjusted the baggage, placing his own suitcase on top impatiently. He was one who always expected those serving to anticipate his slightest unexpressed wishes. He swung savagely around to Arla stranded pitifully by the door, her arrogance and initiative all gone now, nothing but a frightened look in her eyes. She knew his moods. She understood that her time had come to pay for what she had done.

"Well, if that's what you wanted, there you have plenty of it!" he said waving his hand toward the gifts. "Enjoy it while you can. It'll probably be the last you'll see of this sort of thing. If you could only have made up your mind to wait awhile we might have had all this and more!"

The frightened look faded from Arla's eyes and lightning came instead. Her lips grew thin and hard. She turned away from him haughtily and busied herself removing her gloves. She looked very handsome and angry as she stood there not listening to him. He could not but see how smart she looked, how becoming her costume. She knew how to dress. If only he could weather this crisis somehow things might not be so bad after all. She really knew how to wear her clothes just as well as Sherrill, could perhaps make an appearance to suit his pride. And of course she was beautiful, of much the same type as Sherrill. That was what had attracted him to Sherrill in the first place that she had reminded him of Arla. And perhaps Arla could learn. She could get rid of her provincialism. She had learned a lot already. But the money! If he only could be sure—!

He swung around and began to fumble with the baggage, stowing one big suitcase that contained his wedding garments, back under the bed. Swinging another down and shoving it after. Of course the steward would attend to all that presently, but it suited him to be stirring, throwing things around. This was an awkward moment, various emotions were striving within him.

Arla stood where she had first entered, pulling off her long gloves deliberately, finger by finger, smoothing them carefully, thoughtfully. She was struggling to keep from bursting into tears.

The steward tapped at the door and Arla made no

move to answer it, but moved away and stood staring out of the porthole at the panorama of harbor lights. Already they were moving out into the stream and she had a strange dreadful feeling that she was heading out into the midstream of life, leaving behind all that she knew, all that she had hoped, going into a wild lonely sea of problems and perplexities and going utterly unprepared and unloved.

Carter had gone to the door. She heard the conversation vaguely, as if it had nothing to do with her. It was something about a radio message. The operator wished to speak to Mr. McArthur. Carter went out and Arla wondered idly why he was sending a radio message now, on his wedding night, but she was filled with indifference concerning it.

Carter had left the door unlatched as he went out and the draft from the open porthole cooled her hot cheeks. She turned to fasten the door, realizing that she was alone, a brief breathing space, and looked about her again.

Those flowers! How wonderful it would have been if they had been hers! If she had been a girl with friends who could send farewell greetings in such a costly style! Why all these gifts, the wedding that had preceded them, had been but the fulfillment of her childish fairy dreamings, all the things she had most wished for in life, and now they had come and how empty they were! How one's heart could starve in the midst of plenty!

She went about the room stealthily examining the cards, removing them with frightened hasty fingers. She would put them out of sight before Carter returned.

Some of the names she recognized as belonging to people who had been down the line and been introduced to her such a little time ago. They had gone through the motion of friendship with her but that would be all. She would likely never see them again. For a brief moment she had walked with the elite and been recognized by them, but she was not a part of them, never would be. They were not of her world! Her highest dreams had been realized and yet had brought her no joy. Emptiness and sawdust! How she hated it all! How she wished for the old sweet simple days when she went to high school in pretty gingham dresses and Carter carried her books for her, looked down adoringly into her eyes, told her how lovely she was!

Oh, what had she done, how had things gone wrong, that they had come to this night? She remembered the look he had given her as he waved his hand toward the flowers and told her to enjoy them while she could, that it was probably the last of that sort of thing she would see. She shivered with anguish as she felt his contempt all over again, and realized that he was not the Carter of her happy school days, not even the whimsical lover who had sent for her to be his secretary. She must face that fact and not give way to sorrow. Then her lips set with determination, and she stepped calmly to the bell and rang for the stewardess.

When the woman presented herself Arla waved toward the flowers.

"I would like you to take all those away," she said coldly. "They sicken me. Take them down to the steerage, please, and give them to the old women and the little children."

When Carter came back the flowers were all gone. The boxes of expensive confectionery were gone. There was left only the basket of fruit from the office standing alone on the dresser.

"Why,—where—what—?" asked Carter looking about and sensing the emptiness.

"I told the stewardess to take them down to the

steerage and give them to people who could enjoy them," she said in a cold steady voice.

Carter looked at her half startled. He had had so many startling things flung at him already this long terrible evening that one more or less made little impression. Then his eyes swept about the room again and he noticed the fruit.

"Why not that one too?" he asked his lips settling into their habitual sneering curve.

"Because that one is yours!" she answered steadily. "Because *I* paid for that myself!"

"You paid for it yourself?" he exclaimed looking at her in astonishment.

"Yes, I paid for it myself!" she answered, folding her gloves smoothly together again, and laying them out on the table.

"But—*why—?* Why should you pay for them? Why not the others? Who got up the idea?"

"It wasn't gotten up. I did it all. They don't even know about it. They hadn't any money to put into gifts. They have all they can do to keep from starving. Johnny's mother is likely dying to-night. He won't be able to get any flowers for her funeral! Smelton's wife has had a relapse and one of his children has a broken leg, the only child who had any job at all. Miss Gaye needs all her salary for gum. Who would you think would send you fruit from the office if I didn't?"

"But why *you?"* he asked again a strange incredulous look in his eyes.

"Why I?" answered the girl with a flash of her tear drowned eyes, and a sudden quiver of her lovely lip, "Why *I?* Because I was a *fool!* Because I'll always be a fool I suppose where you are concerned! Because I *thought* I loved you, and wanted you to have all the honor there was, even from an office like ours! It was just after you told me that I had always been—Oh, what's the use! I won't say those empty words over. I had a spirit of self-sacrifice. I thought I loved you enough to sacrifice myself! That was before I found out I couldn't stand it! It was before I told your other bride that I'd go through hell to marry you. It was even before I understood what hell was like!"

"Did you tell her that?" His face was white with anger and a strange wild remorse.

"Yes, I told her that when she said she wouldn't marry you after what she'd seen, and asked me if I would, and I said I'd go through hell to marry you! But, I didn't know what hell could be like then, even at the beginning. I thought I was in it then, but I *wasn't.*"

A wave of shamed color swept over his face leaving it white as death. He almost staggered and put out his hand to steady himself against the wall.

"You don't care that you're putting me through hell, do you?" he whined impressively.

She gave him a withering glance.

"You deserve it," she said fiercely, "I don't! I've always tried to be as decent as you would let me. I never played fast and loose with you. I've loved you always,—and—I love you—now! God help me! Why do I love you? Oh, why? You are despicable! You know you are! How could anybody love a little handsome selfish beast like you? And yet I do! Oh, what a wedding night!"

She threw herself suddenly down upon the bed and wept bitterly. And he, trembling, almost ashamed, filled with passionate remorse and angry retaliation, turned the light off and crept humbly to her side kneeling, groping for her hand. Her words had lashed him through fury into a sudden brief fleeting vision of himself.

"Arla!" he said, reaching after her in the dark, "Arla! Don't cry that way! I do love you!"

SHERRILL awoke in the morning with a gorgeous sunlight streaming across the lovely old blue rug, lighting her familiar room cheerfully.

Then instantly, as if someone had struck her across the heart with a club, there came to her a remembrance of all that had happened since she awoke in that room so joyously yesterday morning. The future, drab and desolate, stretched itself away before her, a dreary prospect.

Sherrill's soul turned sick at her own desolation, and all the horror of her situation rushed over her with a realization of details which she had not had time for last night in the sudden stress and need for immediate action.

And now of course the first thought that occurred was, had she done right? Was her action too hasty? Had there been any other way? What would other girls have done? *Could* she have married him knowing the truth about him?

Of course if there had been the least doubt about it, if there had been any chance at all that she was misjudging him, she would have been wrong not to have given him an opportunity to explain, to clear himself if he could.

But she had heard his own words. She had seen him clasp that other girl and kiss her with the same passionate fervency that he had kissed her. She had seen his face as he took her in his arms. She could never forget it. Yes, she had heard his own confession that he still loved the other girl, and that after his marriage and wedding trip they would be freer than ever—! *Ah!* She caught her lips between her teeth with a trembling breath. How that sight, those words had stabbed her! Oh, no, there was no possibility of doubt. He was false-hearted. He had *meant* to be false!

If he had just been weak and fallen into this situation one could forgive. Forgive, but not marry. She could never marry a man whom she could not trust.

But he had been deliberately false, and she could scarcely be sorry for him. No, she could only be sorry for that poor desperate girl who had been willing to go through hell to have him.

Well, there was such a thing as hell on earth of course. Her own present outlook seemed not far situated from such a location, and yet she knew if she had to go through even a mild kind of hell for the rest of her life she would rather take it alone than tied up to a man whom just a few short hours before she had been joyously preparing to marry. No, she must be thankful that a kind Providence had even in such a tragic moment prevented her from marrying Carter McArthur.

And yet though all that was true, Sherrill Cameron lay with wide desperate eyes staring out at a sunlit desolation.

She closed her eyes again and tried to wish herself back to sleep, but the eyes flew open like a doll's that had lost their weights. She knew that she was definitely awake for the day, and could not drop back into merciful oblivion again even for a brief space. She must face what was before her.

So she lay staring about her room that had sheltered so much of her joy and happy anticipation, and suddenly from every wall and corner things started out at her that had been connected with her courtship. A great bunch of dried grasses that she and Carter had gathered the day they took their first walk together. It filled a thin crystal vase on the mantel and made a thing ethereally lovely. Gemmie never would have known that it was a reminder of dear dead days.

High over her white marble mantel was fastened a pennant. It spoke of the first football game she had attended with Carter, less than a year ago! Gemmie wouldn't have realized that the pennant spoke eloquently of a lost past.

Knotted carelessly on the corner of a signed etching on the opposite wall, for no apparent reason at all, was a bow of scarlet ribbon, a memento of last Christmas, kept because Carter had tied it about her hair the morning they were skating together, and then had drawn her face back and kissed her, behind a sheltering hemlock tree that hid them from the view of the other skaters on the creek. And that was another memory that she must cut out and throw away. It did not belong to her and never had belonged it seemed! Gemmie had no idea what that red ribbon meant.

Over on her desk that bronze paper weight! Gemmie never had known that it had been on his desk the day she first went with Carter to his office. She had admired it and he had given it to her. That was before Arla came to be his secretary! Ah, but he had known and loved Arla first! He loved her enough *afterwards* to have sent for Arla. And yet he had gone right on with his intimacy with Sherrill! The bronze too must go into the discard!

And over on the bureau, that little ivory figurine! Gemmie had always admired that. But she did not know that Carter had bought it for her in a curio shop the day they went together to New York.

Oh! She could not bear these memories! She must not! She would give way and weep. And weeping was not for her to-day! She must keep a mask of happiness on her face. She must not let anyone suspect that her life was shattered by that wedding as it had come out last night. They must think it was all planned, or at least that a definite and friendly change was made before the ceremony. She could not go around and explain the whole thing as it had happened. Even if she were willing on her own part, she could not explain what involved others' secrets. No, she must play her part through to the end and keep a brave, cheerful, even merry face. How was she to do it?

Then suddenly she could not bear the sight of those things on her wall and she sprang up and dashed the bunch of grasses down, sweeping them into the fireplace where Gemmie had carefully laid a fire.

The vase was only a plain little thing from the five-and-ten-cent store, but it seemed to understand what was expected of it, and as Sherrill lifted the grasses swiftly from it, it toppled, and rolled slowly, deliberately down upon the hearth and smashed into a thousand pieces.

Sherrill stood for an instant looking at it regretfully, almost as if it had a personality. Poor fragile thing! Too bad for it to lose its existence through no fault of its own. It had been part of a lovely bit of beauty, but at least now she would not have it around to remind her of the grasses and the day that they were picked!

She stooped and swept the pieces quickly with her little hearth broom into a newspaper, and wrapped them carefully, putting them into the wastebasket. Now they were gone. Even Gemmie wouldn't be reminded to ask where the grasses were.

Then she touched a match to the fire and it swept up and licked the grasses out of existence in one flash.

Sherrill turned to the room again. She mounted a chair and pulled down the pennant, stuffing it fiercely into the wastebasket. She snatched the bow of ribbon from the picture frame and dropped it into the fire. She caught up the bronze paper weight. That wouldn't burn! Nor the ivory figurine! What could she do with them? Give them away? They might somehow come back to face her some day, and she wanted to be utterly rid of them. Ah! There was one place where she would never be likely to see them again. She might send them to Carter's office. But no, that would be only to bring back to his mind the days they had had together and that she did not want. She wanted only to sever all connection with him, to wipe out from both his memory and hers, in so far as was possible, all thought of one another. Then only would she be able to lift up her head and breathe freely again.

She unlocked a little secret drawer in her desk to put the bronze and ivory out of sight, and came on a packet of notes and brief letters from Carter. There hadn't been many because he had been right there to see her every day. She had almost forgotten these letters and some programs and clippings. She seized them now and flung them into the middle of the fire, closing her eyes quickly that she might not see the flames licking around her name in that handwriting that had been so beloved, turning her back lest she should repent and snatch them out to read them over again. She must not! No, it would unnerve her! It would make her heart turn back and lash her for what she had done in giving her bridegroom over to another girl. She must not because he never had been hers! He was not worth the great love she had given him.

And now she remembered how unworthy she herself had felt to marry him, and how she had prayed, and wondered. Was this awful thing that had happened in some mysterious way an answer to her prayer? Oh, it was all a mystery! Life itself was a mystery. Joy one minute and awful sorrow and desolation the next! Sorrow! Sorrow! Sorrow!

Suddenly from the next room through the closed door there came a burst of wild sweet song:

"When I have sorrow in my heart,
What can take it away?
Only Jesus in-ah my heart
Can take that sorrow away."

It was Lutie, the fresh-cheeked young girl who came in certain days in the week to help with the cleaning. Lutie had the windows of the guest room open and was beginning her weekly cleaning. Sherrill's windows were open too and that was why the words came so distinctly. But how strange that such words should come to her just now when she was so filled with sorrow!

Lutie was banging things around, drawing the bed out, and the bureau, setting chairs out of the way and running the vacuum cleaner over the floor. Sherrill could hear the thump as the cleaner hit the baseboards now and then. And Lutie's voice rang out clear again in the next verse:

"When I have fear in-ah my heart,
What can take it away?

Only Jesus in-ah my heart
Can take that fear away."

Sherrill began slowly, languidly to dress, listening to the song. Fear in the heart. She considered herself. Did she have fear in her heart? Yes, she recognized a kind of dread of the days that were before her. Not fear of anything tangible perhaps, but fear of gossip, criticism, prying eyes. Fear of having to face all that would come in the wake of that wedding that was hers and yet was not. Fear of a drab future, a long lonely way ahead, no home of her own. She could never have a home of her own now, nor anyone to care for her and enjoy life with her. For she would never dare trust a man again, even if she ever found one whom she could love.

"When I have sin in-ah my heart—"

piped up Lutie joyously,

"What can take it away?
Only Jesus in-ah my heart
Can take that sin away."

Sherrill was not especially interested in sin. She had never considered herself to be much of a sinner, and her thoughts wandered idly considering her own case more than the song as she listened to the lilt of Lutie's voice in the closing verse:

"When I have Jesus in-ah my heart,
What can take Him away?
Once take Jesus into my heart
And He has come to stay!"

There was a pause in the singing and the sound of voices in the hall. Thomas the house man had come up to get the rugs to give them a good cleaning in the back yard. Lutie was demurring, but finally tapped hesitantly at Sherrill's door.

Sherrill in her negligee opened the door.

"Miss Sherrill, Thomas was wanting to get your rug for cleaning but I guess you aren't ready yet, are you? I wasn't sure whether you were in your room or not."

"That's all right Lutie," said Sherrill, stepping through into the next room where the girl was at work, "tell him to go in and take it. I can finish without a rug."

Sherrill went to the guest room bureau and began to arrange her hair and Lutie came back after helping the man roll up the rug.

"That's a curious song you were singing, Lutie," said Sherrill pleasantly. "Where in the world did you get it? It sounds like a negro spiritual."

"I don't guess it is, Miss Sherrill," said the girl pausing in her dusting, "I got it down to our Bible class. It is pretty words, isn't it? I like that part about Jesus taking your sorrow away. I sing it a lot."

"But you've never had any sorrow, Lutie," said Sherrill wistfully, eyeing the girl's round rosy cheeks and happy eyes.

"Oh, Miss Sherrill, you don't know," said Lutie sobering suddenly. "I've had just a lot! First my mother got awful sick for two whole years, and then when she got better my sister just older'n I died. And my little brother has hurt his hip and they don't think he'll ever walk again."

"Oh, Lutie," cried Sherrill in dismay, "that is a lot of trouble!"

"Oh, but that's not all," said the girl drawing a deep sigh. "My dad got some steel filings in his eye about nine months ago, and they think he's going blind, and now they've laid him off the job so my brother Sam and I are the only ones working, except Mother now and then when she can get a washing to do. And our house is all mortgaged up and the bank closed last week where we had our money saved to pay the interest and now we'll maybe lose the house; and Mother needs an operation only she can't stop working to go to the hospital. And—" the girl caught her lip between her little white teeth to hold it from trembling, and Sherrill could see that there were tears in her eyes, "and—then—my boy friend got mad and started going with another girl because I wouldn't run off and get married and leave the family in all that mess!"

The big tears rolled out now, and down the round cheek, and Lutie caught a corner of her apron and brushed them hastily away.

"Excuse me, Miss Sherrill," she said huskily. "It just sometimes gets me—"

"You poor dear child!" said Sherrill putting down her hairbrush and coming over toward her. "Why, you poor kid you! I never dreamed you could have all that to bear! And *yet* you could sing a song like that!" She regarded the girl earnestly. "You certainly are brave! But Lutie, you know a boy friend that would do a thing like that isn't worth crying after." Sherrill said it, and suddenly knew she was speaking out of her own experience.

"I know it!" gulped Lutie, "I know he ain't, but sometimes it all just comes over me. You see I was right fond of him."

Then she flashed a smile like a rainbow through her tears and brightened.

"But I don't feel like that much now since I got Jesus in my heart like the song says. He really drives the sorrow away, and I'm mostly glad just to let Him have

His way with me. If it wasn't fer Him I couldn't stand it. He really does take the sorrow away you know. I guess you likely know that yourself, Miss Sherrill, don't you? But you see I haven't known Jesus so long so I just have to talk about Him and sing about Him most all the time to keep myself reminded what a wonderful Saviour I've got."

Sherrill turned a searching, hungry look upon the little serving maid.

"Where did you get all that, Lutie?"

"Down at our Bible class, Miss Sherrill. I been going there about a year now. We got a wonderful teacher down there. We study the Bible, and it's just wonderful what he makes us see in it. I just wish you'd come down sometime and visit, Miss Sherrill, and see what it's like."

"Maybe I will,—sometime," said Sherrill slowly still studying the girl as if there were some strange mystery about her.

"It ain't a very grand place," said Lutie apologetically. "Maybe you might not like it. It's just a plain board floor, and the walls are cracked and the seats are hard. It ain't like your church. The windows are painted white because they look into an alley. Maybe you wouldn't think it was good enough for you. But I'd like you to come once and see. The singing's just heavenly, and the teacher's grand! Everybody loves it so they just can't bear to go home."

"Why, I wouldn't mind things like that!" said Sherrill earnestly. "Indeed I wouldn't. I'll come sometime, I really will. I'd like to see what it's like. When do you meet?"

"Monday evenings!" said Lutie with dancing eyes. "Oh, Miss Sherrill, if you'd come I'd be that proud!"

"Why of course I'll come!" said Sherrill heartily, relieved that she could do anything to make Lutie's eyes shine like that, half curious too to see what it was that had made this simple girl happy in the face of such terrible troubles.

Sherrill carried the memory of the girl's face with her as she went back to her room to finish her dressing. What a light had come into her eyes when she said what a wonderful Saviour she had! Saviour! Saviour from what? Her sorrow? Her fear? Her sin? Lutie couldn't be such a great sinner. It was probably just a lot of phrases she had picked up in some evangelistic meeting, poor thing, but if she thought she was comforted by it there must be some good in it. Anyway Sherrill decided she would go and find out. If there was any cure for sorrow surely she herself needed it. And she drew a heavy sigh and went downstairs to face the morning after her own wedding day without a bridegroom.

She tried as she walked down the broad front stairs to forget how that other bride had looked, smiling and proud, holding her head high. And how Carter had looked, haughty, handsome, carrying it all off just as if it had been planned that way.

Carter! What had he thought? How had he taken it? Strange that he had not shown a sign, nor spoken a word to her. Did she fancy it or had there been a furtive look of fear in his eyes? Anyhow it was plain enough that he had avoided looking straight at her. Not once had he looked her in the eyes. Not once attempted to draw her aside and speak to her. She did not know from his looks whether he was very angry or only relieved to have had things work out this way.

Her heart was very heavy as she thought of this. It seemed to blot out the happy days of the past, to make Carter into an utter stranger. Yet, of course it was better so. That was what she wanted only somehow the awfulness of his attitude overcame her anew as she came down to the setting of the last act of that tragedy that had ended her high hopes. How was she going to bear the future?

And then, suddenly, just at the foot of the stairs she remembered the emeralds! The emeralds and the stranger! And down upon her like some gigantic bird of prey swept her fear of the night before!

MISS Catherwood was already at the breakfast table looking as fresh and chipper as if she had gone to bed at nine o'clock the night before. She was opening her mail and there was a smile of satisfaction on her face. She gave Sherrill a keen look as she came into the room.

"Well, I'm glad to see you're still a good sport!" she said with her funny twisted grin. "But you didn't sleep very well, did you? There are dark circles under your eyes. Sit down and eat a good breakfast. Oh, I know you think you don't want a thing but a cup of coffee, but that's not the way to act. You've got a few hard days before you and you've got to keep your looks through them or people will say you are mourning after that sap-head, and you don't want that. Come, set to work. We've got to get at sending back those presents. You'll feel better when they are out of the house."

Sherrill gave a little moan and dropped her face into her hands.

"Oh!" she groaned, "How impossible it all seems! But if I could only find the necklace I wouldn't mind any of the rest!"

Aunt Pat flung a wise glance at the bowed head.

"That'll turn up all right," she said, "Come, child, chirk up. I've been wondering. Can you think back and be sure when you last had it?"

Sherrill shook her head.

"No. I've been trying, but I can't be sure. If I only could it would take a big load from my mind."

"Well *I* can!" said Aunt Pat. "You had the necklace on when you sat in the dining room eating your supper after you came in from outside. I know for I sat and watched the lights in those stones and I remember thinking how well they became you, and how they brought out the color in your cheeks and the gold in your hair."

Sherrill's head came up suddenly with a light of hope in her eyes and a soft flush on her cheeks.

"Are you *sure* you saw them on me at the table, Aunt Pat? Perfectly sure?"

"Perfectly sure," said Aunt Pat steadily, studying the girl quietly.

"Well, that's something!" said Sherrill with a sigh of relief. "At least I didn't lose it—in the garden!"

"No, you didn't lose it in the garden," said Aunt Pat with a wicked little grin. "Now don't think anything more about it. Let's get at those presents. First you sit down and work out a little model note sweet and gracious that will fit all the presents and not tell a thing you don't want known."

Sherrill presently brought it to her aunt for her approval.

"My dear—

The sudden change in our plans for the wedding has left me in an embarrassing situation, having in my possession a lot of lovely gifts which do not by right belong either to me or to Mrs. McArthur. I am therefore of course returning all the gifts and apologizing for having been the unintentional cause of so much trouble to the donors.

But I do want to add just a little word of my appreciation for your beautiful gift, and to thank you for your delightful intention for my pleasure. It is so wonderful to see such gracious evidence of friendship.

Very sincerely,
Sherrill Cameron."

"I think that is quite a nice bit of English!" said Aunt Pat with satisfaction when she had read it. "It says all that needs to be said and tells nothing. It ought to be published. It would be so helpful to other girls caught in like predicaments."

Sherrill broke into hysterical laughter.

"Oh, Aunt Pat! You're a scream! As if there was ever another girl caught in such a predicament!" she said.

"I don't know," said the old lady dryly, "You can't tell how many girls have had a situation like yours, only most of them likely didn't have the nerve to handle it the way you did yours. There must have been some girls who were too great cowards to back down from a church full of wedding guests, and the wedding march just on the tiptoe to begin. They probably paid afterwards, and paid double too. Surely Sherrill you aren't the only one who ever found at the last minute that her lover was made of coarse clay. Don't ever fancy, no matter how hard a thing you have to go through, that your experience is unique. This old world has been going on a good many hundred years and there are precious few situations that haven't happened over and over again. Cheer up, child, that's a model letter and you're a good little sport!"

Miss Catherwood handled the return of the presents in a masterly manner. Her secretary and Sherrill wrote the notes while Gemmie and the butler under her supervision repacked the gifts. It was amazing how quickly the things were marshaled from the tables into their neat original packages each with its dainty note attached. Sherrill grew so interested in seeing how much she could accomplish that she almost forgot her anxiety about the emeralds.

It comforted her greatly that the necklace had not been lost while she was out with Copeland. But later in the day something occurred which brought back her uneasiness and that nameless fear again. Oh, to know certainly, who, if anyone, was connected with the disappearance of the jewels!

It was late in the afternoon and Miss Catherwood had just said they had done enough for to-day and must stop and rest. Just then the hall door opened timidly and Lutie showed a deprecating face.

"Please, Miss Catherwood, might I come in and speak to you a moment?" she asked shyly.

"Why of course, Lutie. Come right in," said the old maid cheerily. "What is it?"

"Why, Miss Catherwood, I found something," she said earnestly, holding her two hands cupped, the one in the other. "Maybe it isn't much account, but it looked to me as if it might be something real. It's only a little thing, and I thought if I gave it to any of the other servants they might laugh, but I knew you would know whether it was valuable or not."

Lutie dropped a delicate bit of brightness into the old lady's hand and stood back waiting shyly.

Aunt Pat held the bit of jewelry in her delicate old hand for an instant and examined it carefully. Then she looked up at the girl.

"Where did you find this, Lutie, and when?"

"Just now, ma'am, in the little back room off the servants' hall. It was on the floor just under the edge of the little writing table, and I most swept it up, but then I saw it glittering, and it first looked like a bit of Christmas-tree tinsel, but when I looked closer it seemed like something real."

"H'm!" said Aunt Pat significantly, and looking up at Sherrill added: "It's from the emerald necklace, Sherry, a whole inch of the chain and part of the clasp!"

Sherrill gave a startled exclamation, and the old lady turned to Lutie again.

"Thank you, Lutie, for bringing it straight to me. Did you speak to any of the other servants about it?"

"No," said Lutie. "I was afraid they'd laugh at me. They tell me I'm fussy about little things."

"Well, that's a good trait sometimes," said the old lady. "I'm glad you brought it straight to me. Yes, it's valuable. It's part of something we had lost. You might keep your eye out while you're cleaning to see if you find any more of it. Now, suppose you come and show us just where you found this." They followed Lutie to the little room in the servants' hall.

"Thank you, Lutie," said Miss Catherwood when she had showed them the exact spot, "I shan't forget this!"

"Oh, that's all right, ma'am. I'm glad you weren't angry at my bothering you."

Lutie withdrew with a shy flame blazing in her cheeks.

Aunt Pat turned to Sherrill who was searching the room over, vainly hoping to find more of the necklace.

"Now, Sherrill," said Aunt Pat, "tell me just who was in this room and where each one stood. What were they here for anyway, in this back room?"

"They came to get the license fixed up with the right names," said Sherrill half shivering at the memory, "We sent for the clerk and he sat right there in that chair all the time he was here."

"And where did you stand?"

"Most of the time over there by the door. Once I stepped over to the table while I was explaining to him that I had changed my mind about marrying Carter."

The old lady gave her a swift look.

"Where was Carter at the time?"

"He stood just back of me."

"H'mm! How did he look when you explained that you had changed your mind about marrying him?"

"I didn't look at him. I was trying to keep my voice from trembling."

"Did he say anything or make any motion that seemed like a protest?"

"He cleared his throat in a nervous kind of way. I had a fancy that he was afraid I was going to tell more than I did. He stirred uneasily."

"And didn't he speak at all?"

"Only to answer the questions that were put to him by the clerk. Of course Mr. Copeland had explained the situation to the clerk in a general way and the questions that were put were mere form. He just assented to everything. Mr. Copeland had really made it very easy for us all."

"H'mm!" said Aunt Pat thoughtfully, and then reverted to the bridegroom.

"And Carter assented to all the questions did he? He made it very plain that he was marrying that other girl by intention? He didn't make any protests nor attempt any explanations?"

"Not a word." Sherrill's voice told how deeply that fact weighed upon her.

"Little whippersnapper!" ejaculated the old lady indignantly. "Well, it's just what I would have expected of him! He hasn't the backbone of a jellyfish. He was born a coward! Perhaps you can't blame him so much. He probably had ancestors like that. Well, now, tell me, how long did you stand there?"

"I stepped away immediately after he had answered his questions and made a place for her,—for the bride—to stand."

"And did you watch Carter's face while she was being questioned?"

"I wanted to, but just then he dropped his handkerchief. He acted very nervous and he stooped over to pick it up. It seemed to take him a long time. He didn't seem to want to look at me. I tried to make him. It seemed as if I must make him look at me just once so that we could get adjusted to things. Just a look from him that he was ashamed, or that he felt I had done the right thing, would have made it so much easier. I felt so unhappy and frightened!"

"I know you did, dear child. Of course! But don't have any question but that you did the right thing. Well, who else was there? Carter and that girl and the clerk and you? Was Mr. Copeland in the room?"

"Not at all," said Sherrill quickly. "He stood outside in the hall every minute. I'm sure of that."

"He didn't even step back into the room when you all came away?"

"No," said Sherrill with assurance. "I'm positive of that for he waited for me at the door and walked across to the middle room with me, and Carter and Arla were behind us. The clerk went ahead, down the back hall and to the back stairs the way he had come. He went out of the room before any of us left it."

"Who was in the room last?"

"Why, Carter—and his—that is—the—bride!" she finished with a quick sharp breath.

"You're sure?"

"Yes, I looked back and called to her to follow me and I would help her get ready. Carter was just behind her. He had apparently dropped his handkerchief again and was stooping to pick it up."

"H'm! What did he do with it?"

"Why, I think he put it in his pocket."

"And he didn't look up even then?"

"No." Her voice was grave and very sad. "He seemed as if he was ashamed. He almost looked—well,—frightened!"

"Probably was," said Aunt Pat dryly, "ashamed and baffled. He had been hoping to get a lot besides a bride in marrying you. I didn't tell you, but I came on him looking at the emeralds the morning I gave them to you. He seemed tremendously impressed with them. In fact he looked as if he were just gloating over them. He didn't know I saw him. He thought he was alone. But I can't help thinking if he'd got them he'd have pawned them before the night was over."

"Oh, Aunt Pat!" exclaimed Sherrill in dismay. "Why,—he—really spoke very beautifully about them. He said he was so proud that I should have regal jewels. He said he only wished that he were able to give me such things, but he hoped some day he could."

"Oh yes, he could talk!" sniffed Aunt Pat. "He was mealy-mouthed. But don't try to defend him Sherrill. I know it hurts to have him turn out that way but you might as well understand the truth at once and not go to getting him up on a pedestal again. Now, I've got to think what to do for Lutie. I like to encourage the sort of thing she did, bringing that bit of chain straight to me. She's a good girl, and probably needs help. I wonder if I should give her money?"

"Did you know that she has a little lame brother, Aunt

Pat?" asked Sherrill, "And her father is going blind and her mother needs an operation?"

"Mercy no!" said Aunt Pat looking up from the bit of chain she was examining. "Why, how did you find that out? We must do something for them right away."

"Yes, they are afraid they are going to lose their house too. They can't pay the interest on their mortgage. The bank closed where they kept their savings, and she and her brother are the only ones working."

"Well, for mercy's sake!" said Aunt Pat greatly disturbed, "And to think they never said a word! Why wasn't I told of this sooner? When did you find it out, Sherrill?"

"Just this morning," said the girl thinking back through the day, "I heard Lutie singing in the next room to mine where she was cleaning. She was singing about what to do when you had sorrow in your heart, or something like that. I asked her where she got the song and said I guessed she never had a sorrow and then she told me all about it."

"H'm!" said Aunt Pat thoughtfully.

Then she opened the door and called to Gemmie who was never very far away from her mistress' call.

"Gemmie, go see if Lutie has gone home yet. If she hasn't tell her I want her a minute."

Then she turned back to her niece.

"Sherrill, this is the setting of one of the tiny emeralds from that chain, see, one of the wee ones up near the clasp. Now, where do you suppose the rest of it is? You know the clasp used to be weak, but I had it fixed, at least I supposed I had. I sent it to the jeweler's before I gave it to you. See! This evidently has been stepped on, or else yanked from the chain! How the links are crushed! Now, the question is, where did the necklace drop, and who was there when it happened?"

Sherrill looked up with troubled eyes, the haunting fear coming back to her soul, but Lutie came in just then and she had no opportunity to answer her aunt.

"I sent for you, Lutie," said Miss Catherwood pleasantly, "because I want to tell you that there is a reward for finding this chain and for bringing it straight to me."

Lutie had been a bit troubled at being sent for, but now her face showed great relief and swift protest.

"Oh, no ma'am," she said breathlessly, "I couldn't think of taking anything for just doing my duty."

"Well, you're not, I'm giving it! That's different! I'm giving it because I'm grateful, and you've done me a big favor, one that no money can pay for. You've given me one little clue to something valuable and cherished that I've lost. And now, listen. I've just found out that you've got a lame brother, and your father has trouble with his eyes and your mother needs an operation. In that case I want to help. Yes, it's my right! You don't suppose we were put into this world to be pigs with what God gave us, do you? I want to see your mother on her feet again, and if there's anything that can be done for your father and brother I want to help do it. Sometimes operations will do wonders with eyes you know. Another doctor might put your father where he could go to work again."

"Oh, Miss Catherwood! You're too good!" began Lutie, tears of gratitude rolling down her cheeks and her lip trembling into a big smile like a rainbow upside down. "I don't know as my mother would think it was right to take help from anyone, but it's wonderful of you to suggest it."

"She'd think it right to take it from God, wouldn't she?" snapped the old lady crisply. "Well, this is just God's money and He told me to give you what you needed. There's no further use in discussing it. I'm coming to see your mother in a very few days."

"Well, maybe—" hesitated Lutie, her eyes shining with the great possibility, "if you'd let us work afterwards and pay it off when we can."

"Pay it back to somebody else then, not me," chuckled Aunt Pat in full form now. "I don't want you to have that on your mind. If you ever get able just help somebody else out of trouble. I tell you God told me to give you what you need, without any strings to it! And, oh yes, Lutie, if you should find any more of this just bring it to me at once no matter how busy I may be. It was a necklace and it had green stones in it. Big ones and little ones."

Lutie's eyes grew wide.

"I wonder if that green bead I picked up was one!" she exclaimed. "It was just a tiny little bit, looked like glass. At first I thought it was a bead, but then I thought it was glass, and I swept it up with the dust. It hadn't any hole like a bead in it."

"Where did you find it, Lutie? What did you do with it?"

"Why I found it in the big crack between the floor boards over under the bureau. I had to pry it out with a hairpin. I gathered it up with the dust when I thought it wasn't anything but glass and put it in the waste for Thomas to burn. Wait, I'll run down and see if I can find it. Thomas went down to the grocery for cook. I don't think he's burned the trash yet!"

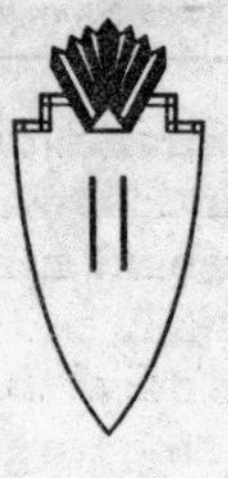

LUTIE sped on swift feet and was presently back again, her eyes shining, a tiny green particle held in the palm of her hand.

Miss Catherwood examined it carefully and Sherrill drew close.

"It is, *it is!*" cried Sherrill. "It's one of the wee little stones by the clasp, Aunt Pat!"

"Yes," said Aunt Pat grimly, "Whoever got away with the rest of the stones missed this one anyway."

Then the old lady turned to Lutie.

"Well, you've done me another favor, Lutie. Here's a bit of money I happen to have in hand. Take it and run home now and get something extra nice for supper just for my thanks offering. Tell your mother I'll be over soon."

When Lutie had finished her happy and incoherent thanks and gone Sherrill came and put her arms around the old lady's neck.

"You are wonderful, Aunt Pat!" she said and kissed her tenderly.

"Nonsense!" said the old lady with an embarrassed

grin. "Nothing wonderful about it! What's money for if it isn't to help along your fellow men and women? And besides you don't know but I may have my own selfish reasons for doing it."

"A lot of people don't feel that way about it, Aunt Pat!"

"Well, that's their lookout!" she answered. "All I've got to say is they miss a lot then."

"But Aunt Pat, aren't you going to do anything more about this now? Aren't you going to call the police and report the loss, or—ask anybody, or anything? Aren't you even going to tell the servants?"

"I've already told the servants that someone who was here last night lost a valuable necklace, and offered a good-sized reward for finding it, but only Gemmie knows it was your necklace. Gemmie would miss it of course when she came to put your things away. She was always very fond of those jewels and was pleased that I was giving them to you. She would have to know. But Gemmie won't say anything."

"But dear Aunt Pat! I do want everything possible done to find it even if it makes a lot of unpleasantness for me. I'd rather have it found. To think that you should have had the keeping of it all these years and then I should lose it the very first time I wore it! Oh, Aunt Pat, I must get it back to you!"

"Back to *me!*" snorted the old lady quite incensed. "It's not mine any more. It's yours, child, and I mean to have it back to you if possible of course, but if not there's nothing to break your heart about. Stop those highstrikes and smile. You are just as well off as you were last week. Better I think, for you are rid of that selfish pig of a lover of yours!"

Sherrill suddenly giggled and then buried her face on her aunt's shoulder.

"Aunt Pat," she said mournfully, "Why do you suppose this had to happen to me? Why did I have to be punished like this?"

"I wouldn't call it punishment, child," said the old lady patting Sherrill's shoulder. "I'd say it was a blessing the Lord sent to save you from a miserable life with a man who would have broken your heart."

"But if that is so," wailed Sherrill, "why didn't He stop me before it went so far? Before it would hurt so much?"

The old lady was still a minute and then she said:

"Perhaps He did, and you wouldn't listen. Perhaps you had some warnings that you wouldn't heed. I don't know. You'll have to look into your own life for that."

Sherrill looked at her aunt thoughtfully, remembering little happenings that had made her uneasy. The time Carter had gone away so hurriedly back to his former home without explanation. The letter addressed to him in a girl's handwriting that had fallen from his pocket one day which seemed to embarrass him but which he put back without a word. The telegram he sent her to say he was called to New York when afterward she discovered he had been West again, and when she innocently asked about it he gave but a lame excuse. The conversation she had overheard about him on the trolley calling in question his business principles. The queer way he had acted about not wanting to purchase her necklace at a certain store where she had admired a string of pearls, but had insisted on choosing one from another place. Oh, little things in themselves, but they had made her vaguely uneasy when they happened. Had they been warnings? Perhaps she should have sifted them. But she had been so reluctant to believe anything against him, so determined to shut her eyes to any fault of his!

There was that day, too, when she had come to the

office unannounced and found Arla sitting very close to Carter, her hand in his, her head on the desk, crying. They had jumped apart and Arla had gone quickly out of the room with her handkerchief to her eyes. Carter had been angry at her for coming in without knocking, and had explained that Arla's mother had just died and he had been comforting her, there was nothing else to it. That incident had troubled her greatly and they had had more than one discussion about it, until her own love and trust had conquered and she had put it away from her mind. What a fool she had been!

She had argued afterwards that of course he was not perfect and that when they were married she would help him to overcome his faults. He seemed so devoted! Then there would surge over her that feeling of his greatness, his ability and good looks, his many attractions, and she would fall once more under the spell of wonder that one so talented as he should love her.

Sharply, too, there came to memory the night before when she had stood looking into her own mirrored eyes wondering and shrinking back. Was that shrinking the result of those other fears and warnings? Oh, what a fool she had been! Yes, there had been plenty of warning. She was glad of course that she was mercifully delivered from being married to him, but oh, the desolate dreariness of her present situation! A drab life of loneliness to be looking forward to. To have thought herself beloved, and then to find her belief was built on a rotten foundation!

They had come out now, crossed the servants' hall, and the back sitting room where Carter had dressed for his wedding, and paused at the head of the stairs for a moment. Sherrill slipped her arm lovingly about the old lady's shoulders, and Aunt Pat patted her hand cheerfully. Then as they stood there they heard the doorbell ring and some packages were handed in, two great boxes.

"More presents!" gasped Sherrill aghast, "Oh, if there was only something we could do to stop them!"

"Well," said the old lady with a grin, "we might send out announcements that you were not married and 'please omit presents' at the bottom of the card."

Once again Sherrill's tragedy was turned into ridicule and she gathered up her courage and laughed.

"You're simply wonderful, Aunt Patricia! You brace me up every time I go to pieces. That's just what—!" Sherrill stopped suddenly, and her cheeks got red.

"That's just what what?" asked the old lady eyeing her interestedly.

"Oh, nothing! You'll laugh at me of course. But I was only going to say that's just what that stranger did last night. He seemed to know exactly how I was feeling and met me at every point with a pleasant saneness that kept me going. I shall always be grateful to him."

"H'm!" said Aunt Patricia approvingly, "Well, I thought he had a lot of sense myself."

Then Gemmie came forward with more boxes.

"We're not going to open them to-night, Gemmie, no matter what it is," said Miss Catherwood decidedly. "We're just too tired to stand the sight of another lamp or pitcher or trumpet whichever it is. We'll let it go till morning."

"But it's flowers, ma'am," protested Gemmie. "It says 'Perishable' on them, Miss Catherwood!"

"Flowers?" said the old lady sharply, giving a quick glance at Sherrill as if she would like to protect her. "Who would be sending flowers now? It must be a mistake!"

"It's no mistake, ma'am, there's one for each of you.

This small one is yours, and the big one is Miss Sherrill's."

She held the two boxes up to view.

Sherrill took her box wonderingly. It seemed as if this must be a ghost out of her dead happy past. For who would be sending her flowers to-day?

She untied the cord with trembling fingers, threw back the satiny folds of paper, and disclosed a great mass of the most gorgeous pansies she had ever seen. Pansies of every hue and mixture that a pansy could take on, from velvety black with a yellow eye down through the blues and yellows and purples and browns to clear unsullied white. There were masses of the white ones arranged in rows down at the foot of the box, with a few sprays of exquisite blue forget-me-nots here and there, and the whole resting on a bed of delicate maiden hair fern.

The fragrance that came up from the flowers was like the woods in spring, a warm fresh mossy smell. Had pansies an odor like that? She had always thought of them as sturdy things, merry and cheery, that came up under the snow and popped out brightly all summer. But these great creatures in their velvet robes belonged to Pansy royalty surely, and brought a breath of wildness and sweetness that rested her tired eyes and heart. She bent her face to touch their loveliness and drew a deep breath of their perfume.

The card was half hidden under a great brilliant yellow fellow touched with orange with a white plush eye. She pulled it out and read the writing with a catch in her breath and a sudden quick throb of joy in her heart. Why should she care so much? But it was so good to have flowers and a friend when she had thought all such things were over for her.

"I hope you are getting rested," was written on the card just above his engraved name, Graham Copeland.

A sudden chuckle brought Sherrill back to the world again, the warm glow from her heart still showed in her cheeks, and a light of pleasure in her weary eyes.

"The old fox!" chuckled Aunt Pat.

"What is the matter?" asked Sherrill in quick alarm.

"Why, he's sent me sweetheart roses! What do you know about that? Sweetheart roses for an old woman like me!" and she chuckled again.

"Oh, Aunt Pat! How lovely!" said Sherrill coming near and sniffing the bouquet. "And there are forget-me-nots in yours too! Isn't it a darling bouquet?"

"Yes, and the fun of it is," said Aunt Pat with a twinkle of sweet reminiscence in her eyes, "that I had a bouquet almost exactly like this when I went to my first party years ago with my best young man. Yes, identical, even to the lacepaper frill around it, and the silver ribbon streamers!"

Aunt Pat held it close and took deep breaths with half closed eyes, and a sweet faraway look on her face.

In due time Patricia Catherwood came out of her brief trance and admired the box of pansies.

"Aunt Pat," said Sherrill suddenly, her great box of sweetness still in her arms, as she looked down at them a little fearfully, very wistfully, "he wouldn't have sent these if he had—"

"No, of course not!" snapped the old lady. "I declare I'm ashamed of you, Sherrill Cameron. Can't you ever trust anybody any more just because one slim pretty man disappointed you? Just get on the job and learn how to judge real men and you won't have any more of that nonsense. Take those flowers to your room and study them, and see what you think about the man that sent them."

"Oh, I trust him perfectly, Aunt Pat. I'm quite sure he is all right. I *know* he is! But I was afraid you would think—!"

"Now, look here, if you are going to keep charging me with all the vagaries that come into your head 'you and I will be two people!' as an old nurse of my mother's used to say. For pity's sake, forget those emeralds and go and put your flowers in water. Unless perhaps you'd rather Gemmie did it for you!" she added with an acrid chuckle.

"Oh, no!" said Sherrill, quickly hugging her box in her arms, her cheeks flaming crimson. "Look, Auntie Pat. Aren't they dear? And yours are dear too. Almost as dear as yourself."

There was a tremble in her voice as she stooped and kissed the old lady on the sweet silver waves of hair just above her brow, and then she hurried away laughing, a dewy look about her eyes.

It was so nice not to feel utterly forgotten and out of things, she told herself as she went to her room with her flowers. It was just like him and his thoughtfulness to do this to-night! This first night after that awful wedding that was not hers! Somehow as she took the pansies out one by one and breathed their sweetness, laid them against her cheek with their cool velvety touch the weariness went out of her. It seemed to her as if by sending these blossoms he had made her understand that he knew this was a hard night and he was still standing by, although he could not be here, helping her through. She thought the joy that bubbled up in her heart was wholly gratitude.

"Pansies for thoughts!" she said to herself and smiled with heightened color, "Is that why he sent them? Forget-me-nots! Oh—!"

She rang for a great crystal bowl and arranged the

flowers one at a time, resting on their bed of ferns, and she was not tired any longer. She had lost that sense of being something that was flung aside, unwanted.

She got herself quickly into a little blue frilly frock for dinner, and fastened a few pansies at her breast, pale blue and white and black among the fluffy frills. She came down to find the old lady in gray chiffon with a sweetheart rose at her throat, and the bouquet otherwise intact in a crystal vase before her.

It was after all a gay little meal. The two had lost their sense of burden. They were just having a happy time together, getting nearer to each other than they ever had been before, and the hazy forms of a youth of the past dressed in the fashion of another day, and a youth of the present very much up to date standing in the shadows behind their chairs.

"I've been thinking of that question you asked me, why all this had to come to you," said the old lady, "I wonder—! You know it might have been that God has something very much better He was saving for you, and this was the only way He could make you wait for it!"

"I shall never marry anybody now, Aunt Pat, if that's what you mean!" said Sherrill primly though there was a smile on her lips.

"H'm!" said Aunt Pat smiling also.

"I could really never again trust a man enough to marry him!" reiterated Sherrill firmly, nestling her chin against the blue velvet cheek of the top pansy.

Aunt Pat replied in much the same tone that modern youth impudently use for saying "Oh yeah?", still with a smile, and a rising inflection, "Ye-*es?*"

"This man is just a friend. A stranger sent to help in time of need," explained Sherrill to the tone in Aunt Pat's voice.

"H'mmm!" said Aunt Pat. "It may be so!"

ARLA'S triumph was brief. She found Carter anything but a lover the next morning. He was surly and crabbed to her at breakfast, found fault with her attire and her make-up, told her her lips were too red for good taste, even went so far as to say that Miss Cameron never stained her fingernails. Arla felt as if she had been stabbed. She could scarcely finish her breakfast.

But because she had determined to make this marriage a success she bore his criticism, even ignoring his reference to his other bride though the tears were not far away, and a smouldering fire burned in her eyes. Was this other girl to be held up to her as a paragon the rest of her days? Oh, he was cruel!

She studied his sullen face, his selfish lips and saw these traits in him for the first time!

And she, by marrying him in that underhanded way, had forfeited a right to protest against such words. She could not flare out at him and tell him he had loved her enough to marry her and therefore he need not compare her with another. He had not married her by his own initiative, she had married him, and taken him as it were unaware, where he could not help himself.

The cold flamed into her face and then receded leaving it deathly white and making the redness of her lips but the more startling!

Then when they went on deck almost the first person he sighted was a man from whom he had borrowed largely but a few days before on the strength of his marriage into the Catherwood fortune.

Without explanation he dashed around a group of deck chairs, upsetting one in his haste, colliding with a man and swinging around to the other side of the ship without any seeming reason at all.

Arla followed him breathlessly, trying not to appear to be running a race. She was nonplussed. What was the matter with Carter? She had never seen him act in such a crazy way.

When she at last brought up panting at the secluded hiding place that he had selected she watched him in dismay. His face was actually lowering.

"What in the world is the matter with you, Carter?" she asked, almost tenderly. She began to think perhaps all that had happened yesterday had unsettled his mind.

"Everything in the world is the matter with me!" he said in a harsh tone. "Everything terrible that could happen to a man in any position!"

Arla studied him, still with that troubled look in her eyes, knowing that he would presently explain himself. She had not been his secretary for some months without knowing his habits.

"That was Mr. Sheldon that we passed as we came up the companionway. Didn't you recognize him?" He turned and glared at her as if she were responsible for Mr. Sheldon being on board.

"Sheldon? What Sheldon?" asked Arla in a pleasant tone, "I don't know any Mr. Sheldon, do I?"

"No!" said Carter, "You don't *know* him, socially of course, but it's not many hours since you witnessed his signature on some papers in the office!"

He paused impressively.

Arla looked puzzled and waited again, but Carter was still trying to impress her. At such time he could take on a fairly ponderous look, though he was not a large man, by merely swelling up proudly and looking down at her.

"Well, what of it?" asked Arla half impatiently after she had waited a reasonable time for explanation.

"What of it? And *you* can say what of it! You who wrote out those papers for him to sign, you who heard the whole conversation, and know that it was on the strength of my expectation of being able to raise a large sum in the near future that he loaned me the money I needed to finance—" he stopped abruptly, conscious that this very wedding trip was a part of the business he had to finance, the ring that sparkled on her finger, the pearls she had worn to the altar. He couldn't quite tell her that! Even in his present state of mind he couldn't be as raw as that.

"Well—?" she said again almost haughtily, watching him narrowly. His whole attitude toward her, his very tone had become offensive.

"Well? No, there is nothing well about it!" he snapped. "That man is a friend of the Catherwoods. He knows the Catherwood lawyer intimately. And he knows Sher—he knows Miss Cameron by sight. I have been with her when we met him. Don't you realize—? You can't be so blind as not to know that it would be nothing short of disastrous for him to know what has happened! Why, it's even conceivable that he might stop payment on that check now. He could radio a message

to his bank you know. And then I'd be in a worse hole than I'm in already. You know as well as I do."

"Well, but he couldn't possibly know what had happened from merely meeting us together on deck!" said Arla haughtily.

"Couldn't he? You don't think he's sharp enough? Well, let me tell you he's keen. How long do you think it would take him to cancel his agreement if he discovers that instead of marrying an heiress I am tied to a penniless secretary?"

The words cut to the quick! Arla caught her breath and set her lovely teeth sharply in her red under lip, trembling with humiliation and anger.

He cast a furtive glance at her and grew only the more hateful, realizing perhaps to what depths he had descended.

"Well, you needn't cry-baby about that!" he said sharply, "You might as well understand what kind of a hole you've put me in!"

"I've put you in—!" said Arla fiercely. *"I!"*

"Yes you!" said the man, now beyond all bounds of self-control. *"I* didn't do it, did I? It was *you* who came to the Catherwood house fifteen minutes before the hour set for the wedding and got hysterics all over the place and drove me crazy so that I didn't know what I was doing! It was *you* that staged a scene with Sherrill and got yourself married to me wasn't it? I didn't know anything about it, did I? What could *I* do?"

There was an ominous silence while Arla struggled to control her voice. Presently she spoke in a tone of utter sadness as if she were removed from him by eons of time.

"Then all you told me last night was untrue!" she said. "Then you lied to me about your great love that you said you had for me!"

Suddenly the man grew red and shamed looking.

"I didn't say it was a lie!" he said. "This has nothing to do with that!"

"No, but I did!" said Arla. "And it has everything to do with that! I went through agony and humiliation to save you from marrying a girl you did not love because I believed you still loved me, and had only fallen for her because you needed her money. I was trying to save you from yourself, to save our love that in the past has been so sweet and true. And this is what I get! You tell me I have put you in a hole! Well, I'm in the same hole! What do you think it is for me to be married to a man that talks that way? Do you think I'm enjoying a wedding trip like this?"

"Well, it was none of my doings!" said the man shrugging his shoulders angrily. "I told you what kind of a fix I was in. I explained the whole matter to you didn't I?"

"Not until you had failed to get me to go out west on a vacation where I couldn't find out about it until afterwards! Not until your wedding invitations were about to come out," said Arla steadily.

"Well, I *tried* to tell you before. I tried to let you know by my actions—!"

"Yes, you tried to be disagreeable to me!" said Arla. "I suppose I ought to have understood you were trying to cast me off like a wornout garment. But I didn't! I thought you were worried about your business. I forgave everything because—I—loved you!"

The man gave an angry exclamation.

"There you are bawling again! Oh, women! They do nothing but make trouble and then they weep about it. A man is a fool to have anything to do with women!"

Arla lifted angry eyes.

"You would have talked that way to your paragon of

a Sherrill Cameron, I suppose?" she said, dashing away her tears.

He gave her a furious look.

"Can anything be more tantalizing than a jealous woman?" he sneered. "Well, I think we've gone far enough. I didn't come up here to listen to the kind of talk you've been giving me. I wanted to make you understand that we're in a very critical situation and we've got to do something about it! We've simply got to avoid meeting people, at least together."

"Just what do you mean by that?"

"Just what I said! We can't afford to have Sheldon get onto this. And he isn't the only one on board that knows us. I met Bixby this morning in the smoking room. He asked after Sh—, he asked after the bride of course and made some silly joke about having admired her first, and I had to tell him you were seasick, that you were a bad sailor and might not be able to appear at meals during the voyage. He knows Sheldon you know, is a sort of a henchman of his, and it won't do to have him talking. I think that's our best bet anyhow to save complications, just you stay close in your cabin, except late at night we can slip out and take a walk on deck where the rest don't usually come."

A wave of indignation passed over Arla's beautiful face.

"So that is the way you intend to treat me on my wedding trip!" she said bitterly, "keep me shut up in my room! Your bride! Well, I'll know how much to believe the next time you tell me you love me! How about you staying in and letting me do the talking?"

"But don't you see that wouldn't do? They all know Sh—, that is they all knew Miss Cameron."

"I see that you are perfectly crazy about money. You love money better than honor or decency or me."

"Now, you're being unreasonable!" said the man irritably, "I've told you our fortune hangs upon what happens in the next few days. I can't help it, can I, that my investments failed? Everybody else is having the same trouble. If the wedding had gone through as planned there wouldn't have been any trouble about money. I could have got around the old lady and got a loan of a hundred thousand or two to tide me over. But now—"

"But now, since she found you out, and the fortune isn't available you mean to take it out on me! who really is the wronged one from the beginning. Well, I won't stand for it, that's all! I'm not going to stay shut in and have you roaming around perhaps with some handsome brunette who has another fortune lying around!"

Her eyes were blazing wrathfully. Her tone was low but very angry. He watched her furtively. It wouldn't do to let her get started on that line. She could mess things up a lot more if she chose to.

"Look here, Arla!" he swung around upon her. "Be sensible! Haven't I told you that my business will go under completely and leave me utterly bankrupt if I can't tide over the next six months and pay my indebtedness. And now, just when I think I'm going to be able to swing it you get childish and balk at helping me."

"I'm not childish and I don't balk at helping you when it's right and reasonable. But I won't be lied about, and I don't intend to allow anybody to mix me up with the girl you didn't marry, not to save twenty businesses. Besides, I don't see what a mere fifty thousand matters. Even if Mr. Sheldon does refuse to pay the twenty-five thousand now, and the other twenty-five thousand in two or three months you still have a lot more thousands that you can't do anything about. You can't save your business anyhow you try, and it's better to realize that and give it up. Just let them take over what you have and don't try to launch out. Begin again in a small way and I'll help you!"

"Ah, but there's where you are mistaken, Arla! I've found a way. I'm sure I've found a way to swing the rest of that. Just last night a way came. I can't tell you about it yet, but it's sure! And we shall be on easy street yet, my girl! Just have a little patience. A day or two after we've landed on the other side I shall have everything all fixed up."

His eyes narrowed and he looked at her cunningly.

She gave him a quick furtive glance.

"And suppose you didn't? Suppose you are mistaken?" Her breath came sharply. "Don't you know you are throwing away something sweeter and finer than any money or any business that you could ever have?"

Perhaps because her words went deeper than she understood they angered him the more.

"Get out of my way!" he roared, forgetting he was on an ocean liner. "If you're my wife take my orders then! Don't you dare to stir out of the cabin again in daylight unless I say you may. Go! I don't want to see you any more, you make me tired! Talk about wedding trips? *I'm* having a glorious one!"

"Hush!" said Arla imperatively in a low controlled voice, "There's your Mr. Sheldon just below you coming up the stairs!"

Carter turned and saw the puffy red face of the financier advancing pompously up to where he stood, but when he turned back to give Arla a warning scowl she was not there. There seemed no way that she could have gone, but she was gone. Carter was left embarrassed and awkward to meet the dignified scrutiny of the man he wished to placate. He wished frantically that he knew how much of his conversation had been overheard.

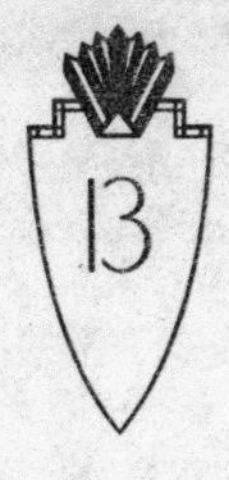

BY a way that her need had discovered to her in the sudden crisis Arla had fled to her stateroom. Having locked her door she stood for an instant with clenched fists down at her sides, her teeth set in her trembling underlip, fighting back the tears that filled her eyes, fighting down the anger, the remorse, the dismay that threatened to overwhelm her. Then she began to walk up and down the small room like a young lion in a cage.

Suddenly her mood changed. She grew calmer. She took a book and a warm coat, went out on the deck and found an out-of-the-way nook where Carter would have to hunt to find her, and sat down, pretending to read, but really thinking out the way before her step by step. If she had to go back twenty-four hours would she have been willing to marry Carter? She refused to answer that question. It was too late. She must go forward!

She stayed in her hiding place until long past the lunch hour, subsisting on the cup of broth that was brought around on deck in midmorning. Still Carter had not found her, or perhaps had not chosen to seek her. Then soon after lunch time a young man came breezily by her chair, paused, hesitated, and then cried out:

"Great Caesar's ghost! If this isn't Arla Prentiss! Say, now, what do you know about that? I'm in luck, aren't I?"

Arla looked up, dismay in her soul, for there before her stood the soda clerk from her home town drug store, crude and breezy and familiar as ever. He had known her all her life, had bestowed various boxes of candy upon her, had attempted to pay her attention sometimes, though she had always been able to laugh him off. Still, he was genuine and somehow the real hearty admiration in his eyes now warmed her heart, even while she was wondering what Carter would say when he found that Hurley Kirkwood was on board.

But there was no dismay in Hurley Kirkwood's heart. He was joyously glad to see her. He had been somewhat like a stray cat till he sighted her, having no acquaintances on board, and being adrift in the world for the first time in his life.

"Say, now, this is great!" said Hurley, quickly drawing up a camp stool and settling down to enjoy himself. "Say, now, Arla, are you alone? Taking a trip to Europe alone? Say, now, if I can be of any service!"

Arla gave a little shiver.

"No, I'm not alone," she smiled, "my husband is around here somewhere! I'm on my wedding trip, Hurley!"

"Boom! Just like that!" said Hurley slapping his hands together noisily. "Hopes busted at the first word! Well, I congratulate you, Arla. But say now, when did it happen? You kept it mighty still, didn't you? Didn't any of the home folks come to the wedding? Your Aunt Tilly wouldn't have missed it I'm sure if she'd known."

Arla suddenly realized that there was another part of her world yet to be dealt with.

"Yes, it was rather sudden," said Arla, "You see Carter found he had to go abroad and of course it made a splendid wedding trip. I had practically no warning whatever. We just got married and rushed off to catch this boat."

"Well, you certainly put one over on the home town," said Hurley. "Sorry I didn't know about it. You might have wired. There's about a dozen I know would have come on to see you off. And me, why I could have made it easy. I been in New York three days just bumming!"

Arla tried not to shudder again at the thought. It seemed to her that nothing could have been more perfectly the last straw at that terrible wedding of hers than to have had Hurley Kirkwood appear on the scene. She registered a distinct thanksgiving that she had been saved so much at least.

And yet, as he talked on, giving her homely items of domestic interest about her Aunt Tilly's rheumatism, old Mrs. Pike's having lost all her money when the bank closed and going to the poor house, Lila Ginn's latest escapade of running away with a drummer, and the party the high school kids had at a road house that made all the school board sit up and take notice, somehow Arla felt the tension in her taut nerves relax. After all it was comforting just to hear of home folks and home town and things that happened in the years before Carter had loved and tried to marry another woman. It was good to forget if only for a few minutes the problems and perplexities of her own present situation.

Hurley Kirkwood made a good soda clerk. He knew how to kid everybody in town with a special brand of kidding for each individual. There was something vivid and interesting about Hurley in spite of his crudeness, and presently Arla forgot herself so far as to be laughing heartily at some of the stories Hurley told.

Hurley had saved up his money, and he was just explaining to Arla how he had always wanted this trip to Europe and mapping out the course of travel he had planned for himself, when suddenly a stern and forbidding Carter arrived on the scene. He fairly glared at the poor soda clerk whom he had never liked, mainly because he presumed to be friendly with Arla. Carter had never approved of Arla's being friendly with Hurley. Just because she had gone to school with him did not give a mere soda clerk the right to take the girl of a man like himself to *anything!* Not even a ball game in the early evening played in his own neighborhood! Not even if he started out alone and just *met* Arla and sauntered with her to the grandstand and bought her peanuts, which is what had happened one summer evening when Carter's interest in Arla was in its initial stages.

Therefore Carter glared at Hurley and gave him a passing:

"Oh, Hurl, you here! Not serving in your official capacity as drink slinger on board are you?"

There was utter contempt in Carter's tone. All the venom and fury that he had been holding in his heart for Arla during the morning because she had not obeyed him, and had been evading him, he vented in that one contemptuous sentence.

And Hurley, gay, crude, a bit obtuse, not easily hurt, could not but recognize the unfriendliness and grew red and embarrassed. He attempted to rise to the occasion by slapping the dignified Carter on the shoulder and offering congratulations in his native style.

"My sympathy, Cart!" he said with a guffaw, "I hear you been getting tied! Only wish I'd been there to be best man. I'd have given you a great send off! But say now, isn't it great we both got on the same little old boat together! My word! I got something to write home to the little old home town now! Mebbe that won't make 'em all sit up and take notice! Cart and Arla got tied at last! We been looking for news and an invite this long while and then you went and done it on the sly! But say now, I certainly do wish you a lotta happiness!"

Carter's face had grown more and more stern during this harangue and now his tone was like a slap in the face as he made another attempt to put this boo from home in his place.

"I am sure Mrs. McArthur and I are greatly obliged to you for your interest," he said disagreeably, and then turned to Arla sternly.

"My dear, I shall have to ask you to come down to the stateroom at once. There is a matter I must discuss with you."

But Arla was resenting her husband's attitude. A sudden loyalty for the home town and the people and things that used to be dear to her surged over her. Carter had no call to insult this well meaning but ignorant youth who stood there red and hurt and wondering over the unnecessary coolness in Carter's tone. She knew that Carter was venting upon him all the injury and indignation he felt for her, and she turned lightly away from the command and answered:

"All right, Carter, I'll be down presently. I want to finish my talk with Hurley first. He's been telling me all about the people at home."

Carter could scarcely believe his senses. Arla was standing out against him. He stared at her in consternation a moment with an icy look, then turned on his heel and marched away.

She did not look after him as he went. She did not

dare to think what effect her attitude would have upon him. It was the first time in her acquaintance with him,—which had dated from her very young childhood,—that she had ever defied him. She had pled with him, she had wept, she had been sweet and submissive, but she had never openly defied him before and she was trembling over it. She found herself almost panic stricken. Perhaps he would never speak to her again. Perhaps he would divorce her. Yet it was what she had resolved in those morning hours of meditation that she would do, defy him, show him that he could not order her about. Would she be able to carry it out?

For another half hour she asked questions about the people at home, questions in which she had not the slightest interest, but which she knew would bring forth voluble answers, long enough to protect her from having to say much back. Hurley was delighted. In all his acquaintance with her taken altogether he had never had this much speech of her. He admired her greatly, and was tremendously flattered that she had stayed to talk with him. He was so flattered that he forgot Carter's insulting tone.

When Arla had finally ceased to tremble and felt that she had sufficient control of herself to carry out the program she had planned for herself she arose sweetly.

"Well, now, I really must go to that longsuffering husband of mine," she said smiling, "It's been so nice to meet you again, to hear all the news from home, and to know you're going to have such a lovely trip." And then she was gone and Hurley knew that he was dropped as definitely as she had always dropped him in the old days when he brought her candy and she accepted it graciously, but always had a reason why she couldn't go to the movies with him.

Hurley went and stood by himself staring off at the sea

and wondering why it was. Here he had been having as nice a time with her as anyone would need to ask to have, and all of a sudden he was out of it, just out! That was all! He knew as well as if she had told him that he wouldn't likely come in contact with either of them the rest of the voyage. Oh, maybe meet and bow or something like that, but nothing more. And here he had been fool enough to fancy that now that he had money enough to take a trip abroad they would be friendly and he would have somebody to talk to now and then, just be friendly with any time he liked! Well, maybe it was just his imagination. He decided he'd forget it. Probably they'd be all right the next time he met them. Maybe he'd try to get at their table and then they'd have to be friendly.

When Arla reached the stateroom Carter was not there. She was likely being punished. So she put on one of Sherrill's prettiest negligees and lay down to rest. That is her body was resting but her mind was madly working. She was looking life in the face, realizing all sorts of possibilities. Well, that other girl had been right. It was no enviable path she had chosen for herself, but having chosen it, being married, the thing she had so much desired, she must make it a success if that were a possible thing to do. She had not attained her wish unless she was able to hold him. And she saw keenly enough that this was the crucial time. What she did now would count through the years. Oh, for wisdom to know what was the best thing to do!

Carter did not return to the stateroom until it was nearly time for dinner. He found Arla attired in black lace and looking fairly regal, putting the last touches to her facial expression. She turned an indifferent glance at him and in spite of his smouldering anger he was startled at her beauty. Sherrill had never been more beautiful!

Arla certainly was a stunning looking woman. There was some satisfaction in that for the future. If he ever pulled through this hard time he could be proud of her. There was an air about her that he had never seen before, a certain smartness that he had always admired in Sherrill. He did not realize that Arla was wearing one of Sherrill's costumes which was the work of an artist and had cost a fabulous sum. He simply saw that Arla was looking more wonderful than he had ever seen her look before. For a moment he was almost ready to forgive her and take her into his arms. Then she turned and gave him a haughty indifferent glance and his anger boiled again.

"What are you all rigged up like that for?" he snarled, even while his eyes gloated over the lovely curves of her throat and white shoulders. "You're not planning to do what I forbade you to do?"

"Forbade?" said Arla with slightly uplifted eyebrows. "Really! I shouldn't recognize any such word as that between us! That isn't what marriage means. Not in this age and generation! If you mean am I going down to dinner, I certainly am. If you don't want to go with me that's entirely up to you. I am sure Hurley Kirkwood will be delighted to take me in to dinner. I can tell people you are seasick you know. But as this is the first ocean voyage I've ever had, and may be the last one I'll ever get, I intend to enjoy every minute of it in spite of your disagreeableness."

"You don't care what happens to me and my business then? I thought you professed to love me!" he said after a long silence during which he went and stared out the porthole.

"Why, I supposed I did too," said Arla lightly, "but as for caring what happens to you and your business at such a price as you demand, I'm not so sure that I do."

He was still a much longer time now, staring out at the endless waves of the ocean.

"Then do I understand that you refuse to comply with my request and stay out of sight during the voyage."

"Yes, I do!" said Arla coolly, taking up her hand mirror and examining her profile carefully and the wave of her lovely gold hair.

"But why, Arla? You have always wanted me to get on. You know I want it for you as much as for myself—!"

"Oh!" interrupted Arla in a surprised voice, "no, I didn't know that!" Her tone was sweet and innocent. "Did you want it for me as much as for yourself when you were going to marry Sherrill Cameron?"

He gave a quick angry exclamation.

"Can't you leave her out of the question now we're definitely done with her?" he asked desperately.

"I'm sorry," said Arla, "I'd like to, but the trouble is she somehow won't be left out. You see she was there, and I'm not so sure she's definitely out of it either."

"Well, then, if you must bring her in, yes, I did do it for your sake as much as my own. I thought an alliance with her would bring the needed funds and position, and later, well,—there are such things as divorces you know!"

She turned a steely eye to him.

"Carter, if you had been brought up in the social world of to-day there might be some excuse for your daring to say a thing like that to me, but both you and I had decent mothers who didn't believe in such things, and when you say that you are insulting both Miss Cameron and myself. You said something of that sort last night I remember, just before you flung me off in the corner and went out to marry your other bride. I don't know how I ever forgave it in you enough to be willing to marry you except that I thought you were beside yourself and didn't realize what you were saying. It was preposterous you know! And if I didn't think you were still rather beside yourself I certainly wouldn't stay here with you now and listen to such talk."

"Very well, now, if you are so interested in me and my business," he said at last, "what would you suggest that we do? You know the facts, that I need a large sum of money to tide me over and if I can get it I can keep my business floating till this depression is past. If I don't I either have to give up and lose everything or else probably go to jail!"

"I would *not* go to jail!" said Arla. He gave her a sudden quick startled look. But Arla went steadily on talking, not looking at him. "I would take the next boat back as soon as I landed and arrange to give over my business interests in such a way that while it might be a total loss of all that has been gained through the last three years, your name would be cleared and you could go honorably into some more modest business and have a chance of making good. You will remember I happen to have been present in the office when an offer was made to you which would have made that possible!"

"Oh!" exclaimed the man angrily, "I'm not an utter fool!"

"Are you sure?" asked the woman. "Sometimes I wonder!"

After a long silence the man spoke again in a voice of smouldering wrath:

"Well, come on, I suppose you've got to have it your way and go down to dinner even if it wrecks everything! It was bad enough before, but now that the situation is further complicated by the appearance of that country bunkum from home I don't see how we can possibly get by without trouble. How in the world are you going to explain him to people if he chooses to barge in on us?"

"I don't expect to explain him or anybody else we may happen to meet. This is not a private boat and anybody has a right on board who pays his fare. Please remember that I had nothing whatever to do with his being here. As far as I am concerned I see no reason why we shouldn't go about our business as anybody else does. If your business was on an honest basis we could go about freely and enjoy ourselves without watching out for what people think."

"Women know nothing about business!" glowered Carter. "Well, come on, let's get this over."

So Arla in Sherrill's costly lace gown from an exclusive Paris house walked regally beside her husband and never showed by the flicker of an eyelash that she had recognized across the saloon another two people from home, a young man and his wife who had been in the same class in high school with Carter and Arla. It would be time enough for Carter to know they were on board when he had to meet them. They would be another element in this problem she was trying to solve.

THERE was a sense of peace in Sherrill's room next morning. The fragrance of the pansies pervaded the place. The delicate perfume spoke to her at once even before she opened her eyes. It brought the memory of the pleasant stranger, as if his presence were still lingering not far away to help.

Then she opened her eyes to see the pansies on the low bedside table where she had placed them. She reveled in their soft brightness, and was glad they were just pansies, not any of the more conventional flowers. They seemed to emphasize the simple frank friendship that had begun on the street, just plain honest friends helping one another. Pansies might grow in anybody's garden, only these of course were sort of glorified pansies. But it was a comfort that they did not recall the bridal bouquet nor any of the flowers in the church. Just simple pansies that she might love and lay her face against.

She reached out for the card that lay beside them on the table. Somehow that hastily penned line seemed to have a deeper meaning than just a wish that she was rested physically. It seemed to carry a desire that she might be healed in spirit from the deep hurt to her life that he could not help knowing that wedding must have been to her.

Little memories of the kindness in his eyes, merry eyes that yet held tenderness, came back to her; the turn of a sentence that made her laugh when he must have seen the tears were very near to coming; his pleasant grin. They all filled her with a warmth and comfort that was restful and almost happy.

She lay there thinking about him. How kind he had been! She was rejoicing in the presence of the pansies in their lovely fern setting when Gemmie tapped at the door and entered with a breakfast tray.

"Miss Patricia said you better eat before you get up," she announced, setting her tray down on a low table and drawing back the silk curtains.

Gemmie brought her negligee and put it about her, adjusted her pillows. Then she bustled over to the hearth and lighted a fire that was ready, though it was scarcely needed that bright spring morning. Sherrill began to perceive that Gemmie had something on her mind. She never bustled unless she was ill at ease. But Sherrill was too comfortable just at that moment to try and find out what it was, so she let Gemmie go on setting things straight on the dressing table and then setting them crooked again. At last she spoke.

"It's right awful about that necklace being gone, Miss Sherrill!"

Boom! A great burden of stone seemed suddenly to land back again in Sherrill's heart, just where it had been the day before, only a trifle heavier if possible.

"Yes," quavered Sherrill pausing in her first comforting swallow of coffee.

"Seems like we ought to do something about it right

away," went on Gemmie. "Seems like we oughtn't to let the time get away with us."

"Yes, Gemmie," said Sherrill distressedly, "but Aunt Pat wants to work it out in her own way. I think she has some idea about it, though she doesn't want to tell it yet. We are not to tell anybody about it you know."

"Yes, I know," said Gemmie severely as if she disapproved greatly. "But Miss Sherrill, it doesn't seem reasonable, does it? That necklace didn't have legs. It couldn't run away of itself, could it?"

"Not very well, Gemmie." Sherrill lay back against her pillows with distress in her eyes.

"There was only one stranger there, wasn't there, Miss Sherrill? I was wondering if you knew him real well. Was you right sure about him?"

"Stranger?" said Sherrill coldly. "Did you mean the clerk who came in to witness the license papers signed?"

"Oh, laws! No! Not him. I've known him for years. He used to live next door to my best friend, and he wouldn't steal a pin. He's too honest, if you know what I mean? But wasn't there a stranger there, Miss Sherrill? I came across him in the back hall just after I got back from the church. I went up to leave my hat and coat and I found him wandering around trying doors all along the hall."

"Oh, you mean my friend Mr. Copeland," said Sherrill with elaborate coolness. "No, I brought him there, Gemmie. He'd just come from the train and brought his suitcase to change here. I met him at the church. He's from out near my old home in the west you know, Gemmie. I put him in that little end room where we afterwards signed the papers. He's quite all right!"

Sherrill explained it all out slowly, her voice growing more assured as she went on, and ending with a ripple of laughter, though she felt that awful haunting doubt creeping into her mind again with the accompanying heaviness of heart.

"You know him right well do you? You're sure he wouldn't yield to temptation, are you? You know those stones are wonderful costly, Miss Sherrill!"

"Oh, for pity's sake, Gemmie! What an awful suggestion to make about a friend and guest of ours! You'd better not say that to Aunt Pat. She certainly would not be pleased. Of course he is entirely above suspicion. Why he is a friend, Gemmie!"

"Well! I didn't know how well you knew him," said Gemmie offendedly, "I never heard you speak of him before and I didn't know but what he might be somebody you hadn't seen in a long time, and didn't know how he'd turned out now he's growed up."

Sherrill managed a real laugh now and answered:

"No, Gemmie, nothing like that! Now, if you'll take this tray I'll get up. I want to get at those presents again. We got a lot done yesterday, didn't we?"

"Yes, Miss Sherrill, but you've not eaten your breakfast, and Miss Patricia will be all upset."

"All right, Gemmie, I'll eat a little more if you'll run and see if the morning mail has come yet. I'm expecting a letter. Aren't my flowers lovely, Gemmie? Mr. Copeland's the one that sent them to me."

Gemmie eyed the flowers half suspiciously.

"Yes," admitted Gemmie reluctantly, "for flowers that aren't roses, they're above most."

Then Gemmie, leaving a mist of insidious doubt in her wake, swept firmly out of the room, and Sherrill had a silly feeling that she wanted to throw the whole breakfast after her and burst into tears. How outrageous of the stupid old thing to get such a notion and try to rub it in! Of course her kind stranger friend was all right! She would not let such sickening doubts creep into her mind. Aunt Pat didn't think any such thing. She didn't herself. As she remembered the fine merry countenance and wide frank eyes she felt that it was utterly ridiculous to suspect such a man even though he was a stranger. Yet there was that heaviness planted for the day again, planted in the very pit of her stomach just like yesterday. Then she suddenly put her face down into her pillows and cried a few hot tempestuous worried tears till she remembered Gemmie would soon return with the mail and she mustn't have red eyes. So she stopped the tears and before Gemmie could come into the room again she sprang up and buried her face in the dewy sweetness of the pansies, touching her lips to their coolness hungrily. Oh, why did evil and suspicion and sin have to come in and spoil a world that would otherwise be bright? She would not, *would not* believe or entertain the slightest suspicion against Graham Copeland. They had made a compact of trust and friendship, and she would abide by her own intuition. Yes, and by Aunt Pat's judgment also.

And so when Gemmie entered Sherrill was bending over her flowers touching them delicately with her finger tips, lifting a pansy's chin lightly to look better into its face, and smiling into their gay little faces with a whimsical fancy that some of them were grinning just as their donor had done.

But Gemmie wore an offended air all that day, and went about poking into corners everywhere trying to find that necklace.

"I don't see why Miss Patricia won't have the police up here!" she declared. "I shan't be happy till that necklace is found! Who was that girl anyway, that bride? Did you ever see her before? Seems to me this is the queerest doings that ever was had about this house. I don't understand it myself. We never had doings around here that was out of the ordinary before. I mus' say I don't like it myself. Did you know that girl, Miss Sherrill?"

"Oh, yes, Gemmie," said Sherrill summoning a brave tone. "She was an old friend of Mr. McArthur's. In fact they had been sort of engaged for several years, and—then—well, they got separated—"

Sherrill's voice trailed off vaguely. She knew she was treading on very thin ice. How was she to make this all quite plausible to this sharp-eyed, jealous servant who loved her because she belonged to her beloved Miss Patricia, and yet not tell all the startling facts?

"You see, Gemmie," she went on bravely, taking up the tale and thinking fast, "she came just after you left with a message for Mr. McArthur and I happened to find out about it, so we had a little talk and fixed it up this way. It was rather quick work getting us dressed all over again, but I think we got by pretty well, don't you?" Sherrill finished with a little light laugh that sounded very natural, and Gemmie eyed her suspiciously.

"I ought to have stayed here!" she declared firmly. "I knew I oughtn't to've gone when I went. That was *your* wedding dress, not hers, and she had no business with it!"

"Oh, that!" laughed Sherrill gayly, "what did that matter? You see she didn't happen to have her own things with her, so we fixed it up that way, and I thought everything came off very well. She looked sweet, didn't she?"

"I didn't take notice to her," said Gemmie sourly. "When I saw it wasn't you I was that put out I could hardly keep my seat. I didn't think you'd be up to any tricks like that, Miss Sherrill, or I wouldn't have left you. If I hada been here I'd not have let her by having your wedding dress, not if she never got married. And your wedding, too. It was a shame!"

"Oh, no, Gemmie, it was lovely! Because you see when I found out a few things I didn't want to get married myself just then, so it turned out quite all right. I wouldn't want to marry a man who loved another woman, would you, Gemmie?"

"I wouldn't want to marry any man that lives!" sniffed Gemmie. "They're all a selfish deceiving lot. Not one good enough for a good girl like you."

"There you are, Gemmie! You think that and yet you are angry that I let another girl marry him!"

"Well, he was yours by rights after he'd went that far!" sniffed Gemmie getting out her primly folded handkerchief and dabbing at her eyes.

"Well, I didn't happen to want him when I found he really belonged to another girl," said Sherrill soberly, and wished that her heart didn't give such a sick plunge when she said the words. They were true of course, and yet her soul was crying out for the lover she had thought she had, though she didn't intend that this sharp-eyed woman should find it out. "And now, Gemmie, keep it all to yourself and let's forget about it. I'm back here to stay awhile, and I'm going to have the best time a girl can have. Do you happen to know where that little pale green knit dress of mine is, with the white blouse? I think I'd feel at home in that. Hasn't it got back from the cleaner's yet?"

"Yes, it came back three days ago but I put it away in the third floor closet. I didn't think you'd be needing it yet awhile."

"Oh, get it for me, Gemmie, will you? That's a dear! It's just the thing for this morning."

Sherrill hurried with her dressing and when Gemmie came back with the dress she slipped into it and with a gay little wave of her hand hurried down stairs, looking much brighter than she felt.

The next two days were full of hard work. It seemed that Miss Catherwood was in a great rush to get those presents out of the way.

But there does come an end to all things, even unpleasant ones, and Sherrill finally came to her aunt and laid a neatly written envelope in her lap.

"There, Aunt Pat, that's the last one of those awful notes I have to write. The very last one! And I'm glad! glad! glad! Now, what next?" and she looked drearily out of the window across the wide sweep of lawn and garden.

"Next we're going to get rested," said the old lady leaning back in her chair with a gray look about her lips. "I believe I'm tired, and I know you are. I've watched you getting thinner and thinner hour by hour. You've been a good sport, but now we've got to rest a little."

Sherrill sprang into alarm at once.

"You dear precious Aunt Pattie!" she cried, and was down on her knees beside her aunt's chair with her arm about her, looking earnestly into the tired old face.

"Oh, it's nothing," said Aunt Pat crisply, trying to rouse herself. "I just want a nap. I guess I've caught a bit of a cold perhaps. You need a nap too, and then afterwards we'll plan what we'll do next. How would you like to take a trip somewhere? You can be thinking about it while you're going to sleep."

THE next day was Sunday. Sherrill had been dreading it. Aunt Pat always went to church. Sherrill would be expected to go also, and she shrank inexpressibly from entering that church again, the church that had been decorated for her wedding, the church in which she had gone through that horrible experience, watching her bridegroom given to another woman. She almost decided to beg off, say she had a headache or something, only she knew a headache would bring alarm to the dear old lady and perhaps bring on a lot more complications that might be even worse than going to church. But oh, how she dreaded the soft lights from the stained glass, the exquisite music that would stir her soul to the depths and make her remember all the lovely things she had dreamed of and lost.

A dozen times during the early morning she thought of new excuses to stay at home, and even after she had her hat and gloves on and was on her way down stairs she had half an idea of telling Aunt Pat plainly how she longed to escape this experience, just this one Sunday anyway.

But when she got down stairs she found that the old lady was already in the car waiting for her and there was such a pleasant light of expectancy in her eyes that Sherrill had not the heart to suggest that she would not go.

"I got to thinking," said the old lady almost shyly, "I'd like to go to an old church where I went once with my best young man. Would you mind, Sherry?"

"Oh, I'd love it of course," said Sherrill deep relief in her voice. It would be so good to go to a new place where she would not have to go through that awful wedding again all during service. So good not to have to face the battery of eyes that would be watching to see just how she was taking life without her bridegroom. It would be such a relief not to have to sit and feel them wondering about her, thinking up things to say about her when they got home to their various dinner tables. Oh, many of the people in the home church were friends, nice pleasant people that she liked, but it was good not to have to be watched this first Sunday after her world had been turned upside down.

Dear Aunt Pat! She had known of course that she would feel like that, and had planned this to have something different.

"You see," said Aunt Pat suddenly, right into the midst of her thoughts, "James and I went out to this church a great many years ago. We started quite early Sunday morning for a walk to get away from everybody else for a while. We didn't plan where we were going,—or at least, maybe James did—he was like that, he thought of nice things and planned them out ahead—but we just started along the road."

Sherrill turned bright interested eyes on her sweet old aunt.

"We took hold of hands," confessed Miss Patricia with

a little pink tinge stealing into her soft roseleaf cheek. "It was very early when we started and there were no people about, not even a carryall on the road. We had a wonderful time. I had some caraway cookies in my silk bag that hung from my arm by little velvet ribbons. Soon there was dust on my best slippers, but I didn't care. We stopped before we went into church and James dusted them off. There were narrow velvet ribbon laces to my slippers, crossed at the ankle and tied in a little tassel bow."

Aunt Pat's eyes were sweet and dreamy.

"We talked about what we would do when we were married," went on the sweet old voice. "We planned a house with pillars and a great window on the stairs. I was going to do my own work. I had written down a list of things James liked to eat and I was learning to cook them."

"Oh," said Sherrill, bright-eyed, "it's just like a story book."

"Yes, it was," said Aunt Pat. "I was very happy. We walked a good many miles, but I wasn't tired. I didn't get tired in those days of course, but James slipped my hand through his arm, and that made it like walking on clouds!"

"Dear Aunt Pat!" breathed Sherrill.

"When we came to that little white church we knew we had come to the place we had been looking for, though we hadn't known what it was or where it was. But it was our church. We both exclaimed over it at once."

Sherrill nestled her hand in her aunt's hand.

"It was still early when we got there. The old sexton was just ringing the first bell, and it sounded out over the hills like music. The bell may have been out of tune but it sounded sweeter than any orchestra has ever seemed to me. We went and sat on a flat grave stone in the little cemetery under a tall elm tree and ate our seed cakes, and James put his arm around me and kissed me right there in the graveyard. It made me glad with a deep sweet gladness I had never felt before. It seemed just like heaven. And a bird high up sang a wonderful song that went through my heart with a sweet pain."

The little old lady had forgotten for the moment that Sherrill was there. Her eyes were dreamy and faraway.

"People ought never to get married unless they feel like that about each other, Sherry."

"No?" said Sherrill as if it were something she had just found out and were considering.

"You didn't feel like that about Carter McArthur, Sherrill."

"No," said Sherrill still gravely, "I don't think I did. I was just happy. Having a good time!"

There was a long minute of stillness, then Sherrill said shyly:

"Tell the rest, please, Aunt Patricia."

"Well," said the old lady, her eyes still on the faraway, "after a while the people began to come. They drove up in buggies and carryalls and phaetons, and a few in old farm wagons with boards across the sides for seats, and carpet on the boards. Then we got up and walked around among the white stones and read the names and dates until the sexton rang the second bell, and then we went in. A young girl with a pink ribbon and daisies on her hat played an old cabinet organ and I remember they sang 'Nearer my God to Thee,' and God seemed very near to us and we to Him."

"Yes?" said Sherrill nestling closer in a pause.

"We sat in the very last seat back by the door," went on the sweet old voice, "and James held my hand under the folds of my ruffles. I had on a very wide biadere striped silk skirt with three deep flounces, and they flowed over the seat beautifully. I can remember the strong warm feel of his hand now."

The tears began suddenly to come into Sherrill's eyes.

"We sat all through that service hand in hand and nobody the wiser," said Aunt Pat with a bit of her old chuckle, and then a softened light came into her eyes.

"We planned to go back there some day and be married in that church when James had got a good job. We loved that church! But, Sherry, we never went back there again! The next day they brought my James home with the mark of a horse's hoof on his temple."

She paused an instant, looking far away and added:

"Lutie's mother was the little child whose life he saved!"

"Oh, Aunt Patricia!" said Sherrill in a low awed voice. She understood now why helping Lutie's family was so important to Aunt Pat.

"I've never been back till to-day."

"My dear!" said Sherrill softly.

They were at the church now, a little white building set among the trees, with a quaint old graveyard surrounding it. A young sexton was tolling the bell. He would be perhaps the grandson of the old sexton who was there when the young Patricia walked up those steps with her James.

There were smart cars parked in the old sheds where farm wagons drawn by plow horses, and buggies and carryalls drawn by the family horses, used to be hitched so long ago. People were coming along the road dressed in stylish modern clothes. But as Sherrill looked at the pleasant white church she seemed to see the young Patricia in her wide hooped skirts with silken flounces and a broad flat hat with streamers, walking with her James up the steps of the house of God, and she had much ado to brush the tears away before she got out of the car, for people were hurrying by them in happy groups eyeing them curiously, as the shining limousine drew up before the flagstone path.

Sherrill watched her aunt furtively as they walked together up that path to the church. Her bright eyes had suddenly grown old and tired looking, and the soft cheeks and lips seemed to sag a little wearily. She walked without her usual spring, and when Sherrill drew her hand within her arm she leaned down heavily upon her as if she were grateful for the support. Her eyes were searching over to the right among the old mossy headstones. Sherrill felt she was looking for the place where she and her young lover had sat so long ago.

They went into the church and found a seat half way up. People stared in a kindly way and whispered about them, pondering who they were. There were quaint windows about the walls made of long panes of clear colored glass put together in geometrical forms like a kaleidoscope. The sun was casting long bright rays through them making quaint color effects of green and blue and yellow on people's chins and noses, and stabbing the old red ingrain carpet in the aisles with a sickly purple and red that did not match. But there was one window, back of the pulpit, high above the head of the minister, a gorgeous window, that was the work of a real master. It pictured an open tomb and an angel in a garden of lilies, with a wondrous blue light in a leaden sky where morning broke the gloom and shed a veil of loveliness over the lilies. Underneath in small clear letters were the words "Sacred to the memory of James and Patricia," and, "Joy cometh in the morning." Then a long ago date in characters so small they were hardly discernible.

Sherrill stared at it startled. So that was what Aunt

Patricia had done! Given this little stranger church a window! A window with a story that nobody understood! Aunt Pat had likely done it through her lawyer, or someone who did not even know her except as a client.

Sitting there in the weird light of stark mingled colors, studying that one lovely window, Sherrill worked it all out; the tragedy, and the sweetness of Aunt Patricia's long lonely life; the patience and utter cheerfulness that characterized her. What a lesson to a whining world! She wondered if Aunt Pat had anything besides her own strong self to rely upon? Did she know Lutie's secret? She was never one to talk religion, or to preach. She went regularly to church at least once a Sunday, and there was a little worn old-fashioned Bible on her bedside stand, but Sherrill had never seen her reading it, had never thought of her as being a strong religionist. Could it be that in her quiet way she too, like Lutie, had something in her heart, some great mysterious power beyond the earthly, that sustained her?

There was a little old wheezy cabinet organ played by a young girl with jingling silver bangles on her arms. The choir sat on a raised platform behind the organ and whispered a good deal among themselves. When they sang it was rousing. Not all the voices were cultured. When they sat down the green and purple from one of the windows played across their features grotesquely. An old man in the pulpit with the young minister prayed plaintively, yet there was something exceedingly sweet and uplifting in it, and Sherrill stole a look at the old lady by her side. There was a look of utter peace upon her face, as if a prayer of her own were winging upward to heaven beside the old man's petition.

The minister was a young seminary student, a bit crude, a bit conceited and greatly self-conscious. His words did not seem to mean much in relation to life. Sherrill was thinking of her aunt, and strangely too of Lutie's mother, the girl who had been rescued from death at such a cost. Now why was that? In all human reason it would seem that the young James with such a bright prospect of life, with such a partner as his Patricia, would have been worth infinitely more to the world than just Lutie's mother, a quiet humble mother of a servant girl. If there was a God supreme above all, surely He would manage His universe wisely, economically. And it seemed such an economic waste to kill a man with great possibilities that humble serving people might live. It did not seem reasonable.

And yet, in the great economy of life was it possible that the servant had some duty to perform, some place in the plan of things, that was important?

It was a baffling question to think upon, and Sherrill had not solved it when she rose to sing the last hymn. She only knew that her soul had been stirred to the depths, but more by Aunt Pat's story than the sermon, more by the great window with its resurrection story than by the service.

Kindly hands were put out shyly in welcome when the service was over as they passed down the aisle and out the door. The stately old lady walked sweetly among them, nodding here and there, smiling with that faraway look in her eyes, loving the gracious country folk collectively, because of one Sunday morning long years ago, and a lad that was long gone Home. You could see that they regarded her almost as if it had been an angel visiting their ancient place of worship. And Sherrill walked humbly in the shadow of that sweet soul's humble greatness.

The people stood back and hushed their chatter to watch the old lady away, but when she was out on the flagged path again she did not go down the walk but turned aside to the graveyard.

"This way," she breathed softly, and stepped on the young spring grass.

She led the way around to the side of the church, far back from the road, under a great elm tree.

"It was there we sat." She said it more as if talking to herself, and indicated with a little wave of her hand a great flat stone with an ancient date almost obliterated by lichens.

Then she turned about but a yard or two to the right, and stood, looking down at a small white stone with a single name "James" cut deep in its side, and a date of a generation ago.

Sherrill stood still startled, looking down at that name, realizing all it meant to her aunt to be standing there this morning, the first time she had come there since that beloved lost lover was laid there.

Just a moment they stood silently, Sherrill feeling the awe of the presence of a funeral pall. Yet there was nothing gloomy about the place. Clear spring sunshine flooding the spot, flicked with shadows of elm branches tossing in the light spring breeze. Birds caroling joyously overhead. The sound of friendly voices of the worshiper was just a few paces away, young laughter, the whirr of a motor starting from the church.

Unquestionably the young lover had not lain there all these years, his body crumbling to dust. He must be somewhere, doing something. Love and bravery and courage did not just blink out. That conviction came to Sherrill as a fixed fact, though she had never thought of such things before. Where was he, this James, and what faith had Aunt Pat that one day joy would come in the morning?

She thought of her own life, blighted right at the start.

Would there be joy, too, in some morning, for a life like hers that had found a lover false-hearted?

The old lady spoke.

"I'd like to have what's left of me put here when I am gone!" she said laying a hand on Sherrill's arm. "There's plenty of room. It doesn't matter of course, only it is pleasanter to think of being here than up under that great Catherwood monument at Laurel Hill. They can put my name there if they like, but I'll lie here. It'll be nice to think of getting up together in the morning."

"Dear Aunt Patty!" said Sherrill struggling with a constriction in her throat.

"I've put it all in my will of course, and the stone's been made ready, just Patricia and the date. But I thought I'd like somebody that belonged to me to understand."

"Of course!" said Sherrill tenderly, catching her breath and trying to steady her voice. "But—you're not going yet, dear—not for a long time. You wouldn't leave me—alone!"

"Why certainly not!" snapped the old lady with one of her quiet grins. "I've got to look after you for a spell yet. Come on, let's walk around. We don't want a lot of people staring at us. There's no need for them to know we're interested in just one grave. Let's walk around the church. There are some curious stones there, very old. James and I found them that day and talked about them. And there's a view,—look! away off to the hills! I think it's a lovely spot!"

"It is indeed," answered Sherrill, and almost envied her aunt for the joyous look on her face. How she had taken her sorrow and glorified it! Sherrill wondered if she, in like situation, could have risen to such heights, and felt how impossible it would have been for her. Felt how crushed she was by this her own sorrow which she recognized at once was so much less than what the old lady had borne for years unmurmuring, and said again to herself that there must have been some sustaining Power greater than herself or human weakness,—even human strength never could have borne it.

There was something glorified in the rest of that day. Sherrill felt that she had been allowed a glimpse into an inner sanctuary of a soul, and life could never again be the trivial, superficial thing that it had seemed to her before.

Aunt Pat was very tired and slept a great part of the afternoon, but in the evening she came down to the living room and sat before a lovely fire that Gemmie had kindled for them. She made Sherrill play all the old hymns she used to love. It brought the tears to hear the quavering voice that still had a note of sweetness in it, wavering through a verse here and there, and Sherrill trying to sing with her felt her own voice breaking.

Yet there was nothing gloomy about the old lady that night, and presently she was joking again in her snappy bright way, for all the world like a young thing, and Sherrill's heart was less heavy. Aunt Pat wasn't going away to leave her. Not now anyway.

SHERRILL needn't have worried about her aunt, for the old lady was up the next morning chipper as a bird, eating her breakfast with a relish.

"We're going to see Lutie's mother right away," she said. "We've got to get that family straightened out before we plan to do anything for ourselves."

"Oh, that will be wonderful!" said Sherrill who had arisen this morning with a great pall over life. Since there was no immediate action necessary she could not get hold of anything in which she was interested. But to help another household who were all in trouble intrigued her. It didn't occur to her either to realize that the canny old lady was wisely arranging to fill her days too full to brood over the past.

So they went to the neat little house where Lutie lived. Sherrill was amazed to see how attractive the little weatherbeaten house had been made. There was lack of paint on its ugly clapboards, lack of grace in all its lines, lack of beauty in its surroundings, for there were slovenly neighbors all about and a great hideous dump not far away to mar what otherwise might have been a bit of landscape.

But the ugly house had been smothered in quick growing vines. The ugly picket fence that also needed painting had been covered with rambler roses now beginning to bud, the yard had a neat patch of well cut lawn, with trim borders where young plants were beginning to give a good showing, and a row of pansy plants showed bright faces along the neat brick walk. The pansies winked brightly up at her like old acquaintances.

An ugly narrow court between houses had been concealed by tall privet hedge trained into an arched gateway, and there were nice white starched curtains at the windows upstairs and down. They might be only cheese cloth, but they made the house stand out like a thing of beauty in the midst of squalor.

"H'm!" said Aunt Pat appreciatively. "Pretty, isn't it? I don't know why I never thought to come here before."

The mother opened the door, wiping her hands on her apron which was an old towel girt about her waist. There was a fleck of soapsuds on her arm, and her face, though the morning was only half gone looked weary and worn.

"Oh, Miss Catherwood!" she said to Aunt Pat, her tone a bit awed.

She opened the door wide and welcomed them in casting a troubled eye over the room behind her to see if it was surely all in order.

"But you oughtn't to be washing!" objected Aunt Pat as she reached the top step and looked into the neat front room. "I thought you were sick. I heard you ought to go to the hospital."

The woman gave a helpless amused little laugh, not discourteous.

"No, I'm not sick," she said rather hopelessly, "I'm not near as bad off as some. I'll be all right when Father gets well. Come in won't you?"

Aunt Pat marched in gayly.

"Now, I'm not going to take up any more of your time than is necessary," she said as she sat down in the big old stuffed chair. "You go and shut off your dampers or gas or whatever it is that's worrying you, and I'll talk to you just five minutes and then you can get back and finish up what you've started. I suppose that's got to be done in spite of everything, but I've got something to say that's even more important."

The woman cast a sort of despairing look at her caller and with a half deprecatory glance toward Sherrill who had settled down on the old haircloth sofa she vanished into the back room where they could hear her turning on water, lifting dripping clothes from one tub to another, pulling a tin boiler across the top of an old fashioned iron range, and slamming the dampers back and forth.

She returned, pulling down her neat print sleeves, and fastening a clean apron over her wet dress.

Sherrill meanwhile had been looking around the little room, noting carefully the pretty trifles that Lutie had used to make the place homelike. There was even a little snap shot of herself that Sherrill recognized as one she had thrown in the waste basket. It was framed in glass with a black paper binding, and stood under the lamp on the small center table. Poor Lutie! Sherrill was deeply touched.

"Well," said Aunt Pat, "I'll get right to the point. My niece found out from Lutie that your husband is sick. How is he? Getting well fast?"

"No," said the woman sadly, "he doesn't improve at all now. He's pretty well discouraged. He said last night he guessed he had got to the end, and the sooner it came the better off we'd all be."

The woman was blinking the tears back, and swallowing hard. Her lips quivered as she spoke.

"Fiddlesticks!" said Aunt Pat briskly. "We'll see if something can't be done about that. Have you got a good doctor? Who is your doctor?"

"We haven't any doctor now," said the woman with a hopeless note in her voice. "We've tried three and he only got worse. He would not hear to having any more bills run up that we never can pay."

"H'm!" said Aunt Pat, "What doctors did you have?"

"Oh, we had the company doctor where he worked first, and he went on for two months and didn't make a mite of difference. And then we got Dr. Green. He was the doctor that examined him for his insurance several years ago, but he said just out plain he couldn't do him any good. And then we tried a specialist somebody recommended at the office where my son works, but he charged ten dollars every time he saw him, and ordered things that cost so much we couldn't get them, and said he ought to go to a private sanitarium for observation where they charge fifty dollars a week, and we had to give that up. Now we owe them all, and Lutie is paying them fifty cents a week, and Sam pays sometimes a dollar when he can spare it, dear knows when we'll get them all paid off."

"Well," said Aunt Pat with satisfaction, "then the coast is clear. That's good. Now, I'm going to send my doctor up to see him. How soon would it be convenient for him to come?"

The woman flushed.

"Oh, we couldn't really afford another doctor," she said in a worried tone. "It's very kind for you to take an interest in us but you see we just couldn't pay him now, and it only worries Father and makes him so he can't sleep."

"Yes, but you see my doctor won't cost you anything," said Aunt Pat. "He does these things as a favor for me. He's an old friend of mine, and he's been our family physician for years. He's very skillful too, and he'll tell me the truth. If anything can be done for your husband we'll find out what it is. And as for money, dear woman, aren't you and I both God's children? I've got some money that is just crying out to be spent somehow. They're after me to build an Art School with it, but if it could make your husband better I'd a lot rather have it used that way. And I take it God would be a great deal better pleased."

"Oh, but Miss Catherwood, I couldn't—! You're awfully good and I'll never forget it—but we couldn't! Oh, we never could!" The woman was crying openly now, into her nice clean blue and white checked apron. Sherrill had a sudden feeling that she would like to go over and put her arms around Lutie's mother and kiss her on her tired seamed forehead. Suppose it had been her mother? Sherrill's mother seemed so very many years away!

But Miss Catherwood was sitting up very straight now.

"Fiddlesticks end!" she said crisply. "As if you'd put pride between when it comes to getting your husband well! Listen! The Lord told me to come over here this morning and see what needed doing and do it. See? And you're not going to block the way. You're just going to be a dear sweet woman and do what you're told. How soon can you be ready for the doctor?"

"Oh!" sobbed the woman, "You're too good to us! Lutie said you were the salt of the earth—"

"Now, look here," fumed Aunt Pat, "Stop that kind

of talk. We don't need any salt around here just now. Wipe your eyes and tell me how soon I can have the doctor stop. Can you be ready for him by two o'clock? I think it likely he could be here about then. And while he's here I'm going to tell him to take a look at the little boy. Lutie said he had trouble with his hip."

"Oh, yes," wailed the mother as if the admission stabbed her to the heart. "They tell me he'll never walk again. He doesn't know it yet, poor kid. He keeps talking about when he's going to get well enough to play baseball with the other boys."

"Well, we'll see what can be done," said Aunt Pat with satisfaction. "And now, is there any way we can help you with this washing? Because you see we want you to be ready to have the doctor give you an examination too, and then we'll know where we stand."

"Oh, but I'm all right!" beamed the mother eagerly. "I don't need the doctor now. If my husband and boy could just get cured I'd be all right. It's just been the worry—"

"Well, that's all right too, but you're going to have the examination and then we'll find out what the doctor says about it. If he says you're all right why then no harm is done, but if he says you need an operation you're going to have it right away."

"Oh, but I couldn't be spared while my two men are sick," said the woman in alarm.

"Oh, yes, you could my dear!" said the old lady determinedly, "and it's a great deal better for you to be spared now than to wait until it's too late to help you. Don't be silly! Here comes Lutie. She'll look after the house and her brother while the three of you are in the hospital."

"Hospital?" said the woman frantically. "But we couldn't afford—!"

"Oh yes you could. It's all fixed I tell you. Here comes Lutie. How about that wash out there, Lutie? Can't you finish that up while your mother gets your father and brother ready to go to the hospital?"

"Oh, Miss Catherwood! Wouldn't that be too wonderful!" cried Lutie her cheeks growing red as a winter apple, and her eyes starry. "Of course I can finish up the wash. Only—" and she paused in consternation, "I'm supposed to go up to your house to help with the ironing at eleven o'clock."

"Well, that's off for to-day. I'll explain to the housekeeper. We've plenty of people there to finish the ironing for this once, and if we haven't it can go unironed. Now go to work quickly and don't let your mother get all fussed up about things."

When they got up to go Lutie looked at Sherrill wistfully.

"I been wondering if you really was going with me to the Bible class to-night," she said in a low tone. "I've been telling the other girls about you and they're so anxious for you to come. But now, I don't know as I can go this week. Maybe I'll be too busy here."

"Bible class?" said Aunt Pat scenting something interesting. "What's that? Where were you going with her, Sherrill?"

"She's been telling me about a class she attends," explained Sherrill. "Why, yes, I guess I can go tonight if you can find you can. I'd be interested to see what it's like."

"Of course you mustn't miss your Bible class, Lutie," said her mother with a wan smile. Then turning to Miss Catherwood she explained, "Lutie's been that taken up with her Bible study, and I'm glad she's got something since things have been so awful bad. But perhaps Lutie you'll be too tired."

"Oh, I'm never tired," said Lutie eagerly, "I'll go. Shall I come round to the house for you, Miss Sherrill?"

"No, I'll call for you with the little car," said Sherrill with sudden inspiration. "Then you won't have to walk when you are tired."

"Oh, that would be wonderful!" said Lutie as if Sherrill were offering her a ride in a chariot of state.

"Here Lutie, help me down these steps. I want to ask you some questions," said Aunt Pat imperatively.

Lutie helped the old lady carefully down the steps and as they walked out to the car Miss Patricia snapped out the questions.

"My niece said you lost some money. What bank?"

Lutie told her.

"H'm!" commented Miss Patricia. "Who owns your mortgage?"

Lutie gave the necessary information.

"H'm!" said the old lady, "I know them. I'll see what can be done. Don't you worry about losing your house. Just get your mother comfortable. And by the way, if your folks all have to go to the hospital you won't have time to work at the house till they get on their feet again, will you? It'll take about all your time to keep house here, won't it?"

"Oh, no! Miss Catherwood!" said Lutie in consternation, "I just couldn't afford not to work. There won't be anything for me to do but get Sam's breakfast and dinner and put up his lunch. I can give you just as much time as you want."

"That's all right then, Lutie. Don't you worry. But if you need to take a vacation for a few weeks why you just come to me and we'll fix it up so you won't lose anything by it. Now, Sherrill, are we all ready to go?"

They drove away amid exclamations of blessing from Lutie and her mother, and Sherrill felt a big lump rise in her throat as she looked back and saw them standing in the doorway, the mother waving her apron.

"That was wonderful of you, Aunt Pat!" said Sherrill eagerly. "That was dear of you! But it's going to cost you a lot of money."

"Well, you see, child, I figured if James gave his life to save Lutie's mother it was maybe my job to look after the rest of the family. And what's money in a case like that? If God thought saving her life was worth a man's life, then surely the least that I can do is to look after her, or somebody else's family if there hadn't been this one. I've you to thank for finding this out for me. I never thought to ask anything about them before, and Lutie never opened her lips. If I thought anything about them at all, I supposed they were all well and hearty and every one with a good job and thrifty. Lutie looks that way. What's this thing you're going to to-night?"

"Why, when she was singing that happy little song the other day I asked her where she got it. She told me about a class where they study the Bible and learn to be glad even when there's trouble. I said I would go with her some time."

"So, she's that kind, is she? Well, I'm glad. Now, here's the doctor's and I'll just run in and give him his orders. I'm hoping he isn't full up every hour today with operations or something. I'd hate to go back on my word."

A few minutes later she was back.

"He's going to see them at three o'clock. It's the best he can do. He's very busy. But I told him all about them and he promised me he'd do his best to put them all back in normal health again. Now, Sherrill, what did I do with the card Lutie wrote that mortgage company's address on? I want to stop and see my lawyer a minute and get him to fix that up and then we can go home and rest awhile. We've done a big piece of work."

"A wonderful piece of work," mused Sherrill. "Oh, Aunt Pat! You've done more with your life than any woman I know!"

"Fiddlesticks end!" said Aunt Pat scornfully, "I've not done the half that I should. Now Sherrill, while I'm seeing my lawyer I'd like you to do a little shopping for those people if you will. They'll need things to go to the hospital with, dressing gowns and kimonos and things, and decent suitcases to carry them in. I want them to be comfortable while they are there. That poor woman doesn't look as if she'd had a day's rest since she was born, and I mean she shall have. Get her a real pretty kimono, and brushes and things. Nice pretty ones. She likes pretty things I'm sure. Look at the way they've fixed up that old ramshackle house with just plants and vines. Not even paint! I'll give you the money and you get the necessary things. And I'm glad you're going to that Bible class. There are a lot of things in the Bible I don't understand, but I believe it from cover to cover, and I'd like to know more about it. I'm too old to study now, but you're not, and you can tell me all about it."

When they got home they found a stack of mail awaiting them. Notes of commiseration and protest from the people who had received their wedding gifts back again. Some letters, intended to cheer up Sherrill in her lonely estate of maidenhood, which made her very angry. A few giving her loving wishes from far off friends who hadn't yet heard of the change in the wedding arrangements.

She looked up listlessly from her lap full of letters and gave a deep sigh. How much more worth while was the world of helpfulness to which she had just been with her aunt, than this social world built around such an unstable foundation. She could sense through all these elaborate phrases that some of her old friends and playmates actually thought less of her because she had allowed herself to be washed up on the shore of maidenhood again, after she had once landed a man and got so far as wedding invitations.

Aunt Pat looked up sharply at the second sigh and handed over a letter.

"Well," she said triumphantly, "they haven't put your emeralds on the market yet, whoever it was that took them. Of course there has hardly been time for anybody to get them across the water. But if they attempt it it won't be long before we know who did it."

"Aunt Pat!" said Sherrill in astonishment. "Then you have done something about it after all!"

"Why of course, child! You didn't think I was a fool, did you? I called up the private detective who was here at the wedding and had a talk with him. He's been quietly watching all the places where they would be likely to be put on the market. They're all registered stones you know. Any jewel dealer of repute will be on the watch for them. Sooner or later they would have to turn up at the right place to get a reasonable price for them. I talked to my lawyer about them too, told him I didn't want publicity, and he's working quietly. So that's that and don't worry! They'll turn up if you were meant to get them back, and if you weren't all the worry in the world won't help you."

After lunch Sherrill went to lie down and had a long restful sleep. She had a sort of feeling when she woke up of being stranded on a desert island, and now that she was coming near to that Bible class that she had promised to attend she found a keen aversion to going. Why had she promised Lutie? Lutie was well enough herself, but Lutie had spoken of other girls who wanted to see her.

They would be common girls without education of course. They would have heard a lot of gossip about her wedding and how she didn't get married after all, and would be watching every move she made.

She half started to the telephone to tell Lutie that she was tired and would go another time, and then the eager look in Lutie's eyes came back to mind and she couldn't quite get the courage to call off the engagement. So she dressed herself in a plain quiet little knit dress of blue wool, and a small felt hat to match. It was one of her oldest sport dresses, and quite shabby now she thought. But she did not want to make Lutie feel that there was too much difference between them.

Miss Catherwood looked at her approvingly as she came into the room at dinner time.

"Some people wouldn't have known any better than to put on evening dress," she remarked irrelevantly, and smiled her queer twisted grin. "Well, I hope you have a good time, and be sure to listen for me."

DUBIOUSLY Sherrill parked her car and followed Lutie into the plain wooden building. If she hadn't promised Lutie she never would have gone to-night. She had lost her first curiosity about Lutie's source of peace, and if she had not seen how eager and pleased Lutie was about taking her she would have invented some excuse.

The building was not inviting. It was old and grimy. There had not been much money for fresh paint, and the floor was bare boards. A large blackboard and a battered old piano were the only attempts at furnishings beside the hard wooden benches, and the only decorations were startling Bible verses in plain print on white cards here and there about the walls.

"All have sinned and come short of the glory of God" was announced on the right; and Sherrill, entering, felt a shade of resentment at being classed with sinners. She had a feeling that her family had never been in that class.

There were other verses but she had not time to read them, for several young girls came up and Lutie introduced them.

One put a hand on Sherrill's arm intimately and with a sweet little smile said:

"We're so glad you have come. Lutie has been telling us about you, and we hope you will like it here. We just love it."

Again there was just the least bit of resentment in Sherrill's aristocratic soul that these girls should think her of their class, and expect her to be coming more than once. Yet there was something so winning about her smile, and so gentle in her manner that Sherrill began to wonder if perhaps she had been wrong. Perhaps these girls were not all in Lutie's class. It was difficult to tell. They wore nice clothes, one had a pretty little pink crepe, and a white beret, like any girl who had been out to play golf or tennis. There was an earnest air about them that made Sherrill like them in spite of herself. Could it be possible that she, Sherrill Cameron, was a snob? She must get out of this state of mind. She would not come here again likely, but while she was here she would be one of them, and do her best to enter into the things. She would be a good sport. She would be in their class, even if they were not in hers. After all, what was her class anyway? She was just a girl by herself who would have had to earn her own living somehow if Aunt Pat had not invited her to live with her. The fact that she had earned it hitherto teaching school instead of cleaning rooms and ironing as Lutie did, really made no difference of course. It was all silly anyway.

So Sherrill put out a friendly hand and greeted all the girls with her own warm smile, and they loved her at once. The strangest part about it was that somehow she couldn't help liking them. They were all so friendly and eager, what was the use of trying to act exclusive?

There was one thing she couldn't understand. She heard one of those girls just behind her speaking to Lutie.

The words came out between the clamor of the people who were gathering. "She's lovely, isn't she? Is she *saved,* Lutie?" And Lutie murmured something very low that Sherrill couldn't catch. Somehow she knew they were talking about her. And then the other girl said, "Well, we'll be praying for her tonight," and slipped away up front with a group of others, and whispered to them. They nodded, gave quick glances back, and a moment later Sherrill could see them off at one side bunched together with their heads bowed. A quick intuition told her they were praying for *her,* and the color mounted into her cheeks. Her chin went up a trifle haughtily. Why should she, Sherrill Cameron, need to be prayed for? And why should they *presume* to do it unasked?

But the room was filling up rapidly now. Lutie led her to a seat half way up and gave her a hymn book. The little group of praying ones had scattered, one to play the old piano, two others to distribute hymn books and Bibles, and suddenly the room burst into song, but she noticed that two or three of them still kept their heads bent, their eyes closed as if they were yet praying.

Sherrill looked around her in amazement. Here was a crowd of people, almost all young people, and they were singing joyously as if it made them glad to do so. They were singing with that same lilt that Lutie had had while she was working, and their faces all looked glad; although some of them obviously must be very poor, if one might judge from their garments and the weary look on their young faces, while others again were well dressed, and prosperous looking.

Presently they began to sing Lutie's song:

"If I have sorrow in my heart
What can take it away?"

and Sherrill, without realizing she was doing so, began to sing it herself, and felt a little of the thrill that seemed to be in the air.

She fell to thinking of her own interrupted life and wondering why it all had to be. Why couldn't Carter have been all right, the perfect man she had thought him? Why did it all have to turn out that way, in that sudden mortifying manner? If it only could have happened quietly! Not in the face of her whole invited world as it were.

But suddenly she felt the audience bowing in prayer, and was amazed to hear different voices taking up petitions, so many young people willing to pray in public! And so simply, so free from all self-consciousness apparently. It was extraordinary. Even little Lutie beside her prayed a simple sentence.

"Please, dear Father, don't let anything in us hinder Thy light from shining through us, so that others may see and find Thee."

Dear little soul! How had Lutie learned all this sweet simplicity? Just a little serving maid, yet she seemed to have something really worth while. What was this mysterious power? Just an idea? A conviction?

One of the prayers impressed her deeply. It came from a girl's voice up toward the front, perhaps one of those who had been introduced to her. It was "Dear Father, if any have come in here to-night not knowing Thee as Saviour, may they find Thee and not go out unsaved." Sherrill had a strange feeling that the prayer was for her although she couldn't exactly understand why she needed saving.

Then the prayers changed into song again, a rousing one:

"I've found a friend who is all to me,
His love is ever true;"

Ah! That was what she wanted Sherrill thought, a friend whose love was ever true. It was almost uncanny as if someone here knew just what she needed.

"I love to tell how He lifted me,
And what His grace can do for you,"

sang the audience, and then burst into that tremendous chorus that thrilled her, though she only half understood its meaning:

"Saved by His power divine,
Saved to new life sublime!
Life now is sweet and my joy is complete
For I'm saved, saved, saved."

Sherrill ran her eye through the rest of the verses and lingered on those lines,

"I'm leaning strong on His mighty arm;
I know He'll guide me all the way."

and experienced a sudden longing. If there was only someone who could guide her! Someone who could take away this utterly humiliated, lost feeling, and make her sure and strong and happy again the way she used to be before all this happened to her!

Then another hymn was called for and the eager young voices took on a more tender note as they sang, just as earnestly, only with deeper meaning to the words than any of the other songs had carried. Sherrill followed the words, and to her amazement found a great longing in her soul that she might be able to sing these words and mean them, every one.

"Fade, fade each earthly joy,"

That was what had been happening to her. The life that she had planned and that seemed all rosy before her had suddenly in a moment faded out.

"Jesus is mine!"

How she wished she might truly say that!

"Break every tender tie,"—

Ah! Her case exactly.

"Jesus is mine!"

rang the triumphant words. She glanced about at the eager young faces, so grave and certain. How could they be certain that Jesus was theirs? What did it mean anyway to have Jesus? Was it just a phrase? A state of mind? She studied several of them intently.

"Dark is the wilderness,
Earth has no resting-place,
Jesus alone can bless,
Jesus is mine!"

The tears suddenly welled into her eyes and she blinked them back angrily. She certainly did not want these stranger girls to think she was soft and sentimental.

The leader arose after the hymn was ended and prayed, just a few words, but it seemed to bring them all to the threshold of another world, an open heaven. Sherrill had never had such a feeling in a meeting before, not even in the solemn beautiful church where Aunt Patricia worshiped. And this was all so simple, and without any emotion except gladness!

There was a little stir all over the room. Everybody was opening Bibles. Lutie found the place and gave Sherrill one, and they all began to read together.

At first Sherrill did not pay much attention to what she was reading because she was so busy watching the others and feeling astonished. But gradually the words began to make themselves felt in her mind. She looked up at the speaker, startled to see if he were looking at her. She almost thought he must have known of her trouble and selected the passage because he knew she was to be here.

"Beloved, think it not strange concerning the fiery trial which is to try you, as though some strange thing happened unto you:—"

It was strange, though, thought Sherrill; how could she pretend it wasn't?

"But rejoice," the voices went on in unison, "inasmuch as ye are partakers of Christ's sufferings; that, when his glory shall be revealed, ye may be glad also with exceeding joy."

Christ's sufferings! How could her trouble have anything to do with what Christ had suffered on earth? He had never had any one go back on Him as she had; He had never been made a public laughing stock by anyone who was supposed to be His special friend—or stay, perhaps she was wrong! Had not His own disciple been the one who turned against Him, betrayed Him, laid the plot that led to His being nailed to the cross before the mocking multitudes?

These thoughts flashed through Sherrill's mind as she looked up from her Bible to give a grudging attention to the speaker.

"Let us see," he was saying, "to whom these words are addressed. Peter was writing a letter to Christians who had fled from their homes because of persecution. At the beginning of the letter he says that they, and himself with them, are 'begotten again' unto a living hope,—" Sherrill winced, her hopes were all dead.

"These words describe those to whom the letter is written. No one else has a right to the promises in the letter except those who are 'begotten again,'—born again. We must understand that clearly before we go on with the letter. If you want the joy that Christ can give even in the midst of suffering, remember that it is for you only if you are a child of God, born into His family by believing that Jesus Christ the Son of God was nailed to the cross because of your sins. He rose from the dead and He can give you life, but your new birth comes from more than just believing this *about* Him! Believing about Christ never saved anyone. It must be believing *in* Him. Believe that He took your condemnation upon Himself, and accept Him as your own personal Saviour."

Sherrill's eyes were fixed on the teacher's face now, utterly absorbed. She had never heard anyone talk like this before. It was quite possible she had sat in church often under sermons which included such doctrines, but they had never been able to reach her heart before, perhaps because her mind was too full of her own plans and thoughts. In fact it was probably the first time in her life that she had even read a portion of scripture with her mind on it. Her mind had always been politely aloof when she entered God's house, or found it necessary to take up a Bible.

A living hope. How she wished she might get one.

This teacher was talking just as Lutie had talked only more convincingly. And these people in the room looked at their teacher eagerly, earnestly, as if they understood from experience what he meant. She looked about on them wistfully. Could she get what they had? The teacher had said it came by believing in Christ, but how could one believe in someone who died so many years ago? How could one believe unless one knew and was convinced?

As if the man had read her thoughts and were answering them he went on.

"Belief is not an intellectual conviction. Belief is an act of the will, whereby you throw yourself on the promise of God and let Him prove Himself true. If someone asked you to take a ride in a new kind of airplane, you might not be able to go over every bit of its machinery and be sure that it was in perfect order, you might not understand the principle by which it worked, not be sure it could carry you safely; you might not even know the man who made it, nor have the wisdom to judge the principle under which it operated, but you could get into the plane and take a ride and let it prove to you what it claimed to be able to do. If you were in need of getting somewhere in a desperate hurry you might not even stop to think very carefully about it. You would say: 'This plane has taken others. I believe it will take me. At least I am going to trust myself to it.' And so you would get into the plane and fly away. Afterward when you have safely reached your destination then you are convinced that the plane can fly, for it has safely carried you. You have experience, but faith comes first. Now turn to Hebrews the twelfth chapter."

The room was filled with the rustling of Bible leaves as heads were bent, and the place was found. Sherrill blundered around among the books of the Bible like a person in a strange city trying to find a street. She was beginning back somewhere near Genesis, and her cheeks were a bit red with confusion. All these young people were turning straight to the right page with confidence. She tried to see over Lutie's shoulder without seeming to do so, to get the number of the page. Surely Bibles had pages didn't they? Why didn't he tell the page? Again that feeling of resentment at being caught in a humiliating position welled up in her. Why did she let herself come here to be made a fool of? All she could remember was Matthew, Mark, Luke, and John and that in connection with some old nursery rhyme.

But Lutie came to her rescue now and made short work of finding the place,—Lutie the little maid who did the cleaning and ironing! Wise in the scriptures!

Then every voice in the room began to read, and Sherrill read too, startled at how the words seemed meant just for her:

"My son, despise not thou the chastening of the Lord, nor faint when thou art rebuked of Him: for whom the Lord loveth He chasteneth, and scourgeth every son whom He receiveth. If ye endure chastening, God dealeth with you as with sons; for what son is he whom the Father chasteneth not?"

The teacher stopped them for a moment.

"The literal meaning of the word 'to chasten' here is 'to train a child.' Although you may be born again, a son of God, you are not to forget your subjection to the will of the Father. I wonder how many of you have been wondering why you have had to pass through some peculiar trial or testing? Have you found out yet that God was giving you that hard thing just to teach you to know Him better? Sometimes we are so taken up with the world, or with our own plans and selves that we haven't given a thought to God and He just had to take away the thing in which we were interested to make us give our attention to Him, that we might know His will, and get the full blessing He has prepared for us.

"I have sometimes seen a mother take away a toy from a little child in order to make him listen to her teaching and God often has to do that for His dearest sons. Go back to First Corinthians eleven thirty-one:

"'If we would judge ourselves, we should not be judged. But when we are judged, we are child-trained of the Lord, that we should not be condemned with the world.' The sons of God, that is believers, cannot be condemned with the world, and if they do not judge their careless and unworthy ways, then the Lord must deal with them and make them experience His chastening."

Sherrill wondered in passing if Aunt Pat had ever studied the Bible in this way. Did she know how the Bible fitted people's daily lives, and that a verse in one book explained a verse in another book?

And then the teacher whirled them back to the Old Testament for an illustration, and Sherrill had to have Lutie's help once more in finding the place. By this time she had determined that before another week—if she decided to come to that class again,—she would learn the books of the Bible.

The teacher was making plain now how God yearned for the love and fellowship of His children. He showed how disappointed God must be in them because they are so filled with themselves, so forgetful of the fact that they are on this earth only temporarily, getting ready for an eternal life.

It was a new view of God. Sherrill had never thought of herself as having any relationship to God at all, and now it seemed one either had to be a son or a deliberate rejector of the wonderful love and grace of God toward sinners. Sinners! As the teacher went on bringing more and more verses to their attention, Sherrill had a view of the Lord Jesus and began to get the realization that everybody was a sinner. She was appalled to think of herself under such a classification.

When the meeting finally closed with another wonderful prayer Sherrill was in a maze of bewilderment. She wanted to get away alone and think. There were so many questions that had come to her mind that, as she watched the young people gather around the teacher eagerly asking questions, she wished she had the courage to join them.

Lutie had excused herself to take a message to a girl across the room, and Sherrill left alone for the moment turned to the book table at the back of the room. What an array of little paper covered books with startling titles! They were all on topics she was in the dark about. A sign above them said they were only fifteen cents apiece. Sherrill picked out half a dozen and got out her purse, paying the pleasant faced boy who had charge of the table.

"Got a Scofield Bible?" asked the youth, waving his hand toward a collection of Bibles in various bindings.

"Why, no, what is a Scofield Bible?" asked Sherrill shyly, and realized at once as the youth stared at her, that she had shown great ignorance.

"Oh, it's the regular text of course," he explained politely, "only it has a lot of helpful notes that make it pretty plain about the dispensations and symbolism and covenants and things. It helps a lot to have them right there on the page with the text, that's all."

"How much are they?" asked Sherrill reaching for a small limp covered one in real leather.

"Well, that's about the most expensive one we have,"

said the boy looking at her with a new respect. "We have cheaper ones."

"But I like this one," said Sherrill, and paid for it feeling as if she had bought a gold mine. Now, perhaps she had something that would answer some of her questions!

When Lutie came back apologetic for being so long Sherrill had a package all done up ready to take home.

"They are wonderful books!" said Lutie casting wistful eyes at the book table. "I've got two or three for my own. We girls get different ones and lend them around among ourselves."

When Sherrill got home she went straight to her aunt's room.

Aunt Pat had gone to bed, but was lying bolstered up with pillows reading, and Sherrill noticed that her little Bible lay on the bed beside her.

"I've been buying some books," said Sherrill half shame-faced. "See what you think of them."

She undid her package and displayed them.

Miss Catherwood took up the Scofield Bible first and examined it curiously.

"I've heard about this," she said thoughtfully, "I'd like to look it over sometime. Maybe I'll get one too. They say it's very enlightening."

Then she went over the other books one by one.

"Yes, I know this one. It's by a president of a theological college, a wonderful man they say. I came across a notice of this book in a magazine. And this I know and love. I used to have a copy but someone borrowed it and never brought it back. But these others I never heard of. You'll have to read some of them aloud to me. I'd like to know what they are. The titles look wonderfully interesting. Well, how did you like the meeting? Was it a meeting?"

"Why no," said Sherrill thoughtfully, "It wasn't exactly a meeting, nor exactly like a school. I don't just know what to call it, but it was wonderfully interesting."

"Begin at the beginning and tell me all about it," said the old lady studying the vivid face before her. Sherrill hadn't worn that look of interest since the wedding night. The desolate haunted expression was almost gone.

After that first night Sherrill began to be fascinated with the study of the Bible. She realized of course that she had only as yet touched the outer fringes of the great truths it contained, but she really longed to know more, and she found that this, more than anything else, was able to help her forget her changed estate.

It was the second Monday night that she lingered till most of the others were gone, and asked a few questions that perplexed her about salvation. For she had come already to see her own need, and she finally in great simplicity said she would accept the Saviour.

When at last the teacher was free and turned to her, she shyly asked:

"Mr. Mackenzie, how can one tell,—does anybody really know—that is," she hesitated—"how would *I* know whether I am all right with God or not?"

She finished in a blaze of embarrassment. She had never spoken to anyone before about the thoughts of her own heart concerning God. She had a feeling it was almost immodest, for the people she knew never did it.

But with Spirit-taught gentleness and understanding the man of God answered her, putting her instantly at her ease, and treating the question as most natural and supremely important.

"Indeed you can know, most positively, Miss Cameron. Let me ask you first, have you ever realized that you—that we all of us—are sinners in God's sight, utterly unfit for His presence?"

"Yes, I have," said Sherrill earnestly. "I never did before, but last week I saw that."

"Then do you realize that you need to have the sin taken away that separates you from God?"

"Yes, oh, yes!" The tears sprang to her eyes.

"Then 'Behold the Lamb of God, who taketh away the sin of the world!' Just look to the Lord Jesus Christ as the One who bore on the cross all the guilt penalty for your sins. God poured out on His own Son all His righteousness wrath against us. 'For all have sinned and come short of the glory of God: being justified freely by His grace through the redemption that is in Christ Jesus.' Do you believe that?"

"I do," said Sherrill solemnly.

"Then read this aloud."

Mr. Mackenzie opened his Bible and pointed to a verse. Sherrill read:

"'Therefore being justified by faith we have peace with God through our Lord Jesus Christ.'"

"Read it again, very slowly please."

Sherrill read it again, very slowly, letting the truth sink deep. Suddenly a radiance broke through the puzzled earnestness of her face.

"I see it now," she said, "It's all right!"

"Then let's thank Him for so great salvation," said Mr. Mackenzie.

The rest had all gone but Lutie, and the three knelt together as Mr. Mackenzie poured out a thanksgiving for the new-born child of God.

So Sherrill went home that night with real news for Aunt Pat that kept that old saint awake half the night praising her Heavenly Father.

PRESENTLY the days settled down into regular normal living again, the lovely pansies had faded, and nothing more had been heard from the stranger.

Sherrill tried to put him out of her mind, tried not to start and look interested whenever the doorbell rang, or a package arrived. She tried to curb the feeling of disappointment each night when she went up to her room, that he had not come that day.

"He has forgotten us long ago," she told herself. "It was a mere incident in his life. He was just a passing stranger. He probably felt that he had done his entire duty toward us by sending those flowers. They were only sort of a bread-and-butter letter, and saved him the trouble of writing one. He has likely gone back to Chicago by this time and got immersed in business again. If he ever thinks of us again it will be to laugh sometime with his friends and tell about the queer wedding he once attended. Why should I be so silly as to keep on watching for him?"

But still she could not forget the stranger. And still there came no word of the lost jewels.

Aunt Pat kept a watchful eye upon Sherrill. She sent for maps and guide books. They studied routes of travel, they considered various cruises, planned motor trips, and betweenwhiles watched over Lutie's family, agreeing that they must not go away anywhere till the operations were all over and the invalids back at home doing well.

When the third Monday night came Lutie was up at the hospital waiting to hear the result of her mother's operation. Lutie's mother was in a very serious condition. Sherrill was restless and finally decided to go to the Bible class alone.

To her surprise the whole loving group of people at the mission knew about Lutie's anxiety and spoke tenderly of her. When the time of prayer came Sherrill listened in wonder to the prayers of faith that went up from many hearts for the life of Lutie's mother. Sherrill was amazed that they dared pray so confidently, and yet always with that submissive "Nevertheless, Thy will, not ours be done."

She had a feeling as she listened that she had been sitting in a dark place all her life, and that during the last three weeks light had slowly begun to break. It seemed that to-night the light was like glory all around her.

These people actually lived with God, referred everything to Him, wanted nothing that He did not send. They were in a distinct and startling sense a separated people, and she was beginning to long with all her heart that she might truly be one with them.

The meeting was more than half over, and the lesson for the evening was well under way when the woman who sat next to Sherrill on the end seat next the aisle, with a whispered word about catching her train, got up silently and slipped out. A moment later Sherrill became aware that someone else had taken her place, someone who had possibly been standing back by the door.

He came so silently, so unobtrusively, that Sherrill did not look up or notice him till he sat down, and then suddenly she seemed to feel rather than see that he was looking earnestly at her.

Startled she glanced up to find herself looking straight into Graham Copeland's smiling eyes!

Then Sherrill's face lighted with a great gladness, and something flashed from eye to eye. He reached quietly over and clasped her hand, just a quick clinging pressure that no one would have noticed, and her fingers returned it. Then something flashed again from hand to hand, some understanding and knowledge of mutual joy.

It was like finding a dear old friend after having lost him. It was the knowledge that everything precious in the world had not been lost after all.

She lifted another shy glance and caught that look in his eyes again, and was thrilled to think he was here. What a wonderful thing was this! Never in all her acquaintance with Carter McArthur had there been anything like this, but she did not think of that now. She was just glad, glad, glad!

He took hold of one side of her Bible when another reference was announced, their hands touched again, and joy ran trembling in the touch. Shoulder to shoulder, their heads bowed over the sacred Book they read the holy words together, and new strength and hope and sunshine seemed suddenly to come to Sherrill. This her friend had come back. He was all right. Her strange unwelcomed fears had been unfounded. Now she knew it. She had looked into his eyes and all was right. She was even gladder for that than that he was here.

This meeting with him might last only a few minutes more, it might never come again; but she was glad that he was this kind of man.

The class was crowded that night, and the chairs were

very close together. The aisles were narrow. Yet the nearness was pleasant, and the fellowship with God's people. She stole a glance at her new friend's face and saw that he was watching the speaker, listening interestedly. He was not bored. He had not come here just to take her away home and make a fashionable call upon her. He seemed to be as glad to be here as she was to have him, and to have entered into the spirit of the hour like any of them. Was that just an outstanding characteristic of his that he could adjust himself to any surroundings and seem to be at home?

But no, she felt he was truly in sympathy here, more even than he had been at that wedding reception. To a certain extent he had been an outsider there, entering in only so far as would help her, but it really seemed as if he belonged here. Or was that just her imagination?

She wondered if she ought to suggest going home. Perhaps he had only a short time. But he settled that by suddenly turning and smiling into her eyes and whispering,

"He's very fine, isn't he?" and suddenly her joy seemed running over so that she could hardly keep glad tears from her eyes. To have a friend like this, and to have him feel as she did about this sacred hour. Why that was greatest of all!

Then it came to her that just the other day she had felt that all the troubles in the world were crowded into her small life, and now all at once they had lifted. What did it mean? Was God showing her that He had infinitely greater joys in store for her somewhere than any she had lost?

These thoughts raced swiftly through her mind while her companion fluttered the leaves of the Bible finding the next reference as if his fingers knew their way well about the greatest book in the world, and then their hands settled together holding it again.

"Well," thought Sherrill, "I seem to be losing my head a little, but I'm just going to be glad while gladness is here." And then somehow their spirits seemed to go along together during the rest of the meeting, flashing a look of appreciation when something unusual was said.

The rest of the hour seemed all too short. It was like a bit of heaven to Sherrill. When it was over Copeland spoke graciously to the friends about her, and greeted the teacher when he came down to speak to them.

"You know we have a great Bible school out in my city too," he said with a smile as he shook hands with the teacher. "I don't get as much of it as I would like. I'm pretty busy. But sometimes I run in there for a bit of refreshment."

Out into the sweet darkness of the summer evening he guided her, his hand slipped within her arm in a pleasant possessive way. He seemed to have already located her car, and as they went toward it he said in vibrant tones:

"I didn't know you were interested in this sort of thing. I'm so glad. It gives us one more tie for our—friendship. I'm sure now that you must know the Lord Jesus."

"And oh, *do you?*" Sherrill's voice was vibrant too. "I've only known Him a very short time and I'm very ignorant, but—I want to learn."

Sherrill's hand was clasped in his now, but she did not realize it till he put her in the car.

"Shall I drive?" he asked, as if he had been taking care of her all his life.

"Yes, please," she said eagerly, "and, tell me, how did you happen to be there? How did you know I—?"

"Your aunt told me the way," he said, anticipating her

question. "I got to the house just after you had left. She told me how to find you and I came at once."

"Then—you had been there some time?"

"Yes. I came in during the singing just before the lesson. They certainly can sing there, can't they?"

"Oh, yes. But I'm sorry I didn't see you. I could have come out—" she hesitated.

"Wasn't it better to stay?" he asked smiling, looking down into her face, "It was a sweet and blessed fellowship and I needed something like that. I've been in a feverish sordid atmosphere ever since I left here and I was glad to get the world out of my lungs for a little while. Besides, I enjoyed watching your face. I got a double blessing out of the meeting from enjoying your interest."

"My face?" said Sherrill in sudden confusion. "Oh!" and she put up a hand to her flushed cheek. "Were you where you could see me? I didn't know there was anything in my face but ignorance and amazement. I can't get used to the wonders of the Bible."

"It was very—" he hesitated, then added, "very precious to watch," and his voice was almost reverent as he spoke.

"Oh!" said Sherrill at a loss for a reply. But he helped her by going on to speak in a matter-of-fact voice.

"I'm glad to get here at last," he said. "I've been going through a strenuous siege of work, in Washington and New York, back and forth, sometimes in such haste that I had to fly. No time to call my soul my own, and then an unexpected business trip to the south which kept me working night and day. I thought I would be able to stop off for a few hours before this, but I couldn't make it. I was afraid you would have forgotten me by this time."

"No," said Sherrill quickly. "I could not forget you. You came to me in a time of great trouble and I shall never forget how you helped me. I'm so glad to have another opportunity to really thank you. I didn't half know what I was doing that night."

"Well, I'm glad to be back at last," he said, "I didn't want to lose this friendship. It seemed to be something very rare sent to me right out of the blue you know."

He gave her a wonderful smile that set her heart thrilling.

"I'm surely losing my head," she told herself. "I mustn't be a fool. But I can't help being glad he is like this even if I never see him again."

Sherrill was sorry when the short ride was over and they had to go into the house and be conventional. She treasured the little quiet talk in the darkness. It was easier somehow in the dark to get acquainted and not be embarrassed at all they had been through together.

Aunt Pat was waiting for them eagerly and Sherrill felt her kind keen glance searching her face as she sat down.

"Now," said Aunt Pat, "before we begin to talk, how much time have we got to get acquainted? What time did you say you had to leave?"

"I think your local train leaves about ten after eleven," answered Copeland. "I have a taxi coming for me in plenty of time so I do not have to keep thinking about that. But perhaps I shall be keeping you up too late?"

He looked eagerly at the old lady.

"Late?" said the old lady laughing. "We're regular night hawks, Sherry and I. We often sit up till after midnight reading. I'm only sorry you have to go so soon."

All too rapidly the brief time fled. He seemed so like an old acquaintance that he fitted right into their pleasant cosy evening. Aunt Pat discovered that they had mutual acquaintances in Chicago and Sherrill sat listening to their talk and wondering how she could ever have entertained that haunting fear about this wonderful stranger. It was such a relief to have the fear gone forever. Not that she ever really suspected him herself, she still loyally maintained to her own heart, but she had been so afraid that others would if it ever came to an investigation.

Then he would turn and look at her suddenly and smile and something would happen to her heart, something wild and sweet that never had happened before. She did not understand it. Never in all her acquaintance with Carter McArthur had there been anything like this. It was like finding an old friend after having lost him. It was knowing that she had not lost every precious thing in the world after all. It was rest and peace and joy just to know she had a friend like that.

The lovely color flooded into her face and joy was in her starry eyes. That pinched look of suffering that Copeland had seen in her face the first night was gone. He looked again and again to make sure. It was not there any more. The glance in his eyes when he turned toward her always with that wonderful smile thrilled her as nothing had ever done before.

In vain she chided herself for feeling so utterly glad just because of his presence. He was only making a call, she told herself. But that gladness would keep surging over her like a healing tide that was washing away the pain and anguish she had received the night she found out that Carter was false to her. He might go away in a few minutes and she never see him again perhaps, but still she would be glad, glad that he had come to-night and reassured her that he was just what she had thought him at first. New strength and life and hope seemed to come to her as the moments flew by.

Aunt Pat took herself off upstairs for a few minutes to

hunt for a book they had been talking about and Sherrill had a little time alone with him.

"You are feeling better?" he said in a low tone, coming over to sit beside her on the couch, scanning her face searchingly.

"Oh yes," she said deeply touched at the tenderness of his tone. "I'm beginning to see some reasons why it all had to be. I'm beginning to understand what I was saved from!"

He reached out and laid his hand quietly over hers for an instant with a soft pressure.

"That is good to know!" he said gently. "You were very brave!"

"Oh, no!" she said, her eyelids drooping, "As I look back I'm so ashamed at the way I played out. It was dreadful the way I let you stand by and go through all that awful reception! But I'm so glad to have this opportunity to really thank you for what you did for me that night. As long as I live I will always feel that that was the greatest thing any man ever did for any woman in trouble. An utter stranger! You were wonderful! If you had been preparing all your life for that one evening you could not have done everything more perfectly."

"Perhaps I had!" he said very softly, his fingers closing about hers warmly again, his eyes catching hers as they lifted to look wonderingly at him, and holding her gaze with a deep sweet look.

Then suddenly Gemmie appeared at the door with her rubber-silent tread bearing a small table and placed it, covering it with a festive cloth. Gemmie, seeming to see nothing, but knowing perfectly, Sherrill understood, about those two clasped hands between them there on the sofa.

Gemmie brought coffee in a silver pot with delicate cups and saucers, tiny sandwiches, cinnamon toast, little frosted cakes and then an ice. Gemmie managed to keep in evidence until Aunt Pat returned with her book. Gemmie watching like a cat!

And the two talked, pleasant nothings, conscious of that touch that had been between them, conscious of the light in each other's eyes, glad in each other's presence, getting past the years of their early youth into a time and place where there was only their two selves in the universe. Wondering that anything had been worth while before, thinking, each, perhaps, that the other did not understand.

Aunt Pat came back with her book and ate with them, a happy little meal. She watched her girl contentedly, watched the young man approvingly, and remembered days of long ago and the light in a boy-lover's eyes. That was the same light or else she was mightily mistaken.

Then all at once Copeland looked at his watch with an exclamation of dismay, and sprang to his feet.

"It is almost time for my train!" he said, "I wonder what has become of my taxi! The man promised to be here in plenty of time."

"Gemmie! Look out and see if the taxi is there!" called Aunt Pat.

"No ma'am, there's no taxi come. I been watching out the window!" said the woman primly with a baleful look at Copeland as if his word was to be doubted. Gemmie thought he likely hadn't told the taxi man to come at all. She thought he likely wanted to stay all night.

"It isn't far, I'll try to make it!" said Copeland. "I'm sorry to leave in such a rush. You'll forgive me won't you? I've had such a wonderful time!"

"Why I'll take you of course," said Sherrill suddenly rousing to her privilege. "My car is right outside. Come, out this side door. We've time enough."

"But you'll have to come back alone!" he protested.

"I often do!" she laughed. "Come, we can make it if we go at once—although I wish you could stay."

"But I mustn't!" said Copeland. "I must get back at once. It's important!"

He took Aunt Pat's hand in a quick grasp.

"You have been good to let me come!" he said fervently. "May I come soon again?"

"You certainly may!" said Aunt Pat, "I like you young man! There! Go! Sherrill's blowing her horn. You haven't any time to waste!"

With an appreciative smile he sprang to the door and was gone. Aunt Pat watched them away and then turned back with a smile of satisfaction to see Gemmie standing at the back of the hall like Nemesis looking very severe.

"That's what I call a real man, Gemmie!" said Aunt Pat with a note of emphasis in her tone.

"Well, you can't most always sometimes tell, Miss Patricia," said Gemmie primly with an offended uplift of her chin.

"And then again you *can!*" said Aunt Pat gayly. "Now, Gemmie, you can wait till Miss Sherry comes back and then lock up. I'm going to bed."

Out in the night together Sherrill kept the wheel.

"I'd better drive this time," she explained as she put her foot on the starter. "It will save time because you don't know the way. You be ready to spring out as soon as I stop, if the train is coming."

Sherrill flashed around corners in the dark and brought up at the station a full two minutes before the train was due.

"I have my ticket, and my baggage is checked in the city," said Copeland smiling, "so this two minutes is all to the good."

He drew her hand within his arm and they walked

slowly up the platform, both conscious of the sweetness of companionship.

"I'm coming back soon," said Copeland, laying his free hand softly over hers again. "Your aunt said I might."

"That will be wonderful!" said Sherrill, feeling that it was hard to find words to express her delight. "How soon?"

"Just as soon as I can get a chance!" he said holding her hand a little closer in his own.

Then they heard the distant sound of the train approaching and had to turn and retrace their steps down the platform.

"I'll let you know!" he said.

Somehow it took very few words to complete the sweetness of the moment. The train thundered up and they stood there waiting, her arm within his.

"I wish you were going along," he said suddenly looking down at her with a smile. "It's going to be a long lonely journey, and there is a great deal I would like to talk to you about, but we'll save it for next time."

Then the train slowed down to a stop and the few passengers from up the road came straggling out.

Copeland and Sherrill stood back just a little out of the way till the steps should be passable, and as they looked up Mrs. Battersea hove in sight through the car door, coming back from an evening of bridge with some friends in the next suburb.

"Isn't that your Battledore-and-shuttlecock lady of the reception?" murmured Copeland with a grin.

Sherrill giggled.

"Mrs. Battersea," she prompted.

"Yes, I thought it was something like that."

The lady brought her heavy body down the car steps and arrived on the platform a few feet from them.

Copeland stooped a little closer and spoke softly:

"What do you say if we give her something to talk about? Do you mind if I kiss you good bye?"

For answer Sherrill gave him a lovely mischievous smile and lifted her lips to meet his.

Then Mrs. Battersea, the conductor just swinging to the step of the car and waving his signal to the engineer, the platform and all the surroundings, melted away, and heaven and earth touched. The preciousness of that moment Sherrill never would forget. Afterwards she remembered that kiss in comparison with some of the passionate half fierce caresses that Carter used to give, kisses that almost frightened her sometimes with their intensity, and made her unsure of herself, and she knew this reverent kiss was not in the same world with those others.

With that sweet tender kiss, and a pressure of the hand he still held, he left her and swung to the lower step which the conductor had vacated for a higher one as the train rolled out of the station.

He stood there as long as he could see her, and she watched him, drank in the look in his eyes, and suddenly said to her frightened happy heart, "He is dear! *Dear!* Oh, I love him! I *love* him! He is no longer a stranger! He is beloved! The Beloved Stranger!"

Then as the train swept past the platform lights into the darkness beyond, with her heart in her happy eyes she turned, and there stood Mrs. Battersea, her lorgnette up, drinking it all in! Even that last wave of the hand that wafted another caress toward her before he vanished into the darkness!

Sherrill faced her in dismay, coming down to earth again with a thump. Then with a smile she said in a cool little tone:

"Oh, Mrs. Battersea! You haven't your car here. May I take you home?"

And Mrs. Battersea bursting with curiosity gushed eagerly, "Oh, Sherrill Cameron, is that really you? Why how fortunate I am to have met you. I've just twisted my ankle badly and my chauffeur is sick to-night. I expected to take a taxi but there doesn't seem to be any."

Then as she stuffed her corporosity into Sherrill's little roadster she asked eagerly: "And who was that attractive man you were seeing off on the train? That couldn't have been the charming stranger who was at the wedding could it? Oh—Sherrill! Naughty, naughty! I thought there was a reason for the changes in the wedding plans!"

Sherrill was glad when at last she reached her own room and could shut the door on the world and shut herself in with her own thoughts and memories. But a moment later Gemmie knocked at the door and brought a message from her aunt that she would like to see her for a minute.

Gemmie looked at Sherrill's lovely red cheeks and smiling lips coldly, distantly. Sherrill felt as if she would like to shake her. But she gave her a brilliant smile and went swiftly to her aunt's room.

"Well," said the old lady from among the pillows of her old-fashioned four-poster, "I hope you see now that he never stole that necklace!"

"Aunt Pat!" said Sherrill in an indignant horrified tone, "I never thought he did! I *knew* he didn't! But I wanted him to come back to prove to *you* that he hadn't! He was *my* stranger. *I* knew he wasn't that kind, but I couldn't expect other people to realize what he was. I was afraid you would always suspect him if he didn't come back."

"H'm!" said the old lady contemptuously. "I know.

You didn't give me much credit for discernment. Thought you had it all. Now, run along to your bed, child. You've had enough for one evening. I just wanted you to know I think he's all right. Good night!"

SHERRILL awoke the next morning with a song in her heart, but while she was dressing she talked seriously with herself. It was utterly impossible, she told herself, that a splendid man like Graham Copeland could care about a girl he had seen only a few hours, and especially under such circumstances. There was that precious kiss, but it had been given half in fun, to carry out the joke on Mrs. Battersea. Men didn't think much of just a good-bye kiss, most men, that is. But her heart told her that this man was different. She knew that it had meant much to him.

Then she told herself to be sensible, that it was wonderful enough just to have a real friend when she was feeling so lonely and left out of everything.

Of course he was very far away. He might even forget her soon, but at least he was a friend, a young friend, to tide her over this lost humiliating spot in her life.

And he had said he would come soon again! Well, she mustn't count too much on that, but her heart leaped at the thought and she went about her room singing softly:

"When I have Jesus in my heart,
What can take Him away?
Once take Jesus into my heart,
And He has come to stay."

The trill of her voice reached across the hall to Aunt Pat's room and the old lady smiled to herself and murmured. "The dear child!" and then gave a little wistful sigh.

It was raining hard all day that day, but Sherrill was like a bright ray of sunshine. It was not raining rain to her, it was raining pansies and forget-me-nots in her heart, and she did not at all understand what meant this great light-heartedness that had come to her. She had never felt toward anyone before as she felt toward this stranger. She had utterly forgotten her lost bridegroom. She chided herself again and again and tried to be sober and staid, but still there was that happy little thrill in her heart, and her lips bubbled over into song now and then when she hardly knew it.

Aunt Pat sat with a dreamy smile on her lips and watched her, going back over the years to an old country graveyard and a boy with grave sweet eyes.

Three days this went on, three happy days for both Sherrill and Aunt Pat, and on the morning of the fourth day there came a great box of golden hearted roses for Sherrill, and no card whatever in them. An hour later the telephone rang. A long distance call for Sherrill.

With cheeks aflame and heart beating like a trip-hammer she hurried to the telephone, not even noticing the cold disapproval of Gemmie who had brought the message.

"Is that you Sherrill?" came leaping over the wire in a voice that had suddenly grown precious.

"Oh, yes, Graham!" answered Sherrill in a voice that sounded like a caress, "Where are you?"

"I'm in Chicago," said a strong glad voice, "I want to come and see you this afternoon about something very important. Are you going to be at home?"

"Oh, surely, yes, all day," lilted Sherrill, "but how could you possibly come and see me to-day if you are in Chicago?"

"I'm flying! I'll be there just as soon as I can. I'm starting right away!"

"Oh, how wonderful!" breathed Sherrill, starry eyes looking into the darkness of the telephone booth almost lighting up the place, smiling lips beaming into the instrument. "I—I'm—*glad!*"

"That's *grand!*" said the deep big voice at the other end of the wire, "I'm gladder than ever that you are glad! Are you all right?"

"Oh, quite all right!" chirruped Sherrill. "I'm righter than all right—*now!*"

"Well, then, I'll be seeing you—shortly. I'm at the flying field now, and I'm starting *immediately!* Good bye—*darling!*"

The last word was so soft, so indefinite that it gave the impression of having been whispered after the lips had been turned away from the instrument, and Sherrill was left in doubt whether she had not just imagined it after all.

She came out of the telephone booth with her eyes still starrier and her cheeks more rosy than they had been when she went in. She brushed by the still disapproving Gemmie who was doing some very unnecessary dusting in the hall, and rushed up to her aunt's room.

"Oh, Aunt Pat!" she said breathlessly, "He's coming! He's flying! He's coming this afternoon. Do you mind if we don't go to ride as we'd planned?"

"Who's coming, child?" snapped Aunt Pat with her wry grin and a wicked little twinkle in her eye, "Be more explicit."

"Why Graham is coming," said Sherrill eagerly, her face wreathed in smiles.

"Graham indeed! And who might Graham be? Graham Smith or Graham Jones? And when did we get so intimate as to be calling each other by our first names?"

For answer Sherrill went laughing and hid her hot cheeks in the roseleaf coolness of the old lady's neck. The old lady patted her shoulder and smoothed her soft hair as if she had been a baby.

"Well," said Aunt Pat with her twisted smile, "it begins to look as if that young man had a great deal of business in the east, doesn't it? It must be expensive to travel around in airplanes the way he does, but it's certainly interesting to have a man drop right down out of the skies that way. Now, let me see, what are you going to wear, child? How about that little blue organdy? You look like a sweet child in that. I like it. Wear that. Those cute little white scallops around the neck and sleeves remind me of a dress I had when I was sixteen. My mother knew how to make scallops like that."

"I'll wear it of course," said Sherrill eagerly. "How lovely it must have been to have a mother to make scallops for you. But I don't know as that is any better than having a dear precious aunt to buy them for you. You just spoil me, Auntie Pat! Aren't you afraid I'll 'spoil on you' as Lutie's mother says?"

"Well, I've tried hard enough," said the old lady smiling, "But I can't seem to accomplish anything in that line. I guess you are the kind that doesn't spoil."

All the morning Gemmie came and went with grim set lips and disapproving air, going about her duties scrupulously, doing all that was required of her, yet saying as plainly as words could have said that they were all under a blind delusion and she was the only one that saw through things and knew how they were being deceived by this flying youth who was about to appear on the scene again. She sniffed at the gorgeous yellow roses when she passed by them and wiped her eyes surreptitiously. She didn't like to see her beloved family deceived.

But time got away at last and Sherrill went to dress for the guest, for they had been consulting flying fields, and had found out the probable hour of his arrival.

Sherrill was just putting the last touches to her hair when Aunt Pat tapped at the door and walked in with a tiny string of pearls in her hand, real pearls they were, and very small and lovely.

"I want you to wear these, dearie," she said in a sweet old voice that seemed made of tears and smiles and reminded one of lavender and rose leaves.

Sherrill whirled about quickly, but when she saw the little string of pearls her face went white and her eyes took on a frightened look. She drew back and caught hold of the dressing table.

"Oh, not another necklace!" she said in distress. "Dear Aunt Patricia. I really couldn't wear it! I'd lose it! I'm afraid of necklaces!"

"Nonsense, child!" said the old lady smiling. "That other necklace is going to turn up sometime I'm sure. Remember I told you those stones were registered, and eventually if someone stole them, they will be sold, will ultimately arrive at some of the large dealers, and be traced. You're not to fret about them, even if it is some time before we hear of them. And as for this necklace, it's one I had when I was a little girl, and it is charmed. I always had a happy time when I wore it, and I want you to wear this for me this afternoon. I like to see you in it, and I like to think of you with it on. You'll do it for me, little girl. I never had a little girl of my own, and so you'll have to have them. I'm quite too old now to wear such a childish trinket."

So Sherrill half fearfully, let her clasp the quaint chain about her neck, and stooped and kissed the dear old lady on the parting of her silvery curls.

Sooner than Sherrill had dared to hope he came. She watched him from behind her window curtain while he paid the taxi driver and then gave a quick upward look at the windows of the house. No, she had not been mistaken in her memory of him. That firm clean, lean look about the chin, that merry twinkle in his eyes. The late afternoon sun lit up his well-knit form. There was a covert strength behind him that filled her with satisfaction and comfort. He was a man one could trust utterly. She couldn't be deceived in him!

Then Gemmie's cold voice broke stiffly on her absorption:

"The young man is here, Miss Sherrill!"

"Oh, Gemmie," caroled Sherrill as she hurried laughing from her window. "Do take that solemn look off your face. You look like the old meeting house down at the corner of Graff Street. Do look happy, Gemmie!"

"I always look as happy as I feel, Miss Sherrill," said Gemmie frigidly.

But Sherrill suddenly whirled on her, gave her a resounding kiss on her thin astonished lips, and went gayly past her down the stairs, looking like a sweet child, in her little blue organdy with the white scallops and pearls, and her gold hair like a halo around her eager face. The small blue slippers laced with black velvet ribbons about her ankles fairly twinkled as she ran down the steps, and the young man who stood at the foot of the stairs, his eyes alight with an old old story, thought her the loveliest thing he had ever seen.

Aunt Pat had managed to absorb every single servant about the place, suddenly and intensively, and there wasn't a soul around to witness their meeting, though perhaps it would not have made the least difference to them, for they were aware of nobody but their own two selves.

She went to his arms as to a haven she had always known she possessed, and his arms went round her and drew her close, with her gold head right over his heart, her cheek rubbing deliciously against the fine serge of his dark blue coat. Dark blue serge, how she loved it! He had worn a coat like that when she first found him!

He laid his lips against her forehead, her soft hair, brushing his face, and held her close for a moment, breathing:

"Oh, my darling!"

Then, suddenly they drew apart, almost embarrassed, each afraid of having been too eager, and then drew together again, his arm about her waist, drawing her into the small reception room, and down to the small sofa just inside the portiere.

The man laughed softly, triumphantly.

"I was afraid to come," he said. "I was afraid it would be too soon, after—after—that other man!"

"You mean Carter?" said Sherrill, and then with a sudden inner enlightenment, "Why, there never was any other man, but you." She said it with a burst of joy. "I thought there was, but now I know there *never* was! At least I thought he was what you are! There has *always* been you—in my thoughts I guess!" and she dropped her eyes shyly, afraid to have too quickly revealed her heart.

"How could I have been so mistaken!" she added with

quick anger at herself. "Oh, I should have had to suffer longer for being so stupid!"

But he drew her within his arms again and laid his lips on hers, then on her sweet eyelids, and then, his cheek against hers, he whispered, "Oh, my precious little love!"

Suddenly he brought something from his pocket, something bright and flashing, and slipped it on her finger. Startled she looked down and saw a great blue diamond, the loveliest she had ever seen, set in delicate platinum handiwork.

"That marks you as mine," he said with a wonderful look into her eyes. "And now, darling, we've got to work fast, for I haven't much time."

"Oh!" said Sherrill in instant alarm, "Have you got to go back again right away?"

"Not back again," he laughed, "but off somewhere else. And I don't know what you'll think of what I've come to propose. Maybe you'll think it is all wrong, rushing things this way when we've scarcely known each other yet, and you don't really know a thing about me or my family."

"That wouldn't matter," said Sherrill emphatically, without even a thought of the emerald necklace, though Gemmie at that moment was stalking noisily through the hall beyond the curtain.

"You precious one!" said Copeland drawing her close again and lifting one of her hands, the one with the ring on the third finger, to his lips.

"Well, now, you see, it's this way. I'm being sent quite unexpectedly to South America on a matter of very special business. It's a great opportunity for me, and if I succeed in my mission it means that I'll be on Easy Street of course. But I may have to stay down there anywhere from six weeks to six months to accomplish my purpose,—"

"Ohhh!" breathed Sherrill with a sound like pain.

He smiled, pressed her fingers close and went on speaking.

"I feel that way too, dearest. I can't bear to be away from you so long when I've only just found you. And I've been audacious enough to want to take you with me! Do you suppose you could ever bring yourself to see it that way too? Or have I asked too much? I've brought all sorts of credentials and things with me."

"I don't need credentials," said Sherrill nestling close to him, "I love you." And suddenly she felt she understood that other poor girl who had said she would marry Carter McArthur if she knew she had to go through hell with him. That was what love was, utter self-abnegation, utter devotion. That was why love was so dangerous perhaps to some. But this love was different. This man knew her Christ, belonged to him. Oh, what had God done for her! Taken away a man who was not worthy, and given her one of His own children!

His arms were about her again, drawing her close, his words of endearment murmured in her ear.

"You will go?" he asked gently. "You mean *you will go?*" There was an awed delight in his voice.

"Of course!" said Sherrill softly. "When would we have to go?"

"That's it," he said with a bit of trouble in his eyes as he looked down on her anxiously. "I have to go *to-night!* Would that be rushing you too much? I'd make it longer if I could, but there is need for great haste in my business. In fact if it could have waited until the next boat I wouldn't have been sent at all, a senior member of the firm would have gone in my place. But just now neither of them could get away so it fell to my lot, and I had no chance to protest."

Sherrill sat up and looked startled.

"To-night!" she echoed. "Why, I could go of course,—but—I'm not sure how Aunt Patricia would take it. She's been wonderful to me I wouldn't like to hurt her. I ought to ask her—!"

"Of course!" said Copeland. "Where is she? Let's go to her at once! I'll try to make her see it. And—well—if this thing succeeds I'll be able perhaps to make it up to her about losing you so suddenly. It might just happen that I would be put in the east to look after a new branch of the business. We could live around here if that would make it pleasanter for her."

"How wonderful!" said Sherrill, "Let's go up to her room! I know she'll be kind of expecting us."

So they went up the stairs with arms about one another, utterly unaware of Gemmie, peering out stolidly from behind the living room portieres.

They appeared that way in Aunt Pat's doorway when she had bidden them enter, for all the world like two children come to confess some prank.

"I see how it is with you," said Aunt Pat with a pleased grin as they stood a second, at a loss how to begin. "I expected it of course."

"I know you don't know a thing about me," began the lover searching around in his legal mind for the things he had prepared to say, "but I've brought some credentials."

"Don't bother!" said Aunt Pat indifferently. "I wasn't quite a fool! You didn't suppose I was going to put my child in danger of a second heart-break did you? I looked you up the day the first flowers came."

"Why, Aunt Pat!" said Sherrill aghast. "You said you

trusted him utterly! You said you knew a man when you saw one!"

"Of course I did!" said Aunt Pat not in the least disturbed, "I knew he was all right. But when it was a matter of you, Sherrill, I knew I had to have something more than my own intuition to go on. I wasn't going to go and give you away to every stranger that came along with a nice face and a pleasant manner. Some day I expect to go to heaven and meet your father and mother again, and I don't want them to blame me, so I called up my old friend Judge Porter in Chicago and asked him to tell me all he knew about this young man. Don't worry, young man, I made him think it was some business I wanted to place in your hands. But I found out a lot more than your business standing, and I knew I would, thanks to my old friend George Porter. I went to school with him and he always was very thorough in all he did. So, it's all right, young man. You have my blessing!"

Copeland's face fairly blazed with joy, but before he had time to thank the old lady Sherrill spoke.

"But there's more, Aunt Pat! He wants us to be married right away!"

"That's natural," said Aunt Pat dryly, with her wry smile.

"Yes, but Aunt Pat, he's being sent to South America and he has to go to-night!"

"To-night!" said the old lady alertly. "H'm! Well it's fortunate you have a wedding dress all ready, Sherrill."

"Oh," said Sherrill with a quick look of astonishment, "I hadn't thought about it. Could I wear that? I could just wear my going-away dress of course."

"No," said Aunt Pat. "Wear your own wedding dress! Don't let yourself be cheated out of that just because you had to lend it to another poor girl for a few minutes. Get your mind rid of that poor fool who would have married you and then made you suffer the rest of your life. Don't be foolish. It was *your* wedding dress and not hers. And she couldn't have hurt it much in that short time. Don't you think she ought to wear a real wedding dress, Graham?" asked the old lady briskly, turning to the young man as if she had known him since his first long trousers.

Copeland's eyes lighted.

"I'd love to see you in it!" he said, looking at Sherrill with adoring eyes.

"Oh, then I'll wear it of course," said Sherrill with starry eyes. "It was really awfully hard to give up wearing it, it was so pretty."

"Of course!" said Aunt Pat bruskly, "and why should you? Forget that other girl, and the whole silly muddle. Now, young man, what is there to do besides getting her suitcase packed? Have you got the license yet?"

"No, but I know where to get it and I'm going for it right away."

"Very well," said Aunt Pat, "I'll have the chauffeur take you. Sherrill, what about bridesmaids? Yours are all scattered."

"Do I have to have them?" asked Sherrill aghast.

"I don't see why," said her aunt. "I suppose we'll have to ask in a few friends, a dozen perhaps, just Cousin Phyllis, and her family and maybe the Grants, they're such old friends. I'll think it over."

"And I wouldn't have to be given away or any of that fuss either, would I? It all seems so silly," pleaded Sherrill. "I thought before that if I had to do it over again I'd never want all that. Couldn't Graham and I just walk down stairs together and be married without any elaborate extras?"

"You certainly could," said Aunt Pat. "If your Graham doesn't feel that he is being cheated out of his rights to a formal wedding."

"Not on your life!" grinned Graham Copeland. "I'd hate it all! But of course I'd go through a good many times that and worse to get her if it was necessary. All I want is a simple ceremony and your blessing."

"Blest be!" said Aunt Pat. "Now, get you gone and come back as soon as possible. Sherrill, send Gemmie to me and tell her to send up the cook. We'll scratch together a few green peas and a piece of bread and butter for a simple little wedding supper. No, don't worry, I won't do anything elaborate. What time do you have to leave, Graham? All right. She'll be ready!"

Sherrill stayed behind after her lover had gone, to throw her arms around her aunt's neck and kiss her many times.

"Oh, Aunt Pat! You are the greatest woman in the world!" she said excitedly.

"Well, you're getting a real man this time, and no mistake!" said the old lady with satisfaction. "When you have time I'll show you the letter my friend Judge Porter wrote about him, but that'll keep. You had better go and get your things together. I'll send Gemmie to help you as soon as I'm done with her."

So Sherrill hurried to her room on glad feet and began to get her things together. She went to the trunk room and found her own new suitcase with its handsome fittings, still partly packed as it had been on that fateful wedding night. She went to the drawers and closets and got out the piles of pretty lingerie, the lovely negligees, dumped them on the bed and looked at them with a dreamy smile, as if they were long lost friends come back to their own, but when Gemmie arrived stern and disapproving still, she had not got far in her packing.

"Miss Patricia says you're to lie down for half an hour

right away!" she announced grimly, "and I'm to do your packing. She says you're tired to death and won't be fit to travel if you don't."

"All right!" said Sherrill with a lilt in her voice, kicking her little blue slippers off and submitting to be tucked into her bed, blue organdy and all.

Gemmie with a baleful glance at her shut her lips tight and went silently about her packing, laying in things with skillful hand, folding them precisely, thinking of things that Sherrill in her excited state never would have remembered. And Sherrill with a happy sigh closed her eyes and tried to realize that it was really herself and not some other girl who was lying here, going to be married within the next few hours.

But there are limits to the length of time even an excited girl like Sherrill can lie still, and before the half hour was over she was up, her voice fresh and rested, chattering away to the silent woman who only sniffed and wiped a furtive eye with a careful handkerchief. It was all too evident that Gemmie did not approve of the marriage. But what could one do with such a woman who had been perfectly satisfied with a man like Carter? She was beyond all reason.

Sherrill went over to see her aunt for a few minutes and have a last little talk.

Aunt Pat invited just a very few of their most intimate friends, and some of those couldn't come on such short notice. "Just to make it plain that we're not trying to hide something," she said to Sherrill with her twinkly grin. "People are so apt to rake up some reason to gossip. But anyway what do we care? The Grants are coming and they are the pick of the lot, and Cousin Phyllis. She would never have forgiven us if she hadn't been asked. She did complain about the shortness of the time and want it put off till tomorrow, but I told her that was impossible."

Then Sherrill told her what Copeland had said about the possibility of his being located in the east when he returned, and Aunt Pat gave her first little mite of a sigh and said with a wistful look like a child:

"Well, if he could see his way clear to coming here to this house and living it would be the best I'd ask of earth any longer. It'll be your house anyway when I'm gone, and I'd like you to just take it over now and run it any time you will. I could sort of board or visit with you. I'm getting old, you know. You speak of it sometime to him when it seems wise, but don't be hampered by it of course," and Aunt Pat sighed again.

"You dear!" said Sherrill bending over her and kissing her tenderly, "I'd love it, and I'm sure he would too. Now don't you worry, and don't you feel lonesome, or we'll just tuck you in the suitcase and take you along with us to South America."

Aunt Pat grinned and patted Sherrill's cheek smartly. "You silly little girl! Now run along and get your wedding frills on. It's almost time for the guests to be here, and you are not ready."

So Sherrill ran away laughing, and had to tell Gemmie to please bring the big box containing the wedding dress.

"You're not going to wear *that!*" said Gemmie aghast.

"Certainly I am, Gemmie," said Sherrill firmly. "It's my dress isn't it? Hurry please. It's getting late!"

Gemmie gave her a wild look.

"I should have been told," she said coldly. "The dress should have been pressed."

"Nonsense, Gemmie, it doesn't matter whether there is a wrinkle or two, but there won't be. You put tissue in every fold. Anyway, you can't press it. It's too late!"

Gemmie brought the great pasteboard box, thumped

it down on the bed unopened and stalked into the bathroom, pretending to have urgent work there picking up damp towels for the laundry.

Sherrill, feeling annoyed at the stubborn faithful old woman, went over to the bed and lifted the cover of the big box.

There lay the soft white folds of the veil like a lovely mist, and above them like blooms among the snow the beautiful wreath of orange blossoms, not a petal out of place. Gemmie had done her work perfectly when she put them away. And beneath the veil Sherrill could see the gleam of the satin wedding gown. Oh, it was lovely, and Sherrill's heart leaped with pleasure to think she might wear it again, wear it this time without a doubt or pang or shrinking!

She turned away humming a soft little tune and went about her dressing.

Gemmie had laid out all the lovely silken garments and it was like playing a game to put them on, leisurely, happily.

When she was ready for the dress she called Gemmie, and then Aunt Pat came in, ready attired in her soft gray robes, looking herself as lovely as any wedding could desire.

"I'm glad I can have a little leisure this time," she said settling into a big chair and smoothing her silks about her, "last time I had to be hustled off to the church when there were a hundred and one things I wanted to attend to at home. I don't know that I care much for church weddings anyway unless you *have* to have a mob."

Gemmie's eyes were red as if she had been weeping and she came forward to officiate at the donning of the dress with a long sorrowful look on her face.

It was just at that moment that there came a tap at the door and the waitress handed in a package.

"It was special delivery," she explained. "I thought maybe you'd want it right away."

"You might a known she'd no time to bother with the like of that now," said Gemmie ungraciously, taking the package from the girl.

"Oh, but I want to see it, Gemmie," cried Sherrill. "Thank you, Emily, for bringing it up. I want to see everything. You don't suppose anybody is sending a wedding present, do you, Aunt Pat? Don't tell me I've got to go through all that again!"

"Open it up, Gemmie!" ordered Aunt Pat. "It might be something Graham has had sent you, you know, Sherrill."

With something like a sniff Gemmie reached for the scissors and snipped the cords.

"It'll not be from him!" she said tartly, "It's from across the water!"

"Across the water?" said Sherrill and reached for the package.

"H'm! across the water!" said Aunt Pat sitting up eagerly. "Open it quick, Sherry. It might be interesting!"

IF Carter McArthur had been told on the first day out from New York that before the end of the voyage he would be almost reconciled to his fate as husband of a penniless bride, he would have been astonished. But it was nevertheless true.

Arla Prentiss had always been a clever girl, and Arla McArthur driven by necessity became almost brilliant in managing her difficult affairs. She had taken the material at hand and used it. Even Hurley Kirkwood and the two old high school classmates became assets in the affair. Before the voyage was over she had even won out with the man Sheldon and used him to her own ends.

How they came to be seated at a table in a pleasant but obscure corner of the dining room with Hurley Kirkwood, Helen and Bob Shannon and a very deaf old man who paid no attention to any of them, was never known to Carter McArthur. He was very angry when he discovered it, and put Arla through the third degree, but in the end he saw it was a good thing. There was nobody at the table they needed to be nervous about. The three old acquaintances had never heard of Sherrill Cameron and her gorgeous wedding at which she was not the bride, and would be very unlikely to hear now, at least before the voyage was over. Moreover they were good company and there was a certain pleasant intimacy that it could not be denied relieved the strain under which both Arla and Carter had been. There was no danger of some embarrassing question coming up.

Carter grew quite genial and like his old youthful self in their company, accepted the stale jokes about his fondness for Arla with the same complacency that he used to do in the old days when they first began to go together, and actually treated Arla with a degree of his former devotion. If he realized that Hurley Kirkwood was sending home daily bulletins of the honeymoon to a devoted group of fellow-citizens, it only filled him with a vague satisfaction. It comforted his self-esteem to feel that his home town still honored him even though Sherrill Cameron had found out that he was a scoundrel.

Besides all this there was a certain amount of protection in having one's own private little clique. It was almost as good as if Arla had been willing to stay in her stateroom and pretend to be seasick.

Then one evening, near the end of the voyage, Carter, coming out on deck to seek Arla where she usually sat, found her walking the deck arm in arm with the great financier, conversing with him vivaciously and seeming to be entirely at her ease.

She was wearing the loveliest of Sherrill Cameron's evening dresses, the orchid chiffon, and with the moonlight gleaming on her gold hair she looked like a dream. Evidently the financier thought she did also, for he was bending graciously to her and smiling.

Carter withdrew to a distance and watched them from afar, his eyes narrowing, his admiration growing for his lovely wife. Either she was going to be his utter undoing, or else somehow she had managed to wrap Sheldon around her little finger.

They had it out that night in the stateroom, very late, in a brief session. Carter poured invectives upon her, to which she listened absently, and then laughed.

"Oh, Carter, excuse me," she said condescendingly, "all that excitement is so unnecessary. You see Mr. Sheldon thinks I am Sherrill Cameron. He told me how much he had always admired my lovely hair and eyes, and said my aunt Miss Catherwood was a marvelous old lady!"

It was some minutes before Carter recovered from the shock of that and asked for details, but before they were finished he actually came to telling Arla that she was a wonderful woman, and that he loved her beyond anything on earth.

"If I had only realized how really clever you are, Arla, I would never have looked at Sherrill Cameron!" he said, and Arla drew a sharp breath and wished he had not said that. Wished that somehow she might get back her illusions about him. Sherrill Cameron had been right of course. One could not be happy with a man who had been torn from his pedestal. And yet, wasn't there some way to put him back there? To keep him from doing the things that made her despise him?

Several times after that Arla walked and talked with the great man, and Carter's temper was improving daily.

It was about three hours before they were expecting to land.

Arla had scribbled a letter to her Aunt Tilly in the home town telling briefly of her hasty marriage, because she knew that Hurley would spread the news widely and her aunt would be hurt if she did not receive some personal word. She had just returned from posting it and found Carter pulling out the suitcases from under the bed. He stacked them up in two piles, the ones that were to be left with the shipping company for the return voyage, the ones they were to take to the hotel with them. His own suitcase was on the top of one of the piles.

Suddenly he remembered some letters he had written which he wished to post on shipboard. He rushed out slamming the stateroom door behind him, and an avalanche of suitcases careened over to the floor. The top one burst open—perhaps it had not been securely latched—and some of the contents flowed out upon the floor.

Arla sprang forward to pick up the things before Carter's return. She had begun to realize that that was to be her perpetual attitude, always being ready to smooth the way before her husband if she wished to live peaceably with him. That was his wedding suit lying sprawled upon the floor. It would not be a wise note to introduce just at this stage, a reminder of that awful wedding.

Arla stooped and picked it up and as she lifted it she felt something slip out from between the loosened folds—or was it out of a pocket, the trouser pocket perhaps?—and slither along the floor.

She looked down quickly. Was it money? No, something bright and sparkling with green lights in it! Something gorgeous and beautiful lying there on the floor before her startled eyes!

She stopped and stared. What was it? Where had she seen that rarely wrought chain before and those wonderful green stones? Emeralds! They were Sherrill Cameron's emeralds. The necklace she had worn the night of the wedding! The necklace that everybody in the room had been talking about and admiring!

For an instant Arla stood there almost paralyzed facing the possibilities of how that necklace got into her husband's pocket. Over her face the whole gamut of emotions played in quick succession. Astonishment, horror, disgust, scorn, fear, and then a great determination.

Frantically she dropped the garments she held and grasped the glittering necklace, cradled it in her hand for an instant, caught the gorgeous lights in the beautiful gems. Was Carter planning to sell these rare jewels to get the fortune that was to have come from the alliance that her coming to the Catherwood house that night had foiled? Was that what he had meant, that he had found a way to get the rest of the money he needed to save his business schemes?

And was he excusing himself by saying that the jewels were a part of the wedding presents and therefore he had a right to take them? She knew that Carter was capable of such quibbling. Her heart sank. Was she also to have a thief as well as a trifler for a husband?

Outside the door she could hear footsteps coming along the passageway. He might return at any moment! A great panic came upon her. He *should not* be a thief! She would foil that as well as his attempt to marry the other girl!

Her first impulse was to hurl those stones from the porthole and destroy the evidence against him, but as she swayed to take a step in that direction she realized what she was doing. Those were Sherrill Cameron's jewels. Hurling them into the sea would not make Carter any less a thief, even though no one ever found it out. And Sherrill Cameron had been wonderful to her, generous in the extreme. She could not do that to her, throw her costly jewels in the sea! That other girl had already suffered greatly through herself, she should not also lose her property. No, the only possible way to undo the wrong that Carter had done was to return them to their owner. Somehow she *must* return them and yet shield Carter! Shield him from going to the penitentiary!

Hastily she wrapped the jewels in a clean handkerchief, tied the corners securely, and hid it in her own suitcase beneath the lingerie. Then she hurried back to pick up Carter's things. If she could only restore them to their place before he returned!

She schooled herself to go carefully, folding each garment without a wrinkle, laying everything smoothly back in its place. It seemed to her that it was hours before that suitcase was fastened and back on the top of the pile where he had left it.

Then she went to her own suitcase and began frantically hunting through it among the various fittings for a suitable container for the jewels. If she could only get them in the mail before it closed! She glanced at her wrist watch. There was a little over half an hour. She must not fail to get them in. She *must* get them wrapped in time! He should not be *allowed* to be a thief! He might have done many crooked things in business, doubtless had, she could not help the past, but in so far as she was able he should not be allowed to steal a lady's jewels! She never could endure life with that over her, that she had helped him to take the necklace of the girl who had given him up to her. It was too low and contemptible! He wouldn't be thinking himself of doing it if he weren't so utterly frantic about money! He had been decently brought up, just as decently as she was. He wasn't naturally a crook. She must protect him against his worst self.

And she must protect the necklace from her own weakness, too, she realized. If he should discover she had it, should look at her with his beautiful eyes, kiss her the way he did last night, ask her to surrender it, could she resist? She doubted her own strength. She must put that necklace where neither he nor she could ever get it again.

She found in the suitcase a little leather case containing lovely crystal bottles of perfume and lotions. She took out the bottles and packed the jewels carefully, swiftly, among soft folds of Sherrill's own fine handkerchiefs. Then scribbled a hasty note.

> *You must have dropped this when you were packing. I found it in the suitcase. I hope it has not caused you any anxiety.*
>
> *Arla McArthur.*

With the leather case wrapped in a bit of silk lingerie and then in paper she went hurriedly out and procured a mailing carton from the stewardess, addressed her package at a desk and was not satisfied until it was safe in the keeping of the ship's mail service.

When she went back Carter was directing the steward about the baggage. She was silent and abstracted putting a few last things in her suitcase. The baggage was all going up on deck at once. The whole ship was in a state of getting ready to land.

Carter too seemed absorbed in his own thoughts. Just before they left their stateroom he remarked briskly that they would go directly to the hotel and he would leave her there for the morning. He had some business to be transacted that must be attended to the first thing. Then he would be free to go about with her if all went well.

All during the slow process of arrival and landing and on the way to the hotel Arla was thinking what to do when her husband should discover his loss. Now that she was safe on land and the package in the return mail was presumably safe on its way to America she felt more sure of herself.

Nevertheless when they arrived and were at last left alone in their room, even before Carter began fumbling with the latch of his suitcase she found she was trembling. She could hardly take off her hat, she was afraid Carter would see that she was shaking.

She busied herself hanging up their garments, putting away her hat, washing her hands. Anything not to seem to be noticing Carter who was frantically flinging his things about on chairs, on the bed, the floor, anywhere, and finally turning his suitcase upside down and shaking out its corners.

"I've lost something!" he said when she came out from the closet where she had been arranging her dresses on hangers, and found him standing amid confusion. "It's something very important," he said, beginning again to pick up things and fling them about, to feel in pockets, poke into the fittings of his bag.

"Can I help you?" asked Arla, trying to steady her voice.

"No! No one can help me!" he said flinging a house coat across to the bed. "I can't find—Oh, it's here somewhere of course! It couldn't have got away! I *know* it's here! I'm *wild!* That's all. It couldn't have got away!" He seemed to be talking more to himself than to her. He seemed almost to have forgotten her existence.

"Oh, to think I had to be forced into such a situation!" he groaned at last flinging himself down in a chair and covering his face with his hands. "Was ever any man tormented as I have been?"

Arla came over and stood beside his chair, laying an icy hand on his bowed head. She was shaking from head to foot, but she tried to make her voice calm.

"I'd like to help you, Carter!"

"Well, you can't help me!" he said flinging rudely away from her. "It's all your fault anyway that I'm in such a situation. You put me here, how could you help me? It's too late! If you had wanted to help me you'd have done what I told you sooner and then everything would have come right—. No, you can't help me. You don't even know what it is I'm hunting for, and if you did you wouldn't understand!"

Arla stood still for a minute and then she went and sat down across from him.

"Listen, Carter!" she said in a cold clear voice, "I understand perfectly what you are looking for and what you meant to do. You are looking for Sherrill Cameron's emeralds and you won't find them because they are on their way back to her!"

He sat like one stunned for an instant and she thought he had not understood her. Then suddenly he sprang to his feet and glared at her. His hair was awry, his face was distraught, his eyes glittered like a mad man's. For an instant she thought he was going to strike her. He looked as if he might even have killed her for that minute, if he had had the means at hand. He was beside himself.

"You—! You—! You *dared!*" he screamed, and poured out upon her a stream of invectives that made her shudder with their cruelty.

But she must not cry. She must not show that she was afraid of him. This was the time she had to be strong. She had saved him from the penitentiary and now she must make him understand what danger he was in. Her courage rose to the necessity.

"Yes," she said steadily, "I dared! For *your* sake I dared!"

"For my sake!" he sneered. "You say you did it for *my sake?"*

"Yes, I did it for your sake. Remember you tried to marry another woman once for my sake. Well, I didn't do a thing like that, but I took away the knife that would have cut your throat. You didn't know what you were doing perhaps, you had been through so much. But afterward you would have realized and been ashamed. And I didn't intend to have a common thief for a husband!"

"Thief?" he cried furiously, "I had a perfect right after all that had been done to me. An underhanded—!"

"Stop!" said Arla coldly, "You are not the one to talk about anything underhanded. And you would not have found your argument would have stood before a court of law."

"It would never have come to a court of law. They wouldn't dream who had them. Besides, I had arranged to sell them at once!"

"You poor fool," said Arla, "didn't you know that that necklace was registered? Those stones were well known stones. I heard them talking about it at the reception. You couldn't have got away with it even if I hadn't interfered. You would have been in the penitentiary before three months were passed."

The man was white to the lips now, and sank back in his chair groaning. It was a piteous sight! Tears filled Arla's eyes in spite of her resolution.

Then he suddenly raised his head and glared at her again with his bloodshot eyes.

"And I suppose you don't think they'll trace your package and come after me to every country in Europe?" he snarled, terror in his face.

"No," said Arla coolly, "I wrote a note inside the box and told her she must have dropped the necklace into the suitcase when she was packing."

He was still, staring at her, the strained muscles of his face gradually relaxing. Then he dropped his head into his hands again and groaned aloud, groan after groan until Arla felt she could not stand another one.

At last he spoke again.

"Everything is lost!" he moaned. "I might as well be in the penitentiary. I can't meet my obligations! I can't ever get on my feet again! I am disgraced before the world!"

"Listen, Carter!" said Arla in a tone that demanded attention. "You are only disgraced if you have done something wrong. I saved you from doing one wrong thing. I'm glad I could. I never could respect you again if you had done that! But it's undone now. The necklace is on its way back, and no harm will come to you but losing your business. I'm glad you're losing that. I hate it! It is what made you forget your love for me and go after another woman. Oh, she may be a great deal more attractive than I am, and all that, but you belonged *to me*. By all that had gone before you were mine and I was yours. You knew that! By your own confession these past few days you know it now. Now stop acting like a baby and be a man! How do you think I feel having a husband like you?"

"What can I do?" he groaned.

"Sit up and stop acting like a madman," said his wife, turning away to hide the sorrow and contempt in her eyes. "If you'll get calm and listen I'll tell you what you can do, and I'll stand by and help you! What you should do is take the next boat back and hand over your business to your creditors. Then let's go Home and start anew. You can do it, and I can help you. Won't you listen to reason Carter, and let us be honest respectable people as our parents were?"

Carter slumped in his chair made no reply for a long long time. Arla sat tense, every nerve strained, waiting. She knew that her words had been like blows to him. She felt weak and helpless now that she had spoken. It was like waiting to see whether someone beloved was going to die or live.

But at last he lifted his head and looked at her. She was shocked at his face. It had grown old and haggard in that short time. He had the terrible baffled look of one who had walked the heights and been flung to the depths. She had never seen him before with the self-confidence stripped from him utterly.

"I could never get back to that!" he said and his voice was hoarse and hopeless.

"Yes, you could!" said Arla eagerly. "If you'd just be willing to give it all up and start over again!"

"Oh, you don't know!" he said still with that hopeless look in his eyes. "You don't know it all!"

"You'd be surprised!" said Arla springing up and going over to kneel beside him with her arm about him. "I know a lot more than you think I know. You left your books out one day and I thought they were the books you told me to look up that old metropolitan account in. I hadn't an idea what I was coming on until it was too late."

He looked at her startled, blanching.

"And you knew all that and yet you married me?"

"Yes," said Arla her voice trembling.

He suddenly dropped his head upon her shoulder.

"I'm not worthy of you," he groaned. "I guess I never was!"

"That has nothing to do with it, Carter!" she said almost fiercely, "I love you and *you shall* be worthy! Say you will, Carter, oh, say you will!"

Her tone fairly wrung the promise from him.

"I'm a rotten low down beast!" he said between his clenched teeth. "I can say I will, Arla, but I don't even know if I can do what I say I will."

"Yes, you can!" said Arla in the tone of a mother

determined to save her young. "You *shall!* I'll help you! I'll make you. When you're weak then I'll be strong for you! I've got to! I'll die if you can't be brought back to be a decent man again!"

For a long time his face was hidden on her shoulder, and his whole frame shook with emotion, but her arms were about him and she held him close, her tears raining down unheeded upon his bowed head.

At last he said in a low tone husky with emotion:

"If you can love me like that after all I've done to you, then perhaps I can! I'll try!"

Then eagerly she lifted his face to hers and their lips met, their tears mingling.

It was sometime after that that Arla spoke, gently, quietly.

"Now, oughtn't we to be doing something about a boat to go back on?"

Carter looked up and his capable business expression came upon him.

"I think first, perhaps, I'd better cable to that man that made the offer about the business. He'll maybe go back on it, or have done something else already you know."

"You're right!" said Arla. "Let's go together. I can't be separated from you now till it's all fixed."

"Yes, come!" he said catching her fingers. "Oh, Arla, there's may be something for us somewhere, when you can love me like this!"

Thus Arla entered on her life undertaking of making a man.

"This diamond," she said thoughtfully looking at the gorgeous ring on her finger, "and those pearls. Are they paid for, Carter?"

She watched him keenly as the slow color mounted to his forehead again and his eyes took on a shamed look.

"Because if they're not," she hastened to say, "Let's

send them back, I mean take them back or something. They're not really mine you know. They never were. You got them for her and I think of it every time I look at them. Some day when we can afford it you can get me some of my own, and I'd like that much better."

Carter went and stood by the window looking out with unseeing eyes. His perceptions were turned inside to himself. He was seeing just what kind of a contemptible failure he had been. Seeing it as nothing else but utter failure could have made him see.

"There's no end to it!" he moaned hoarsely.

"Yes, we'll get to the end of it, only let's make a clean sweep now once and forever. Suppose we sit down while we're waiting for the answer to that cable and write down a list of things that have to go back or be sold or something, and debts that have to be paid. Don't forget anything. Let's just look it all in the face and know where we stand."

"We don't *have* a place to stand!" said the disheartened man. "Every foot of ground under us is mortgaged. That's what you've—what we've—what *I've* brought you to, Arla!"

Arla's eyes had a strange light of hope in them as she looked at him. He hadn't said she had brought him to that. He had started to, but he hadn't said it. He had acknowledged that he had done it himself! There was some hope.

They had about a week to wait for the boat they had decided to take, and they went to cheap lodgings and made little excursions here and there on foot, seeing what they could of the old world in a humble way. Perhaps nothing could have better prepared Carter to go from a life of extravagance into plain homely economy like taking their pleasure without cost. For Arla wouldn't let them spend an unnecessary cent. She had everything down to the last penny now, and was determined that they should get free from debt.

"Some day," said Carter watching a young couple, obviously on their wedding trip, as they entered a handsome automobile and drove happily away, "Some day I'll bring you over here and we'll see Europe in the right way."

"Perhaps not," said Arla, her lips set with determination. "We've got to get over expecting things like that. If we ever get rich it might happen, and then of course it would be great, but it isn't likely, not for a long time anyway, and we're not going to expect it nor fret that we haven't got it. It's wanting things we hadn't got that has nearly wrecked our lives, and we're going to stop it! We're going to have a good time on nothing if we have to, and just be glad."

There was disillusionment in her voice and eyes, but there was cheer and good comradeship. Carter looked at her in wonder, and was strangely comforted.

But Arla turned away her disillusioned eyes and struggled to keep back sudden tears. She was getting on very well it was true. Carter had been far more tractable than she had hoped, and that gleam of self-abasement had been hopeful, yet she knew it was but transient. He was weak. He was full of faults. He would fall again and again. He would lapse back into his old self. The world was too full of temptations and ambitions for her to hope for a Utopian life with him. Hell was there with its wide open doors, and her strength was so small! She suddenly felt like sinking under it all. Just courage, her own courage, just determination, couldn't pull him out of this and make him into a decent man again, a man in whom she could trust, upon whom she could lean. Oh, for some strength greater than her own! Oh, for some power to right their lives! Happiness in such circumstances? She knew it was impossible. A good time on nothing? Yes, if they loved and trusted each other perfectly perhaps, but not when one had constantly to bear the other up.

Oh, she would go on as she had promised, stand by him through everything. She loved him. Yes, she loved him. But there was a desolate desperateness about it all. She knew it. She knew it even while she set her beautiful strong red lips in determination to go on and succeed. She knew intuitively that there was something lacking! Some great need that would come, some need for help outside of themselves. Just human effort couldn't accomplish it.

Would Carter ever come to see that he was radically wrong, not just unfortunate? Would his remorse over his failure ever turn to actual repentance?

Oh for something strong and true to rest down upon! And vaguely even while she tried to set her courage once more for higher attainment she knew that what she was trying to do was just another of the world's delusions. She never by her own mere efforts could save Carter from himself. She might help perhaps, better things in great degree, make life more bearable, more liveable, but still in the end there would be failure! What was it they needed? Oh, there must be something, some way!

So with desperation in her eyes, a vision of a future full of useless efforts, she turned back to her heavy task.

SHERRILL filled with a startled premonition that clouded her eagerness over the package, tore off the wrappings and pulled out the little bundle in its cover of silk, shook out the bit of lingerie, a sort of consternation beginning to dawn in her face. This was her own, one of the things that had been in Arla's suitcase!

Then she recognized the little leather case and snapped open the catch, dropping out the note that Arla had written. It fell unheeded to the floor.

But there were no lovely little bottles in the case! What was this, just handkerchiefs? She pulled them out, just catching the heavy little lump knotted in the handkerchief, before it fell.

With hands that trembled now with excitement she unknotted the corners of linen that Arla had tied so hastily, and stood staring as the gleam of the great green stones flashed out to her astonished gaze.

"Oh, Aunt Pat! It's *come!* My emerald necklace has *come back!* Look! The stones are all here! Gemmie! Oh Gemmie! Where are you? The emerald necklace has come back! It's *found!* It's found! Oh, isn't it wonderful that I should find it just now?"

Gemmie hurried in from the bathroom where she had been pretending to pick up the towels and place clean ones. Her eyes were still suspiciously red, and she came and stood there looking at the jewels, the most amazed, embarrassed, mortified woman that one could find, heartily ashamed at all she had been thinking and doing, almost half suspicious yet.

"Where did they come from?" she asked sharply. "Who took them?"

"What does it matter now?" sang Sherrill, "They're here and I don't have to worry any more! Oh, I'm so glad, so glad!"

"What this on the floor?" said Aunt Pat whose sharp eyes had sighted the twisted note.

Gemmie stooped down and handed the note to Sherrill and Sherrill read it aloud. Read the name too, Arla McArthur, and never thought how that last part was once to have been her own.

"Oh, Miss Sherrill!" Her voice was shaking with emotion. "It certainly is wonderful. And I'm that ashamed! And me thinking all this time—!"

But nobody was listening to Gemmie. Aunt Pat asked to see the note and Sherrill handed it happily over to her. She read it carefully and then with her little wry smile and a twinkle in her eye she remarked, "So, you dropped it in the suitcase when you were packing! Well, it may be so, Sherrill! Of course it may be so!"

Then when Gemmie had gone out of the room on some errand she said:

"Well, Sherrill, I'm glad you learned to trust him before it turned up!" and met with a wicked little grin and another twinkle of her bright eyes, her niece's indignant denial that she had ever done anything but trust him.

An hour later, dressed once more in her wedding satin, with the long silvery folds flowing out behind her, and the soft veil blossom-wreathed upon her head, Sherrill stood before her mirror. The faithful Gemmie knelt beside her arranging the folds of her train.

Someone tapped at the door and handed in a big box.

"It'll be your flowers," said Gemmie in an awe-struck voice. She brought in the box and opened it, carefully taking out the lovely bridal bouquet of wedding roses and lilies.

"It's much, much nicer than the other one, Miss Sherrill," she said in deep satisfaction, as her eyes gloated over the flowers. "They're a better quality of flower, they are indeed! And I like the white ribbons much better than the silver. It comes from the most expensive place in the city, too, it really does. They have all the quality orders—they! They really do!"

"Oh, you dear old silly," said Sherrill affectionately. "But it is lovely, isn't it? I like it better too!"

"Well, I like yer man, Miss Sherrill, I'll say that!" added Gemmie shamefacedly. "And now, I'll just be running over to see if Miss Pat wants anything. And mind you don't go to playing any more pranks on us, slipping in another woman on me fer a bride," she added anxiously.

"No, Gemmie, I'll stay right here this time," laughed Sherrill. "I won't give this man up to any other girl!"

So Sherrill stood before her mirror in her bridal array once more and looked into her own mirrored eyes. Happy eyes this time, without a shade of fear or hesitation in them. Eyes full of trust and hope. And suddenly as she faced herself she closed her eyes and lifted her head and spoke into the silent room: "Dear God, I thank you that you took away what I thought I wanted, even though it hurt, and gave me what you had kept for me. Oh, make me worthy of such joy, and make me always ready to yield to your will."

Silently she stood with bowed head for a moment more, and then with a lovely light in her face she lifted her head and went to meet her bridegroom at the head of the stairs.

The little assembly of congenial guests were waiting for them as the two walked down the stairs. An old musician friend of Aunt Pat's was playing the wedding march on the piano, and the minister stood waiting before a hastily assembled background of palms and ferns. Sherrill walked into the room on the arm of her bridegroom and took her place to be married, her heart swelling with joy and peace.

It was a simple ceremony, few words, solemn pledges, another ring to go with her diamond, and dear people coming up to congratulate her. There was one fine old gentleman among them, a friend of Graham's father, who told her what a wonderful man she was getting, and wished her the simple earnest wishes of a bygone day.

And there were amazing presents. Some of them had been sent her before and returned, and returned again now, laughingly, because their donors had had no time to get something new. And there was a gay happy little time with a few tears at the end. Then Sherrill kissed Aunt Pat and Gemmie too and in her pretty dark blue going-away dress that she had never worn until now, was whisked off in Aunt Pat's car to the airport, and taken in an airplane to New York. An hour later the ship weighed anchor and set sail for South America. It didn't seem possible that all this had happened since the golden hearted roses arrived that morning.

Sherrill and her beloved stranger husband stood at last

on deck in a quiet place alone. They watched the lights of their native land disappear into the distance, looked at the great moonlit ocean all about them, and clung closer together.

"To think that God saw all this ahead for me, and saved me for making such a terrible mistake!" said Sherrill softly.

"He knoweth the end from the beginning," quoted Graham, holding her hand close in his own, and looking down into her sweet eyes.

"Yes, but the best of all is," said Sherrill after a little pause, "that He brought me to know Himself. Graham, if I hadn't been stopped in what I thought I wanted most of all in the world, I would never likely have known the Lord Jesus, nor have found out what a wonderful book the Bible is."

"And I perhaps would never have found a girl who knew my Heavenly Father!" said Graham. "His will is always best."

Then softly he began to sing and her voice blended with his tenderly:

"Have thine own way, Lord! Have Thine own way!
Hold o'er my being absolute sway!
Fill with Thy Spirit till all shall see
Christ only, always, living in me!"

About the Author

Grace Livingston Hill is well known as one of the most prolific writers of romantic fiction. Her personal life was fraught with joys and sorrows not unlike those experienced by many of her fictional heroines.

Born in Wellsville, New York, Grace nearly died during the first hours of life. But her loving parents and friends turned to God in prayer. She survived miraculously, thus her thankful father named her Grace.

Grace was always close to her father, a Presbyterian minister, and her mother, a published writer. It was from them that she learned the art of storytelling. When Grace was twelve, a close aunt surprised her with a hardbound, illustrated copy of one of Grace's stories. This was the beginning of Grace's journey into being a published author.

In 1892 Grace married Fred Hill, a young minister, and they soon had two lovely young daughters. Then came 1901, a difficult year for Grace—the year when, within months of each other, both her father and husband died. Suddenly Grace had to find a new place to live (her home was owned by the church where her husband had been pastor). It was a struggle for Grace to raise her young daughters alone, but through everything she kept writing. In 1902 she produced *The Angel of His Presence, The Story of a Whim,* and *An Unwilling Guest.* In 1903 her two books *According to the Pattern* and *Because of Stephen* were published.

It wasn't long before Grace was a well-known author, but she wanted to go beyond just entertaining her readers. She soon included the message of God's salvation through Jesus Christ in each of her books. For Grace, the most important thing she did was not write books but share the message of salvation, a message she felt God wanted her to share through the abilities he had given her.

In all, Grace Livingston Hill wrote more than one hundred books, all of which have sold thousands of copies and have touched the lives of readers around the world with their message of "enduring love" and the true way to lasting happiness: a relationship with God through his Son, Jesus Christ.

In an interview shortly before her death, Grace's devotion to her Lord still shone clear. She commented that whatever she had accomplished had been God's doing. She was only his servant, one who had tried to follow his teaching in all her thoughts and writing.

Don't miss these Grace Livingston Hill romance novels!

VOL.	TITLE	ORDER NUM.
1	Where Two Ways Met	07-8203-8-HILC
2	Bright Arrows	07-0380-4-HILC
3	A Girl to Come Home To	07-1017-7-HILC
4	Amorelle	07-0310-3-HILC
5	Kerry	07-2044-X-HILC
6	All through the Night	07-0018-X-HILC
7	The Best Man	07-0371-5-HILC
8	Ariel Custer	07-1686-8-HILC
9	The Girl of the Woods	07-1016-9-HILC
10	Crimson Roses	07-0481-9-HILC
11	More Than Conqueror	07-4559-0-HILC
12	Head of the House	07-1309-5-HILC
14	Stranger within the Gates	07-6441-2-HILC
15	Marigold	07-4037-8-HILC
16	Rainbow Cottage	07-5731-9-HILC
17	Maris	07-4042-4-HILC
18	Brentwood	07-0364-2-HILC
19	Daphne Deane	07-0529-7-HILC
20	The Substitute Guest	07-6447-1-HILC
21	The War Romance of the Salvation Army	07-7911-8-HILC
22	Rose Galbraith	07-5726-2-HILC
23	Time of the Singing of Birds	07-7209-1-HILC
24	By Way of the Silverthorns	07-0341-3-HILC
25	Sunrise	07-5941-9-HILC
26	The Seventh Hour	07-5884-6-HILC
27	April Gold	07-0011-2-HILC
28	White Orchids	07-8150-3-HILC
29	Homing	07-1494-6-HILC
30	Matched Pearls	07-3895-0-HILC
32	Coming through the Rye	07-0357-X-HILC
33	Happiness Hill	07-1487-3-HILC
34	The Patch of Blue	07-4809-3-HILC
36	Patricia	07-4814-X-HILC
37	Silver Wings	07-5914-1-HILC
38	Spice Box	07-5939-7-HILC
39	The Search	07-5831-5-HILC
40	The Tryst	07-7340-3-HILC
41	Blue Ruin	07-0349-9-HILC

VOL.	TITLE	ORDER NUM.
42	A New Name	07-4718-6-HILC
43	Dawn of the Morning	07-0530-0-HILC
44	The Beloved Stranger	07-0303-0-HILC
60	Miranda	07-4298-2-HILC
61	Mystery Flowers	07-4613-9-HILC
63	The Man of the Desert	07-3955-8-HILC
64	Miss Lavinia's Call	07-4360-1-HILC
77	The Ransom	07-5143-4-HILC
78	Found Treasure	07-0911-X-HILC
79	The Big Blue Soldier	07-0374-X-HILC
80	The Challengers	07-0362-6-HILC
81	Duskin	07-0574-2-HILC
82	The White Flower	07-8149-X-HILC
83	Marcia Schuyler	07-4036-X-HILC
84	Cloudy Jewel	07-0474-6-HILC
85	Crimson Mountain	07-0472-X-HILC
86	The Mystery of Mary	07-4632-5-HILC
87	Out of the Storm	07-4778-X-HILC
88	Phoebe Deane	07-5033-0-HILC
89	Re-Creations	07-5334-8-HILC
90	Sound of the Trumpet	07-6107-3-HILC
91	A Voice in the Wilderness	07-7908-8-HILC
92	The Honeymoon House	07-1393-1-HILC
93	Katharine's Yesterday	07-2038-5-HILC